THE BOOK OF
CHOICES

VOLUME TWO

WOLF GROVE MEDIA, LLC

Additional Illustrations: Adobe Royalty Free, freepik.com

1st edition, 2024

Print ISBN: 978-1-958329-23-8

E-Book ISBN: 978-1-958329-24-5

CONTENTS

INTERSECTION

BY REDD HERRING

"Warm up?" She held out the coffee pot and brushed a few stray strands of hair back under her bright, yellow scarf. The two old-timers in dusty caps slid their cups across to her. She filled them to the brim, spilling a little on the countertop. Each man returned his cup precisely to the round stain it had previously occupied.

The waitress returned the pot, took a drag from a cigarette resting in a bowl, and wiped the counter. "Ya'll see the new stop light at the intersection there?" Both men nodded as they sipped.

"Yup," the man with the faded red Purina Chow hat replied. "Pretty sure there'll be a wreck soon." He wiped his mouth with the back of his hand. "Ain't no warnin' signs to let ya know it's comin' up."

"Why do ya need a sign, Jake?" the man asked, adjusting his John Deere cap. "It's a stoplight. Ain't that warnin' enough?" He flicked the ash from his cigar onto the floor.

"Well, maybe it is and maybe it ain't, Frank." Jake swiveled his chair around and pointed to the left. "If you're comin' over the rise there," he moved his hand in a sweeping motion to the right, "you ain't gonna see it until just about Wendell's store." The waitress came around the counter and peered along the line Jake was drawing in the air. "Shelly, you see what I'm talkin' 'bout there?"

"Yea, I think so." She squinted at the hardware store.

"What's your point, Jake?" Frank walked around the counter and filled his cup. He held the pot up. "Ya'll want some?" They both nodded. Frank pulled another cup from the stack for Shelly. He filled it and returned to his seat with the cups and coffee pot. "Gimme your cup." Jake handed it over. Frank filled it and gave it back.

"Thanks." Jake pointed out towards the street again. "So, like I was sayin', if you're comin' from there and it's dark, like it is now, you're gonna be on that light before you know it. Hard to stop if you're doing much over fifty."

They all leaned out a little farther toward the street, as if they were pondering one of the great mysteries of life.

"Hmm, could be," Frank ruminated on the idea. Shelly nodded, lost in thought.

"Plus," Jake pushed his hat back, "everyone 'round here is used to a blinkin' yella light for the last twenty years. Most people ain't even gonna notice the change." He swung his seat around. "I'm just sayin', there could be trouble there."

"Yep," Frank agreed, spinning around.

"Yep," Shelly nodded and walked back to the counter.

"Yep," Jake took another sip.

The screech of tires on pavement ripped through the silence, shaking the diner windows. Shelly let out a squeal, dropping the coffee pot on the linoleum. Both men jumped out of their seats and turned to face the front of the building. A black sports car was in the lot, straddling three parking spots. A dust cloud blocked out what little moonlight there was.

A man dressed in all black walked inside, shaking the dust from his clothes. He chose a seat at the counter and nodded to the men. They returned the gesture, mouths hanging open a little in shock. He smiled at Shelly, "Coffee any good here?"

"Uh," she stammered, "most of it's on the floor."

"Strange way to serve it," the man laughed, "but I'm not from around here, so I don't know the local customs."

All three just stared. "Hey," he leaned over to look at the waitress's name tag, "Shelly, you got any 'non-floor' coffee for a city slicker?"

Shelly snapped out of it, "Oh yea, sorry mister. I'll get a fresh pot goin' for ya."

"Thanks." He looked at the two men and pointed to his car. "Crazy intersection. I almost didn't see the light at all. That could have been a bad wreck." They both stared. "Let me ask you two something. Who goes through an intersection on a tractor at," he looked above the pickup window at the clock with *Sunshine Diner* printed on it, "eleven fifteen at night?"

Frank glanced at Jake, "Must be Charlie headin' over to his brother's place."

"I know this is a small town," the stranger grinned, "but you visit each other on tractors?" Shelly placed a cup in front of him. He took a sip, "Oh yea. That's what I needed."

"Charlie's gonna plow the corn stalks under in his brother's field," Jake told the man. "He comes through 'round midnight to avoid traffic. Plus, it's a lot cooler on a tractor at midnight than at noon." He chuckled and took a sip. "We usually roll up the sidewalks 'bout nine here."

"So, what are you two doing up?" The man looked over the pie menu. "And why would a sleepy-town diner be open so late if everyone is in bed?" He tapped the menu,

"Shelly, if you have any of this blueberry, I sure would love a slice." She nodded and went to the back.

"Well, Frank and me usually end up here 'bout four nights a week. When ya get to a certain age, sometimes you don't sleep all that well." He pointed to an old pool table in the corner. "So, we come here and play a few games, drink coffee, and just sort of pass the time. Plus, Shelly likes the company. The diner stays open twenty-four hours for truckers passin' through."

"Seems like the coffee wouldn't help you sleep," the stranger commented.

Jake shook his head, "Not really tryin' to sleep. Just gettin' out of the house so we don't wake up our wives. Not sure where you're from, mister, but 'round here wakin' up the missus in the middle of the night ain't a formula for a happy next mornin'." Frank laughed and nodded in agreement.

Shelly slid the pie to the stranger. "That's beautiful, Shelly. Did you make it?" the man asked.

"Sure did, honey. All I needed was these," she laughed, holding her hands up.

He took a bite and rolled his eyes back. "Oh wow, Shelly! This is the best pie I have ever tasted." Jake and Frank laughed, and Shelly gave them a playful glare.

"What am I missing fellas?"

Frank smiled, "Shelly considers opening the pie box and cutting a slice *'making it'* with her own two hands." He pointed to the street. "The pies come from the bakery over there."

"Shelly might not be a whiz in the kitchen, but she sure can cook up a story!" Jake laughed so hard that he spilled his coffee.

"Oh, shut it, Frank Harris." She popped him with her dish towel. "You'd tell a lie if the truth paid a hundred dollars!" She wiped the counter and refilled Frank's cup. "So, now that you know about us, what's your story, sweetie?"

The stranger lay his fork down and took another drink of coffee. He glanced at the clock on the wall. "Well, I am not sure you're going to believe me, but here goes." He stood and walked toward the door.

"Where ya goin'?" Jake called to him. The man turned and held up a finger as if to say "just a second", then spun around and walked out. They all stared at the door confused. He opened the car door, leaned inside for a moment, then exited with a backpack in his hands. He walked back inside and took his seat again.

"This is why I'm here." He opened the pack and pulled out an old, leather book. He placed it on the counter and let them take it in.

"It looks like it's been in a fire," Shelly reached out. The man pulled the book back quickly. "Sorry."

"It's not a good idea to touch it," the stranger explained.

"Well, you did," Frank pointed to the book.

The man nodded, "I did, and it was a mistake. Now I'm just trying to do what it tells me so I can be done with it."

"What it tells you?" Jake raised an eyebrow.

"I know," he opened the book, "it sounds crazy. But let me tell you all, this book told me to come here tonight." No one made a sound. The pages flipped for a few seconds, then stopped. The man pointed to the words. They looked burned onto the page.

3 And 16 Convene
Sunshine At Midnight
Red, Yellow, Green
Your Choices Are In Sight
One Life You Must Give
Only Then Can You Live

"What's that supposed to mean?" Shelly leaned in a little closer.

"The book sort of talks in riddles, but it definitely tells you what it wants from you."

"How did you end up with this thing?" Frank asked, nervously adjusting his cap.

"I was in this little bar – The Crossroads Cantina it was called. Not even sure how I ended up there." He looked at the clock. "The bartender had the book." He glanced toward the intersection, shifting in his seat. "He told me a customer left it for him, saying the book finds a way to help. He said he had been through hell and back because of it. Then, he handed it over, saying the book was for me next. Shelly, can I borrow your order pad?" She gave it to him. He began writing.

"What you writin', mister?" Jake looked over his shoulder.

"Copying the last two lines. Those were not in the book until I got here. The bartender told me that the book sometimes erases what is written, so I don't want to take any chances." He finished and tore the page from the pad. "I was diagnosed with cancer a few days before he gave me this book, and I wondered if that was what he meant when he said it was for me next." He took a quick peek at the intersection. "It took me almost six months of searching. I hope I have it right."

"What are you talkin' about?" Jake asked. "This stuff don't make no sense."

"I know. Told you it sounds crazy." He pointed to the pages. "Here is what I *think* I know right now." He looked outside again. "I wondered if that first line might be streets or highways. So, I searched and found this place here where Route 3 and Highway 16 intersect. When I looked it up, I saw this place – *Sunshine Diner*. So that's *Sunshine At Midnight*, I think." He pointed to the clock.

"11:51. Almost midnight," Shelly whispered, giving Frank and Jake a concerned look.

"Yes," he continued, "*Red, Yellow, Green...*"

"The stop light," Frank said. The cup in his hand was shaking a little.

"Mm-hmm, the stop light. The next line is *Your Choices Are In Sight*. I don't see anything out there under the light, so maybe it's too early. Those last two lines that just appeared though, they worry me even more."

"So, what now?" Frank looked around the room. "We just wait?"

"I think so." The stranger leaned back and took a sip of his coffee.

Four pairs of eyes alternately stared at the clock and back at the intersection. Shelly, needing something to occupy her, refilled the cups and began wiping the counter. She looked up over her shoulder.

11:54

Jake stood and walked across the room to the pool table. He lined up and took a shot. The smack of the balls on the table made everyone jump. He looked at the wall.

11:56

Frank joined Jake at the table. He picked up the red ball, number three. He turned it over in his hand, then lay it on the felt next to the number one, the yellow ball. He rolled the number six until it touched the number one. 3-1-6 ; Red, Yellow, Green. He pointed and looked up at Jake. The stranger was watching them from his seat. They all looked at the clock.

11:58

Everyone tensed and watched the intersection. Jake, Shelly, and Frank moved to the big front window. The man in black picked up the book and walked to the pool table. He took the three balls that Frank had arranged and rolled them to the other end. They bounced off the cushion. He saw them staring, waiting for what would appear under the light. They were side by side - Jake in his red cap, Shelly with her yellow scarf, and Frank topped with the green John Deere hat. One of the pool balls bumped the man's hand. He looked down – the yellow number one. He heard the clock hands click.

12:00

The man sighed and hung his head. "Yellow." They all turned when he spoke.

The words on the page burned away. Shelly let out a startled scream as she slowly began to dissolve in front of them. Jake and Frank were frozen in place, helpless. The page in the book was blank, Shelly was a pile of ashes on the floor, and the stranger could feel that his cancer was gone.

"I'm really sorry fellas," he closed the book and left it on the table. He stopped next to the two men. "I figure you'll both be fine in a few minutes." He reached up and turned Jake's cap around backward. "The book is yours now. It will help you." He shook his head as he left. "But you'll wish it didn't."

ABOUT THE AUTHOR

Redd Herring has written as long as he can remember but only recently began publishing his work. Maybe he was busy sailing his ship, **Have Mercy**, across the seas of time and space, maybe he just wrote for himself, or maybe he spent too much time in the Crossroads Cantina trading stories for drinks - probably that last one.

Redd listens to metal music or watches sci-fi as he writes and tries his best to sneak in references to his favorites. If you have read "The Red Diamond" in The Golden Gull Anthology, you might be able to catch a nod to Alice in Chains, Mad Season, or Firefly.

Currently, **Have Mercy** is docked at a small farm in Texas, where the crew is learning to grow grapes and make wine before leaving on their next voyage. Redd is also in negotiations with Nemo, the Crossroads Cantina bartender, to get a juke box filled with metal tunes added to his favorite corner near the back door.

You can go to www.reddherring.com for a list of his works or just to send him a message.

BLOOD IS THICKER

BY DEAN ROBERT HOLMES

How can one person accumulate so much crap? Lower back hollering for mercy, Jim hoisted yet another box into the trunk. Throughout his entire life, Jim never saw his dad buy so much as a pair of shoes. But now that he's gone, it seems Big Jim left a mountain of memories behind.

"Ah! Damnit." Reaching into his father's hunting duffle, Jim quickly withdrew his hand. Must've been one of the knives. Moths probably gnawed through the sheath.

Forefinger weeping red, Jim sucked on it and moved over to a stack of books. Between a few dog-eared romance novels and fad diet manuals belonging to his late mother, he spotted a slim, weathered volume.

Perhaps the word *Diary* once existed on the cover. But with the passage of fingers and time, now Jim could barely make out a letter. He plopped down on a box destined for the thrift store and flipped through, but found nothing beyond two scribbled dates from August 1978. Well, except for a rusty dot, the result of his still-bleeding finger making contact. Jim licked a thumb and scrubbed, but the blood smear wouldn't budge. With a shrug, Jim tossed the journal into one of many piles, deciding to tackle his father's fishing equipment.

By the end of the day, shirt plastered to his skin and car full of junk, Jim collapsed on his dad's hideously patterned couch with a beer. A lot could be said about his father. Neglectful, distant, workaholic. But he always kept the kitchen stocked with a brew and a smile.

Sweat drying and head light from the alcohol after a day of neglecting his stomach, Jim supposed he pushed himself too hard out of guilt. In the weeks leading up to his death, Big Jim called every day. *Son, I need to talk to you. Gimme a call back when you get a chance. Love.* His father always ended calls like that. Not, "I love you," or even his wife Gwen's cute little, "Love ya!" Just, "Love." As if he couldn't bring himself to personalize the word, lest he be accused of mushiness.

But even though Jim made a mental note to call his dad back, it never happened. Different justifications meandered through his head. Busy with the new garden Gwen insisted on planting, only to dump the upkeep on Jim once she returned to work after the baby. Tax season at the office putting everyone on edge. Not to mention his own Little Jim, finally big enough to cause chaos with every wobbly step.

No matter what Jim told himself, however, he couldn't justify forgetting to call back. Because, in his heart of hearts, Jim knew, he did anything and everything to avoid talking to his father while he was alive. On the rare occasions he came home for Thanksgiving or Christmas, their celebration consisted of half-frozen/half-molten microwave meals. And aside from a few grunts at the football game, they never discussed anything deeper than the weather.

Maybe Jim should've worried about his new son not knowing his grandfather. But throughout childhood, he didn't know Big Jim, either. His father went to work, came home, drank a beer, and watched TV. He never hit and barely scolded, but after his mother's death, it was Big Jim who became a ghost. So, for all intents and purposes, Jim considered himself an orphan.

But with his father truly gone, something nagged at Jim's gut. Should he have put in more of an effort? Was the moat between them really all his father's fault? Or did he hold part of the blame? His dad may have refused to lower the drawbridge, but even if he had, Jim wasn't convinced he would've crossed to the castle.

So now, can empty and stifling a burp, Jim did what he could to get to know his father through his stuff. And there were a few surprises. A picture of his mother hidden in the bedside drawer. Letters from a mysterious Hilda socked away under the bed, which were more than a little erotic. But for some reason, Jim's brain kept gravitating towards the diary.

Sifting through boxes, he soon located the faded tome. After cracking the spine, at first Jim thought the diary was empty, aside from the two dates almost four decades past. But thumb skimming the pages, he found an entry near the end, labeled two weeks earlier in his father's businesslike script.

Don't know what to do. The scars, the voices. Can't take it anymore. And I need to tell Jimmy. Need to warn him. For almost 40 years now I thought it was over, but apparently not. The words circle around my brain. Like they're making fun of me. There's only one way to get rid of them. I know that. Last week I got the syringe. Stolen from the cart when a nurse wasn't looking. It should be foolproof. No one will see that little prick between my toes. Ha, I just read that again.

Little prick. Guess I should be glad I can still laugh after all this.

Lowering the diary, Jim peered around the room, as if he might find someone to explain. His father? Suicide? Voices? No. Unbelievable.

Maybe it was just a writing exercise or something. Jim never knew his father to try his hand at the creative realm, and he never read anything more complicated than the newspaper. But technically, it was possible. What did the coroner say? Cause of death–pulmonary something or another. Jim had yet to visit the morgue, not exactly thrilled at the prospect of seeing his father's corpse. Those sullen lines carved on his cheeks which surely deepened in death. Lines that silently spoke to his son, *You'll never be good enough.*

But maybe Jim could check...

***

"If I could just have a moment alone with him."

The attendant, a man as gray and lifeless as those he oversaw, nodded and ducked out of the room. Jim turned back to his father, well, what was left of him. Pale. Cold. Still. If not for the Y gouged into his chest, he might've fallen asleep in front of the ball game again. Something in

Jim urged him to pay respect, make amends. But placing a hand on his dead father's stiff and chilled shoulder just made him want to run.

"Sorry, Dad." The words creaked from his mouth like a coffin lid. Brain fuzzy, Jim could think of nothing else to say. A stalemate of silence between them and here he was, carrying on the family tradition.

"Well…" He muttered to himself more than anything before unzipping the body bag. Eyes averted, he quickly went to his father's feet. Bending. Searching.

A little hole. Lurking between two toes, an unassuming intruder. Even if the coroner noticed, he'd write such a tiny thing off as insignificant. An accident.

But staring at that minuscule puncture, Jim knew better. What could drive his father to take his own life? Yeah, after Mom died he went through a rough patch, slugging back whiskey and calling into work. But, eventually, he came around. And, to the best of Jim's knowledge, never contemplated following her to the grave.

Unless his father wrote more as-of-yet-undiscovered memoirs, Jim would have to accept the mystery. Just another sad man, cloaking his pain from the world. Jim understood this better than most, thinking back on his dreary high school years. But he never expected his father to give up so easily.

Thanking the morgue attendant on his way out, questions swirled and pecked at Jim's brain like buzzards, but with no answers on which to feast, they simply cawed in protest. Car guiding him back home, Jim decided to put off the trip to the thrift store until tomorrow. After all, he had more than enough for one day.

In bed, back singing wildly out of key while Gwen snored on the next pillow, Jim ordered himself to relax. *Just go to sleep.* But, as with so many things, the brain rarely listens to its own advice. Rolling over and kicking out a leg in hopes of alleviating his spasms, Jim's mind floated once again to his father's diary.

The scars.

The voices.

Can't take it anymore.

Take what? Jim didn't know. But, finally in a position that let his muscles unravel, at 3:32 a.m., he figured he shouldn't care.

"Kill..."

Shooting straight up in bed, Jim's eyes ricocheted off the shadowed walls. "Who's there?"

Nothing. Heart doing the samba in his chest, he shook Gwen's shoulder. "Honey? Honey, did you hear that? Wake up."

A slurry, "Nnn..." leaked out of his wife before she sank once more into the respite of slumber.

Must've been a dream, Jim told himself, forcing his complaining body back to the sheets. *Yeah, that's all it was. A dream...*

***

After an arduous day of composing wills and begging impulsive yuppies not to squander their savings, Jim wanted nothing more than to go home for a nap. And to make matters worse, his hands hurt. Upon waking, he discovered dozens of cuts on his fingers. Red. Throbbing. Must have happened while clearing out his dad's house, but Jim swore last night his skin was intact. A few band-aids did the trick, though, so no big deal. But, climbing in the car after calling it quits, he spotted the stack of boxes in the rearview mirror and sighed, "Shit." If he put off the errand again, Gwen would certainly complain. And Jim subscribed to the motto: Happy wife, happy life.

Detouring to the thrift shop, Jim opened the trunk. Before he hauled out the first load, he once again rifled through his father's remnants for the diary.

His fingers protested, holding the book with porcelain delicacy. Regardless, ink blots of blood transferred to the ancient spine. But where yesterday existed only one page of writing, now Jim found three.

Didn't want to do it. But Jimmy, that's my boy. My little buddy. Me and Mare tried for years to get pregnant. Six miscarriages and nothing. Until our little miracle came along. And when I found this damned book, he was still so young. So much potential. Maybe if the voices started now, I might've made a different decision. But no, I couldn't do that to Gwen or my grandbaby. As awful as it was, I made the right choice. I had to kill her. Mare had to die.

Mouth agape and injured hands atremble, Jim stood in the parking lot unable to fathom what he read. Did his dad really kill his mom? No. It wasn't possible. Mom had an accident, that's all. Tripped over the carpet and fell down the stairs.

But what if he faked it? An insidious thought jeered in Jim's ear. *What if he killed her and made it look like an accident?*

"No!" Jim said louder than he intended, startling a woman bearing a cart's worth of tchotchkes. She gave him a look, the kind of accusatory scowl that says, *What are you, crazy?*

Murmuring an apology, Jim closed the trunk and got back in the car, leaving tchotchke lady to purse her lips and load her treasures. Sitting in the front seat, he went back to reading.

She lived a full life, after all. Well, half one. And back then, Jimmy was only six. How was I supposed to explain something like this to a child? He wouldn't understand. The sleeplessness, the thoughts. Hell, I tried to tell Mare, and she didn't get it either. Then again, I didn't give her much time to put it together. I couldn't risk her getting away.

What the hell? His father, a murderer? Jim's brain cringed at the idea. The last label anyone would brand his father with is 'psychotic.' Practical above all, his father never made so much as an off-color joke. And in their house, everything had its place. Tools outlined on particle board in the garage. Dishwasher promptly unloaded. And, though he wasn't the most demonstrative dad, Big Jim attended every PTA meeting, every baseball game. Initially, Jim thought his father developed persnickety ways to make up for his mother's absence. Unlike many male households, they never lived in filth. Plus, he maintained a job at the plant for over forty years. Someone like that couldn't be in the throes of madness. ...Could they?

Though the pain in his hands ascended to his wrists, Jim flitted through the rest of the diary. Blank. But returning to the full pages, the ink sheened scarlet.

His mother. Murdered. Should he tell somebody? Rush to the police station and call his father out as a criminal?

No, Jim closed the book. *Not yet, at least.*

After all, what would it accomplish now? With his parents reunited in the hereafter, maybe it would be better to let those left behind believe in their love. Well, better for everyone but Jim.

More than anything, Jim wanted to discuss this with Gwen. His wife possessed a knack for problem-solving. Level-headed and able to see options which often evaded Jim. *Yeah, I'll talk to Gwen*, Jim decided, lugging the boxes into the thrift store, but not until he stashed the diary under the driver's seat. *She'll know what to do.*

Back at home, Jim did his best to project an aura of calm. Perhaps if he treated this like a minor issue, it would be.

"Hey, honey!" Gwen came around the corner, Little Jim on her hip and tugging an auburn dangle of her hair. Both smiling. "How was your day?"

"Hey, actually it was—I wanted to talk to you about—"

But, tongue to the roof of his mouth, the words jammed against his teeth. Gwen placed Little Jim in his playpen and approached, concern furrowed between her green eyes. "Jim? What's wrong?"

Hand spinning in front of his chest, Jim tried. Cheeks puffed. But nothing got past his sputtering mouth.

Cupping his jaw, forever a sympathetic solace, Gwen studied his face. Close. Every fiber of her beauty magnified.

Kill. Kill her...

The Voice. The same voice from last night. But, fully conscious, Jim listened more carefully to the scraping, gravel texture of its tone. How it scuttled up his spine and clamped teeth into his brain. Prodding. Demanding.

"Are you sick or something?" Gwen asked, feminine lilt coaxing him out of a terrible reverie. "You don't look so good."

A sigh burst from Jim, as if the need to divulge boiled from his gut into his constricted throat. Admitting defeat, he shook his head. "No, no, I'm fine. Just a long day. How are you doing?"

While Gwen babbled on about a friend she ran into at the grocery store, Jim mulled. What the hell was going on? Throughout seven years of their marriage, he never hid a thing from Gwen. And now, even when he wanted to confess, some force locked his lips.

Finishing her story up by mentioning the 'sweet as pie' check-out clerk, Gwen handed Jim a cup. Herbal tea, part of his post-work decompression. Fingers grazing, Jim yelped and retracted his hand so rapidly that lemon chamomile splashed his shirt.

"What's wrong with you today?" Head tilting, Gwen dabbed the stain with a dish towel. "You're so jumpy."

But Jim didn't want to explain. About the searing pain when they touched. The image that popped into his mind. Fully formed. Gruesome. And tempting...

"Nothing," He hurriedly responded, setting down the cup. "Just a little on edge with tax season coming up, I guess."

Gwen's hands hovered near his shoulders. "You want me to give you a massage? I could–"

"No!" Jim barked. Seeing her confusion, he stood up and dampened his voice. "I mean, no thanks. I'm okay. I think I'm just going to take a nap."

"Okay, darling. Sleep well. I'll be here if you need anyt hing." Gwen got to her toes and kissed his cheek.

Again. Like a flashbulb in his mind. Gwen. Tongue lolling out and eyes bulged. A noose around her neck. Jim skittered from the thought but still felt the rope biting his palms. That surge of power, radiating from his stomach and out to his fingers. Fingers that could...

No. Laying down, Jim tried to convince himself this was a coincidence. He'd been thinking about his mother dying, so naturally, he pictured the mother of his own child dead. That simple.

But mentally tiptoeing back to the moment their hands met, Jim relived that tortuous scene. Gwen dead. Her broken body in a pool of glutinous crimson. Different from the one he saw after she kissed his cheek. But just as horrific.

In the dim afternoon light, Jim looked at his hands. Had the cuts multiplied? This morning, he thought they stopped around his second knuckle. But now, slashes populated his palms.

And remembering Gwen giving him the tea, Jim realized: She hadn't said anything. A conscientious woman, the smallest injury did not escape his wife's attention. Once Little Jim came home with a bruise on his elbow, and she grilled the babysitter to the point of interrogation. So, of course, she would notice Jim's damaged hands.

But she didn't. Which meant, like the grotesque images, she couldn't see them.

Jim breathed. In and out, in and out. Slow. *This can't be happening*. Eyes on the ceiling and hands tenderly resting on his belly, he swallowed hard. *This isn't real*.

The sting in his fingers, though, was real. The tickle in his brain, returning and dashing away from the idea of Gwen's corpse like a tennis player chasing a ball, was real. And above all, the diary was real. Pages cursed with his father's transgression and calling, calling to Jim.

Kill.

Kill.

Kill.

Sick of sitting in a fog of misery, Jim dragged himself out of bed. In the middle of preparing dinner, Gwen didn't hear as he plucked Little Jim out of his playpen.

"Hey, buddy. How's—*Ah!*"

Letting go of the toddler in a jolt of white-hot agony, Jim watched as his son's head bonked the playpen's corner. For a second, Little Jim seemed no more than stunned. But eyes screwing up, a wail poured from his juice-stained lips.

"Jimmy!" Gwen dropped a bag of frozen corn and ran into the living room, scooping up Little Jim and clutching him to her chest. Coos of, "Oh no, baby, what happened? C'mon Little Man, it'll be okay. I got you," wafted to Jim as if from a great distance. Because though his child screamed, nothing compared to what he just saw.

Bruises and shattered bones. His only son, crumpled. A rag doll. Stuffing knocked out by the bat in his hand.

Gwen's fingers snapped an inch from his nose. "Hello! Earth to Jim!"

Shaking himself back to the present, Jim blinked. "Huh?"

"I said, 'Go turn down the burner so I can get him settled'," Gwen repeated, flapping a hand towards the stove. "Please?"

"Oh right. Right." Pulse rocketing, Jim instructed his legs to go to the kitchen. Left, right. Left, right. Lowering the temperature on his wife's stew.

Turn it up...

Burn them...

Kill, kill, kill!

The Voice needled his brainstem. Orders thumping through his skull as if bellowed by a drill sergeant.

"No!" Jim yelled at the blameless stove and clicked off the burner.

Coming around the corner, ginger hair askew and Little Jim apparently soothed, Gwen rolled her eyes. "I said to turn it down, not off." She adjusted the dial. "What's with you today?"

Jim took a step away from her for good measure and ran a hand across his forehead. "I don't know. Just tired, I guess."

"Well then, you better eat and go straight to bed," Gwen suggested, ladling up a bowl. "You'll feel better in the morning."

"Yeah. I hope so…"

***

Fitful sleep. Balanced on a sliver of mattress, lest he accidentally touch Gwen in the night. Dreams haunted by his deceased wife and son. A hatchet in her forehead, a knife growing from his baby's chest. Over and over and again until Jim gasped awake in a cold sweat.

Kill, Kill, Kill!

Synced to his heartbeat, the Voice chanted. Persistent, permanent. Until, weary and frustrated, Jim rose. Flicking on the bathroom light, he suppressed a shout just in time.

His skin. Shredded to ribbons and oozing. Cuts spiraling up his arms and disappearing into his sleeves. Jim ripped off his shirt and found the marks stopped just short of his heart.

But dabbing them with peroxide, the angry maroon smiles neither stung nor bubbled. No blood on the cotton ball. Despite the gnawing on his skin, they were no more than a figment of Jim's imagination.

It's just stress. Tax season. You're pushing yourself too hard.

A feeble excuse, maybe. But enough to allow Jim to prepare for work. Sneaking out of the house before Gwen stirred, he jotted a note on the counter.

Went in early. Call if you need anything. Love.

Jim stared at the message. *Love.* Just like his dad. Repulsed, he added a quick, 'you,' and crept into the garage.

Once safely in front of Lawrence and Kuddy Tax Services, Jim parked and fished the diary out from under the driver's seat. He remembered what it contained before, those three disturbing entries. But as he opened the diary, a barrage of words greeted. Every page, every line, crammed full.

Jim read. And read. Around the halfway point, he vacated the parking lot and called his boss, plugging his nose and coughing. Sitting outside a bustling coffee shop, he arrived at the last page.

The handwriting. Shakier now. But still undeniably Dad.

Tried to get in touch with Jimmy. I really did. But he won't come. Thought about telling him on the phone, but he'd probably call the men with the butterfly nets before I could get it all out. So Jimmy, if you found this I'm sorry. I had a choice. You or your mom. And I wanted to give you a

fair shot at life. I did everything I could, even tried destroying this thing. Burned it. But the bastard came right back. Sorry but I just couldn't stop myself. I know you'll never forgive me for this and I reckon that's how it should be. But I pray you can avoid this curse. And if you can't, God help you.

Jim sat in the car, eyes seeing nothing. Could he kill himself if it came to that? Envisioning what it might be like choking back a handful of pills or buying a gun; he didn't think so. And even if he could, that might not fix anything. He could blow off half his jaw, or end up in a coma. And what if the diary trapped someone else? What if it ended up in Little Jim's pudgy hands? Would he, too, be damned?

Keyed up and fidgeting, Jim went into the coffee shop and ordered a flat white. The last thing he needed was caffeine, but a notion plagued his thoughts. Did it have to be Gwen or Little Jim? Surreptitiously bumping into a stranger, Jim waited. For the visions of death. That yearning which bubbled up from his stomach to his potent fists.

None came. Thinking it might be dependent on skin contact, when accepting his drink, Jim purposefully stuck out his pinky finger to touch the barista. Still, zilch.

Choose... The Voice crowed with sickening allure. *Choose. Kill.*

Ignoring his father's claims, Jim drove to the seedy part of town. Eyes scanning the streets. Happening upon a bum barrel, he traded a dollar for a lighter from a bedraggled gentleman who smelled of sour milk and lost hope. Diary at the ready, Jim clicked the lighter. Flames crackled, devouring the slim volume whole. Jim stayed. Watched as the pages curled and coughed up smoke. Sifting his fingers through the ash until only specks remained. *It's done*, Jim exhaled in relief. His skin still bore the scars, but they would fade in time. *I'm done.*

Spring in his step as he strolled back to the car, Jim even caught himself whistling. An oldie, a favorite of his father's. As good a tribute as any, since aside from music, they had less than nothing in common.

Behind the wheel, Jim decided to go home. Tell Gwen he got out early and take her to a nice lunch.

KILL!

No. Key in the ignition, out of the corner of his eye Jim saw it. The diary. Sitting on the backseat, innocent, like a dormant snake. Afraid to touch it, for a moment Jim just stared. But eventually, his hands wandered of their own volition.

Words and sentences and paragraphs. Detailing his father's indiscretion. Poisoning Jim's fingers, his body, with an authority unknown.

Jim drove home just the same. Thinking about Gwen. How they met outside of that concert. Two people waiting for a cab and Fate. How she posed questions and her legs. Her intellect, forever tinkering and thinking like no one he knew. Her laugh rich and a tad obnoxious. Illuminating her beauty and brilliance.

They married later in life. Both convinced they'd never find a partner until they stumbled into each other's paths. A true miracle, Jim believed. True love.

But then there was the product of their love. Little Jim. A sweet, sensitive boy who adored his blocks and feeding ducks at the pond. With his carrot-orange hair and his inquisitive eyes, Jim knew his son was destined for greatness. And, more importantly, goodness.

As he turned onto his street, Jim seethed. How dare his father burden him like this? What the hell was wrong with him? *I just won't do it,* Jim resolved. *No, I won't.*

But the Voice lingered. *Choose, kill. Choose, kill.* Drilling into Jim's mind and sparking the fuse. Jim's hands crushed the steering wheel. Picturing Gwen's neck, Little Jim's. Esophagus fracturing under his fingers and light extinguished from their eyes.

Pulling into the garage, Jim scratched at his chest and hissed. He peered down the front of his shirt. Furrows of black led to his heart from all directions. Dribbling noxious muck. Burning.

Pulling out the diary once more, Jim flipped to the beginning. A single, short entry during the summer of 1978.

Aug. 11, '78

I don't know what's happening. I found this diary mixed in with Dad's old Army gear. Though I bet he'd be pissed if he heard me calling it a diary. A journal, then. More manly. That was Pop all over. Made himself feel like a man by making everyone else less of one.

But ever since I picked it up, I've been having these...ideas. Don't even want to write them down, in case someone finds this. But they're upsetting. Awful, even. I don't know, maybe I'm just tired.

For a few pages his father's writing continued, the letters eroding like a beach in a hurricane. Until, three days later, Jim read this:

8-14-78

I can't take it anymore. No sleep. Can't touch my family. Not without those thoughts. Horrible things I never thought I could even dream of. Maybe I've just lost it. Maybe I can't blame this silly little book, and this was always coming. But I don't think so. Up until three days ago I loved my wife and my boy. Still do, I think. But love doesn't hurt. Not like this. Mare, if you can read this somehow, please...forgive me.

Jim traced a finger over the dates. The same mysterious dates that marked the diary from the beginning. Three days. Three days his father endured, before surrendering to sin.

And here was Jim. Sitting in the garage after three days of his own torment. Growing up, Jim always thought of himself as weaker than his father. Too frail to work at the factory, prone to crying jags after Mom died. Whereas Big Jim merely cracked open a cold one and said, "Quit your whining, there's work to do." If he had any feelings of grief, he smothered them along with his guilt.

But now, after 72 hours of anguish, Jim realized he made it just as long as old stone-faced Dad. Not weak, but the same. Every inch his father's son.

Jim replaced his tie and shut off the engine. Burying the diary among a half-opened box of photo albums, he took a deep breath and went inside. *Here we go.*

***

In front of the fridge, Gwen fit a container of strawberries into the crisper. Hearing Jim's steps, she called out, "Hey, honey, what are you doing home?"

"Went in early, so they let me go."

"Hmm, Branson must've been in a generous mood." She searched for a place to put the sour cream and inclined her head towards the groceries on the counter. "Could you help me unpack these, hun?"

"Yeah, sure. Where's Little Jim?"

Gwen sniffed a carton of milk, nose wrinkling and tossing it in the trash to make room. "In the backyard playing with that new toy."

"Okay, I'm just gonna go say hi. Be right back."

Out in the yard. The scene of tossed balls and raucous laughter. Little Jim in the sandbox. Squeezing a plush lamb and giggling up a storm each time it baa'ed.

"Daddy!"

Itty bitty fingers like exploring caterpillars. Making his introduction to the world by shaking his father's hand.

"Hey, buddy." Jim bent down, eyes cloudy and voice comforting rain, a plastic bag behind his back. Big and strong enough to carry sustenance. Or to fit over a small head. "I have something to show you..."

ABOUT THE AUTHOR

Dean Robert Holmes is a queer, trans author living in St. Paul, MN. As a prolific writer of fan fiction, his work often explores psychological themes and the diversity of gender and sexuality.

DEEPEST DESIRES: APOTHECARY AND ALCHEMIST

BY ROXANNE KALINDA

She hummed to herself as she passed the shelves of colour. A rainbow of potions bubbled and swirled like lava lamps, all carefully labelled and categorised. Every hue and shade gleamed from the delicate glass bottles containing tonics for all manner of ailments. Her shop held the largest range of magical life enhancers in the country, a kaleidoscope of desires to suit anyone's secret ambition, and business was good.

Bubble-gum pink: Fond friend to lustful lover.

The sound of rain hammering the concrete streets surrounded her shop. It was peaceful, her small oasis, at this late hour. With this storm she was sure to have several hours peace to perfect her latest creation.

Siobhan chuckled softly to herself as she gathered ingredients for the new concoction: a milky-white deception detector. The cool glass jars were smooth, cradled by her soft hands. It wasn't quite perfected yet, but she suspected that when it was it would rival even her 'revenge on cheating spouse' potion, a delicious fire-engine red with stripes of emerald-green.

Neon green: Dispels rumours and punishes gossips.

She turned towards the sound of delicate chimes as the door opened and a young man stepped inside. His hair was dripping. A glimpse of lightning rent the darkness outside before the door swung shut. He sniffed and ran his free hand through his hair, locking eyes with her as water droplets trailed across the hardwood floor. The company

name 'MagEx' was printed on the pocket of his shirt, the
tagline in swirling letters underneath, "Express deliveries
with magical ease".

Butter yellow: Your house feels like home to all who enter.

'Hi,' he stepped forward, 'got a delivery for Siobhan
Samhain.'

'That's me,' she nodded, taking the rectangular package
from his hands. It was surprisingly heavy. 'Bit late, isn't it?'

He shrugged, glancing at the antique clock on the wall
that showed it was a quarter past two in the morning. 'This
one was priority express.'

Waving his hand in a circular motion, he created a sphere
of blue light. He reached inside and pulled out a small
piece of parchment.

'Sign here, please.'

With a quick flick of her wrist Siobhan's signature
formed on the paper and she nodded her farewell, eyeing
the package curiously. The bell jingled as he left and was
then drowned out by a violent rumble of thunder.

Storm blue: Chaotic truths.

Her eyes scanned the name and address written in a
small, neat hand she didn't recognise. Siobhan turned
the package over in her hands, disappointed to find no
return address. She slipped a finger under the packing
tape and pulled the thick paper away to reveal a chunky
leather-bound book.

Its cover was black and smooth aside from the Celtic design swirling within a broad vertical strip. The wide red letters of the title were clearly not English. She opened the book and flipped through until she reached a piece of paper with a typed note.

Siobhan Samhain,

It is with great pleasure that I enclose this rare and ancient artifact for your perusal. It is a highly sought after piece, perfect for any collection of arcane magical objects. The 'Codex Indevitatus Electus', or Book of Choices, is activated by a single drop of blood and will present the user with a choice that will irrevocably change their life.

Best wishes,

T

The furrow between Siobhan's brows deepened as she stared at the note, waiting for something more to reveal itself. She racked her brain for anyone that might have sent this to her, anyone with a name starting with T. She dropped the book onto the counter in frustration and a boom of thunder reverberated through the shop, glass tinkling in response. An object imbued with blood magic was a powerful thing—perhaps this could fill a need for her customers.

Tangerine: To attract friends with similar interests.

She ran a finger along her jawline, eyeing the book. Her potions were potent—she didn't know anyone with as varied and reliable a stock as the one she created—but there were many things her magic could not do. If this book could give her customers the things that she couldn't, maybe it would be a worthy acquisition. She could feel the tome's power purring and rubbing wantonly against her soul; the magic was calling for her to summon it.

She rubbed her eyes before walking behind the counter and placing the book in a drawer. *Perhaps it is too strong to be available to the public*, she thought. With a tired sigh Siobhan decided to call it a night, packing away her equipment and closing the shop. The book would remain tomorrow's mystery to solve.

***

The next morning the sun shone brightly against the grey pavement and sandstone buildings of the city. Siobhan strode with purpose the few blocks from her apartment building to the shop. She relished the crisp air that the rain had left behind, mindful that in a short time the sludgy odours of human creations and confinement would return.

As she glanced at the sign of her business, hung on the building façade, she spotted a ginger tabby sitting haughtily near the top of the concrete stairs, fixing her with a green-eyed stare. The smell of cold steel lodged in her nostrils and she shivered as a bitter breeze caressed the bare skin of her arms. The monochrome landscape loomed around her, shells of brick and concrete housing hundreds of lives in tiny boxes. Cats were known to be wise though indifferent creatures. The knowing in the tabby's gaze left her wondering what it could tell her if it chose to do so. The cat held her eyes for a moment more before bounding down the stairs and into a nearby alleyway.

Siobhan pursed her lips then shook her head, reaching into her bag for her keys. Her fingers ran along the cold, smooth metal railing as she made her way up the stairs and unlocked the door. The familiar crunch of the lock was followed by the tingle of bells as she entered. Her senses were calmed by the myriad colours and the scent of lavender that permeated the room.

'Morning!' sang her apprentice Elodie from behind the counter.

'Morning,' Siobhan replied, depositing her bag in the small back room. It usually served as a tearoom for staff, but occasionally they offered tarot or palm readings when a reputable reader asked. Charging a small commission was generally worth it as customers rarely left without a potion to aid their future endeavours.

'It's been quiet today,' Elodie informed her, looking up from a stock list, 'just a couple of regulars: Harry, then Vi.'

Siobhan nodded, checking over her shoulder. Satisfied with Elodie's progress she began gathering ingredients. 'Good. There are a few potions here that need to be replenished. When you've finished this, join me in putting them together.'

***

They worked together in companionable silence for several undisturbed hours, a production line of freshly brewed potions covering the long workbench tucked into the side of the shop, each colour carefully measured and categorised ready to be placed on the shelves.

As Siobhan sent Elodie for her lunchbreak a striking woman entered the shop. Her hair held a sprinkling of grey, and the navy dress suit she wore looked perfectly tailored. She immediately seemed out of place in the eccentric shop. Siobhan noticed the brief faltering of her confidence before she approached the counter.

'Good afternoon. How may I help you?' Siobhan kept her tone light and welcoming.

The woman glanced around the shop before granting Siobhan her full attention, 'I understand that this shop supplies what some may call occult substances?'

'You could certainly say that,' Siobhan replied. 'We have the largest collection of magical brews on the continent, probably in the world, as well as an extensive range of rare ingredients for those who prefer to create themselves. Is there something particular you require?'

The woman, again, seemed to hesitate, a slight tremor in her hand as she pushed a lock of hair behind her ear.

'It's...' she sniffed, her finger against her mouth, '...it's my husband. He's in the hospital, intensive care. A massive stroke. The doctors say he can't recover. I just...I thought that maybe there was another way to save him. I'm not ready to lose him.'

A small noise escaped her throat as she fought to keep her emotions in check. She closed her eyes briefly, taking a deep breath, before levelling Siobhan with her gaze. 'Can you help me?'

Siobhan felt the tug of magic before she recognised its source. 'I'm so sorry, I have no potions that will heal an injury that extensive, and it is unwise to risk a soul so close to the veil.'

'Is it possible, though?' the woman demanded. 'I'm willing to risk anything for my Michael.'

Siobhan's hesitation was answer enough, but the woman pushed harder. 'Please, I beg of you. I will pay whatever price you ask for a chance to save him.'

Siobhan clenched her jaw and opened the drawer where the book lay waiting. She could feel its energy shivering in excitement at the prospect of its use. 'This book is imbued with blood magic; a single drop will activate it and present you with choices. I don't know if it will save your husband. I do know that it is incredibly powerful. I do not recommend its use, not knowing what consequences may come from it.'

'Any consequence will be worth his life. I told you—I'll risk anything. I'd give my life for his. Please!' The woman subconsciously reached for the book, her eyes intent on Siobhan.

Siobhan opened a smaller drawer and picked out a small pin. 'Any purchase from this shop entails a waiver of liability from unintended or unforeseen consequences of the use of magic. I have made my recommendation known to you and leave this choice in your hands as an individual over the age of eighteen years.'

The woman barely let her finish before snatching the pin from her grasp and plunging it into the soft flesh of her finger. She opened the book, letting the red liquid drip onto a page. It greedily accepted the offering. Her eyes opened wide as they scanned the page, yet Siobhan could not see the message laid across the parchment for her.

'Save him,' the woman whispered, and the book slammed itself shut.

Siobhan felt an immense energy burst from the book, it writhed and reeled around the room, like electric eels, and left a sour taste in her mouth. It pulsed three times and then dissipated. The woman trembled, smoothing her hands down her suit jacket. They both jumped when a tinny melody rent the air between them. The woman shoved her hand in her pocket and pulled out her phone, her hand shaking as she attempted to answer the call.

'H-Hello, Regina speaking...yes...yes, that's correct...' Her breathing became heavy. 'Are you sure? There's no mistake? Yes! I'll be there right away.'

With a soft beep she ended the call and stared at Siobhan. 'They said he's woken up.'

They both looked down at the book. Siobhan felt a prickling sensation along her spine. Once again, the book called to her, beckoned her to discover her own choice.

Regina sniffed and straightened. 'I need to go! Thank you.' In a flurry she left the shop and Siobhan dragged herself to the tearoom, her body heavy and sluggish.

A short time later, Elodie returned, her usual grin on her face and a coffee in hand for her mentor. She paused in front of the counter and stared at the book.

'What's this?'

'It was sent to me. Apparently, it is called the Book of Choices. I think perhaps I should get rid of it.' Siobhan's voice was weary as her hands gratefully accepted the coffee.

'What's it do?'

'A woman came in looking to save her husband from the brink of death. You know we don't have anything here that would achieve that. I let her use the book, and she said he woke up.'

'But that sounds amazing. Why wouldn't you let people use it?' Elodie sunk into the chair opposite Siobhan.

'I'm not sure I trust the book. We don't know what consequences there might be for using its magic.' Siobhan tried not to get involved in why people used her potions, they were certainly not all rainbows and sunshine, but this felt different.

'You always tell me it should be up to the customer how they use what we offer—the consequences come with their choice, not ours,' Elodie looked at her earnestly. 'Just think of what it could give to people that we can't!'

Siobhan nodded. 'If it can do for others what it did for that woman, perhaps it would be wrong to keep it from people...'

***

Several weeks later a young woman entered the shop quietly, her narrow shoulders shuddering, her mouth full of quick, silent movement.

Siobhan looked up from her work, recognising Aisha Talvert. Her smile quickly faded as she took in the blood-shot eyes and tear-stained cheeks.

'What's happened?' When Aisha only stared at her, Siobhan quickly strode into the aisle, and, placing a hand on Aisha's elbow, guided her to the small private room at the back of the shop.

'Give me a minute, honey. I'll lock up and make us a cup of tea.'

Sky blue: To bring calm to arduous circumstances.

Siobhan waited until Aisha had taken a few sips of the potion-laced tea before she softly implored, 'Tell me what's happened.'

Aisha's lip trembled, tears silently trailing down her cheeks.

'My sister, she lost her baby.'

'I'm so sorry. How did she lose it? Wasn't she nearly due?' Siobhan kept her voice gentle, searching her memory for the small details Aisha had shared with her about her life.

'Thirty-two weeks,' Aisha choked out, her hands wrapped tightly around the warm mug of tea. She sat staring into the cup, frozen like a statue for several minutes.

Siobhan knew better than to push now; she sensed the torment Aisha was working through and waited to learn the source of it.

'It's my fault,' she finally whispered, shaking her head and rocking back and forth in tiny motions.

Siobhan couldn't help the frown that passed over her face. 'How could it be your fault?'

'I made the wrong choice,' her breath blew the steam rising from the tea into a turbulent frenzy.

Siobhan's body stiffened as she glanced out the door at the book, sitting on the counter. 'You used the book?'

Aisha nodded and took a long gulp of the tea as though she was preparing herself for a life-threatening confrontation.

'We've done everything to get pregnant and nothing has worked. The book said, "you may choose to let the seed of life inside you grow while those you love wither, or remain barren forever while the garden grows around you."' Her words were becoming rapid. 'Most of my friends have started their families already. Kysha—she was already pregnant, nearly due. I didn't think it would take that from her! How could it be so *cruel*? How could I have *known* it would kill an innocent baby? She called me, sobbing, telling me how tiny he was, how just a couple of weeks ago they'd done an ultrasound and he was happily bouncing and wriggling inside her. I couldn't tell her I caused this. Couldn't tell her how *sorry* I am. It's all my fault. Just because I couldn't accept that I wasn't meant to have a child of my own.' Her chest heaved as she fell apart, dropping the mug and burying her face in her hands.

With a quick spurt of magic, Siobhan deftly caught the mug and floated it to the nearby table. She breathed out a shaky breath, her mind racing but focused on staying calm for Aisha.

'Did the doctors say why it happened?' She kept her voice soft and soothing.

'Something about the placenta failing,' Aisha choked out between heaving gasps. 'It doesn't matter what they say. I know it was because of me.'

'How?' Siobhan eased herself forward on the plush fabric chair.

Aisha shuddered and wrapped her arms around her waist. 'I took a test this morning... I'm pregnant.'

***

Long after Aisha left, her young body bent with the grief and guilt she was carrying, Siobhan sat in the back room staring at the book. Shaking off it's persistent call she took out her phone. Scrolling through her feed she paused at her business page, a new review was apparently gaining a lot of attention.

Celio Quixote: I used to rave about this shop to friends and family. There is a wide array of potions to fit any need and the staff are always friendly and helpful. However, recently they've added a feature to the shop that frankly should be illegal. I'm sure I'm not the only one that's used the book. Like anyone, I wanted fame and fortune without the effort you usually need to put into it. The book offered me the talent I was dreaming of or a quiet but satisfied life, and of course I reached for the stars. I've been booked out for weeks, got an offer with a major label, I was set to be on TV. I thought my life was finally perfect. Then, awful things started to happen. My cat was killed. My girlfriend started getting threatening phone calls. Her brake line was cut, she could have died, she left me. I started getting creepy letters. The police say I've got a stalker. They won't do anything to help though. Not enough evidence. "The price of fame" they tell me. I thought, maybe I can just back out of my deals, go back to an anonymous life. But no. They're ironclad legal agreements. And the lawyer said I'll be filling obligations for at least the next 50 years. I said that's ridiculous. He said, well you signed it. My life has been ruined by this book. The owner should be ashamed of herself for allowing people to use it!

Muhand Chananyah: You didn't have to use it mate. Live with your choices.

Lukas Maegan: Bit harsh. There should have been a warning.

Muhand Chananyah: No warnings can compete with stupid. It's blood magic. What did he think was gonna happen!??

Lukas Maegan: That's the point though, how could he know what might happen? I've seen that book. It's so creepy. I'd never go near it. But if I had a dream so big, I could never make it happen myself...I mean, wouldn't you try?

Muhand Chananyah: No way, man. You couldn't pay me enough to touch that book. Choices have consequences and magic just makes them bigger. He could've just done the work, like everyone else has to.

Lucia Nova: I hear you. This book should be burnt. I can't even share what it's done to me. It doesn't matter what choice you make. It seems great at first, but that book is a curse.

Siobhan sighed and put her phone down. This was getting way out of hand. It was clear the book had to go, but where? If it was in the shop, it was a temptation that someone would eventually give in to. She was certainly not going to have it in her home. Who was this mysterious 'T' it had come from? Perhaps it was time to find out and return the book to her duplicitous donor.

***

The weeks passed with a frustrating lack of answers. Siobhan enquired with the delivery company, but they refused to give details. When she pushed with a few well-placed magical nudges, they found that 'T' was the only identifier on their records anyway. A mysterious feat that had never been accomplished before – to their knowledge.

She scoured her records, investigating any person with a first or last name beginning with 'T'. There were a couple of connoisseurs of the occult that stood out at first glance, but both were quickly eliminated – their credentials not holding nearly enough sway to procure something so rare and controversial. Widening her search of all her clientele, business contacts and even random enquiries also turned up empty of realistic matches.

Next, Siobhan turned to magic, scrying widely for any hint of the person behind the book. She cast spells for truth-telling and revealing deception at her home, the shop and even upon the book with no success. The book itself remained locked away in a safe at the back of the supplies room. Even there she could feel its magical tendrils reaching out, seeking someone to activate its dark power.

'Still no luck?' Elodie placed a hot chocolate on the counter, watching Siobhan rub her temples. Chocolate was the ideal remedy for magic depletion: tasty, comforting and containing a special spark that nourishes the soul.

'I'm not sure what else to try.' Siobhan sipped the hot drink gratefully. She knew she'd been irritable of late, the frustration slipping into her words and actions, and was grateful Elodie didn't hold it against her.

'Maybe it's time to give it a rest. Come back to it fresh in a few days?' Elodie patted her shoulder and moved back to her work.

Siobhan sighed and picked up her mug, walking wearily to the back room and curling up in a big velvet armchair. The supple fabric cradled her body as she drank slowly, savouring both the taste and the warmth that spread through her weary spirit. Her mind wandered, picking at the problem like a colony of ants, teasing it apart.

She cast her gaze to the small table, set her drink down and picked up the newspaper, hoping to distract herself for a few minutes. Her eyes scanned the tiny print and large pictures. The triumphs and failures of the city spread out before her until she halted at a familiar face.

A smiling woman in a smart business outfit stared at her from the pages, grey dappled hair flowing freely.

'Regina...' Siobhan murmured, a cold fist clenching her stomach as she began reading the article.

Local woman Regina Alberta, 54 years old, was found dead in her home earlier this week. Police have taken her husband, Michael Alberta, into custody, reporting her death as suspicious.

Family and friends say they are shocked by the news. Many stated that Michael was a "good man" who would never dream of hurting his wife. Others confided that they were often fearful that Regina was being harmed in her home. However, she never confirmed that fact. Our investigation found a number of serious hospitalisations had occurred over the couple's 25-year marriage.

The alleged murder is even more confusing after the miraculous recovery of Michael Alberta just a few weeks ago, after suffering what would usually constitute a deadly stroke. Doctors were amazed at his unexpected recovery, Dr. Michelle Guiayib stating, "I have never seen anything like it in all my years practicing medicine. He should be dead."

This comes after a spate of domestic homicides in the local area. Local businessman, Theodore Anulap, claims that he has experienced an increase in women seeking refuge from violence and that police interventions are largely being ignored by perpetrators. He told The Tribute, "Society seeks to chain women to their choices while men receive little-to-no consequences for their violent actions. Violence is a choice that we all suffer for."

Advocates are calling for harsher penalties and more support for those experiencing domestic violence.

Siobhan's eyes prickled with tears. The tightness in her chest made it hard to breathe. She scanned the face before her, a bright, successful woman with plenty of life left to live. How much could she have offered the world if her husband had died as nature intended? Magic brewed within her as she was overcome by her grief and her guilt.

It bubbled like a boiling pot inside her. Even though she hadn't used the book herself, hadn't activated its magic with her blood, she felt tainted by it. Her choice had been to allow people to use it, even though her intuition had warned her against it.

'Are you alright?!' Elodie's eyes were wide as she entered the room, 'I can feel your magic from out there.'

Siobhan grit her teeth against the tide of power inside her, it was much too strong if Elodie could feel it. It had been decades since she was last so out of control of her own magic, priding herself on her steady command of it.

'Regina. The first woman. She's dead. Her husband, the one the book saved, killed her.' Siobhan held the newspaper out for Elodie to read for herself.

Elodie sat heavily on the opposite armchair, scanning the article quickly. Siobhan watched the emotions pass over her face as she read, instantly noticing the crinkle between her eyes as she neared the end.

'What is it?'

Elodie shook her head. 'It's probably nothing.'

'Tell me anyway,' Siobhan pressed.

'It's just... this Theodore... they don't say what his business is, or why he would know about women seeking refuge... doesn't it seem odd to you?'

Siobhan grazed her teeth along her bottom lip. 'Theodore...T... do you think?'

'I don't know.' Elodie shook her head again, 'but it's the only lead we've got.'

***

Icy rain fell in sheets across black tar. Siobhan scampered through the storm; umbrella held close. Light escaped the window of the store, muted by the blur of rainfall. She pushed through the door. A light jingle rang across the dimly lit shop. Its muted tones and occult symbols were an unfortunate cliché. A stark contrast to her own colourful business. She supposed, it must serve its purpose. According to her research 'Le Magick' was doing incredibly well and the owner Theodore had seen a massive spike in popularity in recent months.

'I was expecting you sooner,' a deep voice reached her ears.

Theodore was tall, average build with an unguarded face. No typical welcoming smile graced his face at a new customer. He seemed sombre to see her.

'Why did you send me the book?' Her tone came out sharper than she intended. A distant rumble of thunder mirrored the aching guilt that sat in her chest.

He sighed and rubbed the back of his neck. 'I had no choice.'

Siobhan stepped closer. A spark of anger stirring at the thought of all the damage that book had caused, that she had caused. 'What do you mean no choice?'

'I...' His face scrunched up and he turned away. 'I used the book. I couldn't help myself. Its call was so strong.'

Now, it was Siobhan's turn to sigh, her shoulders slumping. There was no escaping the book's reach. 'What choice did it offer you?'

'Success.' He waved an arm, looking forlornly around the shop. 'My business was floundering. But I knew I could help people here, that they just needed to find me and I could make their lives better. It said I could succeed in my dreams if I sent the book to someone else. I thought it didn't seem so bad, so I sent it to you. A gift...' he trailed off.

'Some gift,' she huffed, crossing her arms.

'I know,' he stammered, his eyes wide and sincere. 'I had no idea. But then Regina came in, so happy her scumbag of a husband had recovered. I'd been working with her for months, she knew what he did was wrong, but she couldn't get past the love-bombing. She always believed he'd change his ways. When she came and told me he was dying, I thought, maybe she can get a clean break. Then his miraculous recovery. I started hearing rumours about a book in your shop. I hoped getting myself in that article might catch your attention.'

'You could have just come to me. Not put me through all this cat and mouse shit.' She clenched a fist.

'I was ashamed. I hadn't meant for any of this to happen.'

Siobhan wiped a hand down her face. Could she really blame him? She'd been just as reckless with the book. Maybe even more so.

'Come. Let's sit,' he suggested, motioning to a door behind the counter.

She followed him into a small room with a kitchenette and a little square table. He turned the kettle on and sat down, gesturing for her to do the same.

'I feel so guilty for doing this to you.' He looked down, unable to meet her eyes.

Exhaustion was setting in. Siobhan felt the weight of the past months upon her shoulders like a dozen elephants.

'Where did the book come from?'

'I wish I knew,' he sighed. 'I came to work one day and it was bundled up on the doorstep. No note. Nothing. I got in touch with a few contacts and one of them suspected what it might be; translated the title for me. At least you weren't stupid like me. You didn't use it yourself.'

Siobhan scoffed lightly. 'Maybe not. But I ruined so many other lives by letting them use it. I wish I'd made the right choice.'

Theodore looked at her, the guilt in his gaze mirroring her own.

'I don't think there are right choices with that book.'

ABOUT THE AUTHOR

Roxanne Kalinda is a secondary teacher with a passion for writing and photography. Her chaotic home comprises of four young children, two border collies, two cats and one very supportive husband. Originally from Melbourne, she is currently enjoying the beautiful Far North Queensland region of Australia and all the inspiration it provides for creative endeavours.

THE FAMILY BIBLE

BY GORDON PHILLIPS

This was the only thing Alice had ever wanted to inherit, and now it was all hers. She held the leather-bound bible tightly to her chest, as though it were a baby, and breathed in deeply the evocative, comforting smell of its cover. She then placed it on the table in front of her and, for the first time ever, opened it to read the inscription inside.

This is the Bible of the Greatorex Family, first acquired by Anne Greatorex, only child of Benjamin and Sarah Barton of Alfreton in the county of Derbyshire. On the holder's death, it should be passed down, not to the eldest son, but to the eldest daughter. I wish it to be the property of solely the female line of this family.

    Anne Greatorex (née Barton)

    December 25ᵗʰ in the Year of Our Lord 1632

Alice's hands trembled at the thought that something so old and so beautiful was now all hers. She traced the index finger of her right hand over the signature. My several-times great grandmother, she said to herself and, as a myriad of family memories rushed into her head, she removed her glasses and placed them on the table.

Alice's mother had long promised her this copy of the King James Bible, and now it had been expressly bequeathed to her in the will. She knew nothing of her maternal line, of the people who had owned the book before her, only that her mother had received it as a girl when her mother, Alice's grandmother, had passed. Aunt Barbara had said she had been hung on the court's orders for murder, something her mother had described as utter nonsense. Alice was forbidden from ever seeing her again, or even to mention her or her grandmother. She knew from the look in her mother's eye that this was not a decision she should challenge and so that was that. Grandmother, who may have died of natural causes or may have been executed, never featured in any subsequent conversation.

How Alice wished she had insisted on knowing more, on asking those vexatious questions. Now she had time in her life to trace the family tree and unearth those long-buried skeletons; this would be her "retirement project", a challenge she would relish. Perhaps clues lay in the Bible but, as she pushed her glasses back on and turned over the page, she was shocked to see the Bible was empty. Where she had expected colourful illustrations and biblical script, there was instead blank page after blank page. They were slightly yellowing, but unmarked. Why had her mother said it would be hers one day, but failed to tell her the pages were blank? Until the day she died, her mother had remained just as enigmatic as the book in front of her.

"Curiouser and curiouser," Alice said aloud, unwittingly quoting her namesake.

She reached out, picked up her landline and distractedly telephoned her daughter with the news.

"Hi, Amy, it's me."

"Hi, Mum."

"I just wanted you to know we've started clearing the house – oh god, what a job and a half that's going to be! – and I've found the Bible I told you about."

"Oh, really," replied Amy, in her usual "twenty-nine year old desultory teenager" tone.

Alice knew her daughter's faults and decided to ignore her studied indifference.

"Yes, and it's beautiful. Leather-bound and smells like it's fresh from the shop. I could sit here for hours, just looking at it and smelling it. Did you know it was first owned by someone called Anne Greatorex in 1632? 1632, can you believe it?"

By way of explanation, Alice then read out the dedication on the opening page.

"Oh right," said Amy.

"Sounds like an unusual name to me. Don't you think? I reckon early retirement is going to be very busy; can't wait to find out who she was and also about all the other women who owned it before I did."

Silence. Alice suddenly became aware that she had warbled on like an excitable child, speaking quickly and tripping over every fourth word, without even asking her how she was or how her granddaughter was keeping. Maybe she should give her monosyllabic daughter a chance to speak.

"Well, what's new with you? How's my favourite granddaughter?"

"She's fine. Playing with Mr. Monkey at the moment."

"Ah, bless her, she's so gorgeous."

Silence.

"And the new job? Going well?"

"Beth is lovely, and the job's fine. But..... It's married life I hate," she spat out with real venom.

Alice froze. She loved her long-suffering son-in-law John and, somewhat disloyally, had raised him to sainthood when he married Amy. How was he able to cope with her petulance and incessant mood swings?

"Amy! Why? What's the matter? What's he done?"

"No, as always he's Mr. Thoughtful, a proper little goody two shoes. I just wish he weren't here."

"Oh God, Amy. You don't mean separation, do you? Are things that bad? What about Beth? Think about her!"

Amy refused to expand, to explain how she felt and to talk through the cause of the problem. As always, she had sown the seed in Alice's head, giving her yet something else to worry about, and then fallen silent.

"Sorry, Mum, I've got to go. Meeting someone for coffee and I'm not even dressed yet."

And with that, the receiver was placed down and the conversation over. Alice hated these moments. Of course, she loved Amy, but she certainly didn't like her. Over the years, she had caused her so much anguish and brought her so little joy. What was she supposed to do now? She could hardly speak to John about it; *"By the way, you're making my daughter miserable. Could you do something about it please?"* She had tried to talk to a couple of girlfriends about Amy, but felt so awful at her own disloyalty. While they both clearly loved all of their children unconditionally, even the ones with the biggest faults, Alice could not forgive Amy for giving her this sense of constant guilt. Had she not shown her enough love as a child? Or maybe she had indulged her too much, and turned a spoilt child into a selfish adult? Whatever the reason, it was bound to be her fault.

This was always the pattern. Every conversation with her was followed by pangs of guilt, deserved or otherwise. Then the rain starts to fall. At first it's a gentle drizzle, then a downpour, followed by the most god-awful storm with flashes of lightning and roars of thunder. She lowered her head, gently massaged her temples and closed her eyes, willing the migraine to go away. Suddenly, a big drop of blood fell onto page one of the Bible and then another. Her eyes shot open.

"Sod it!" Alice moaned and, pinching her nose with her left hand, stumbled to the box of tissues by the fireplace.

"Oh God, I've ruined it. A nearly four-hundred year old Bible and in just one day…. What have I done?"

Alice sobbed inconsolably and wandered through to the bathroom. She reached for her tablets, poured a glass of water and gulped down the doctor's miracle cure. She then tried to make herself presentable with a splash of cold water and the gorgeously scented soap she had treated herself to. She sighed. Thank goodness; this was just a bad headache, not the pounding migraine that blurred her vision and left her totally incapacitated. She wandered back into the lounge to inspect the damage.

What greeted her was not a blood-stained page, however, but a couple of words: "*third*" and "*daught*" (presumably the beginning of daughter). Instinctively she spread the little bauble of blood across the page and more writing revealed itself. "*Every third generation*" and "*daughter will*".

It must be written in some kind of invisible ink that only reveals itself to the reader when liquid is placed on it. It was like one of those magic books everyone had as a child; the ones with secret codes that only water could reveal. She went back into the bathroom and retrieved her glass of water. Excitedly, she gently moistened the corner of her towel and gently stroked the page. Nothing. Of course there was nothing; this vampiric Bible required human blood.

Without thinking, Alice went to her mother's old sewing box – well, now *her* sewing box – and took out a needle and pricked her finger. She cursed the fact that only a small globule of blood appeared and smeared it along the page, as thinly as she could, in order to reveal the maximum number of letters. The letters "*co*" appeared, so she coaxed a little more blood out, by pressing as hard as she could and massaging the cut. Four more letters appeared, "*mmit*".

Alice became so lost in her task that she failed to consider what a surreal experience this was turning out to be. Instead, she pricked another finger and a third, insanely reasoning that each finger would contain its own store.

But the process worked and the book revealed more and more of itself. After some time, she had the first page almost complete in front of her.

This is the curse of the Greatorex family. Anne Greatorex hereby asserts that every third generation - the eldest daughter of the eldest daughter of the eldest daughter - will kill somebody she once loved and will pay dearly for her deed. The solution is in your hands. To prevent this, you must slay your eldest daughter.

What an awful suggestion; this must be a trick. Had someone with a sound knowledge of chemicals created this ridiculous book in order to play with her mind? Alice got up slowly, in a daze, and went to the bathroom to wash her injured hands. She knew the book's revelations could not be dismissed as casually as this, but the idea of her own daughter killing someone could never be entertained. And the idea of killing Amy to prevent her murdering someone else was simply quite ridiculous and too dreadful to countenance.

Two weeks passed and, all the time, Alice dwelled on the contents of the Bible; she could think of nothing else. She tried to dismiss what she had read as an elaborate hoax, but the thought that Amy might kill went round and round in her head. She was tortured by the idea that she, Alice, was being asked to prevent the grisly deed by slaying the person she had given birth to, had brought up, had cared for.... True, she had always been a truculent child and was now a truculent young woman, but she could not kill her on the off-chance that she might be saving another person. Try explaining that to the police, to a judge; I killed my child because I thought she might one day kill someone else.

Alice fell back against the armchair, exhausted, the curse having drained her not only of blood, but also the ability to make rational decisions. She needed to focus. If this was a trick, it was the nastiest trick anyone could play. And, if it were a trick, how did they know about her Bible – and possibly about her grandmother? She put her hand to her mouth, something she always did in moments of fear, as she considered that it may well be true that her grandmother's fate had been to murder and to end up on the gallows. Alice felt frustration that she had not forced her mother to reveal the details, to tell her for certain whether this was or wasn't true, and now it was too late. Why had her mother refused to talk about her father? Was he a murderer too? Or was he the victim?

Tears of impotence came to her eyes, and gradually made their way down her cheeks. She wiped them away and suddenly realised what her thirty minutes of madness had done to her fingers.

"Oh my god, I'm going insane," she told herself, aloud, "these thoughts have to stop."

But they wouldn't. If the rumour about grandmamma were true, then I am the eldest daughter of the eldest daughter. I am the second generation, which makes

Amy the third generation. She may be the most difficult daughter a mother has ever had, but she is not a killer. A mother would know and Amy had never shown any signs. *Murderess* was not, and never had been, written in her stars. Alice was horrified at the thought of ending the curse, of putting an end to Amy. Quite impossible! She cackled. Thank heavens she had not been taken in.

Suddenly the phone rang, making Alice jump with a start. Better that than the doorbell, however; she felt totally unpresentable, incapable of greeting someone from the outside world. But a phone call she would try to handle.

"Mum, it's me!"

"Oh hi Amy," she replied, successfully hiding the shock of hearing her voice and suppressing the thoughts she had had over the last few minutes.

Then the floodgates opened and Amy sobbed into the telephone.

"It's John. He's dead."

Alice clutched the phone as though her life depended on it. She dreaded what she was about to hear.

"I've killed him."

Alice sat dumb, in a haze, unable to formulate a question, while Amy tried desperately to justify what she had done.

***

The trial lasted hardly any time at all. Why would it? There was no disputing the facts; the two had been the only adults in the house, the knife belonged to the couple and, besides, Amy admitted she had killed him in a fit of rage. She wished she could have said in court that he had been cruel and that he had controlled her. But he had not. She accepted he had been a kind, gentle, and loving man, but she hated him simply for being there. Yes, she had loved him once, but that soon turned sour and now she was unsure whether she regretted her actions or not. She simply accepted what she had done and was resigned to her fate.

The jury took only moments to make their decision. The judge needed psychological reports to be compiled: and those she went through with a fine tooth comb before she could pass sentence. Amy was declared to be of sane mind; she had simply killed because she wanted to.

The press intrusion became unbearable. Every journalist wanted to know about Amy's childhood and whether there had been any signs of insanity. The word "evil" was bandied about quite freely, causing the whole neighbourhood to be hungry for every morsel of information.

Alice soon became a pariah. If she crossed paths with anyone who knew her, they either pretended not to see her, or they gave a perfunctory nod and quickly crossed the road. Alice, who had meanwhile adopted her beloved granddaughter, knew they had to move for her own peace of mind. There was no way she could carry on living in the house she had lived in for almost forty years. But where could she run? The fact that her daughter had murdered her husband, and might well remain incarcerated for the rest of her life, would never leave her. She had been literally cursed for eternity.

Alice always confronted her problems full-on; she had never been one to bury her head in the sand and ignore the pain. But what options did she have? She reread the first page of the curse and decided she had to know more. Would the subsequent pages provide a solution? It was an out-of-body experience, when she went to fetch the sharpest carving knife she possessed from a drawer in the kitchen. She made a clean cut along her left forearm, dabbed her right index finger into the magic ink and revealed more.

A torrent of words miraculously burst onto the page. The book was not satiated, nor was she, so she cut again and again and fed the book.

If the eldest daughter of the eldest daughter of a murderess fails to reach the appropriate decision and kill the child she has borne, that child will kill another, and she is indirectly responsible. Now, another choice befalls her. She might still kill her child's eldest daughter and then the curse is broken. A failure to do so will punish generations to come.

Subsequent pages merely provided detail and thus dispelled any doubt she may have had about the curse. Anne

Greatorex had killed her son; her great-granddaughter had killed her sister; and, subsequently, *her* great-granddaughter had killed her father. The list went on. Alice eventually came to the recent past and her own grandmother, Emma. She had indeed poisoned her husband and had paid the ultimate price; she had been hanged at HM Prison Holloway in 1938.

The curse was real, and Alice froze at the choice she faced. Beth was merely a small child, so she took comfort from the thought she could prevaricate; she did not have to make the decision today, but would set herself the arbitrary deadline of deciding within ten weeks. Alice knew her arms soon resembled those of a woman who self-harms - there were cut marks from wrist to elbow - but she was determined to carry on as normal for a while and successfully hid her wounds from Beth and Amy with long-sleeved shirts and cardigans.

Weeks passed and the need to make a decision pressed ever more heavily on her. Should she kill Beth and thus end the curse? Should she take the coward's way out and simply kill herself, leaving the decision to another? In either case, when should she do it and how? If she were to kill Beth, what would become of her after the deed was done? Would anyone believe the Bible was anything but an elaborate hoax? What would be the effect on Amy, as she languished in prison with nobody outside to care about her?

The questions swirled around Alice's head, but remained unanswered and the worst part was that such deliberations could not be shared. If she confided in someone, they would probably have her sectioned or imprisoned. In her more level-headed moments, Alice realised there was no rush, and her self-imposed deadline meant nothing.

All the time, Alice was trying to build a comfortable, new life in a new town, where she could care for her granddaughter, away from the whispering surrounding her dark secret. But even here, she could not stop herself from reading the leather-bound book every night and seeking inspiration for what she should do.

Beth was thriving; she seemed to have largely forgotten her mother and was rapidly changing from a tiny toddler to a young child. Perhaps the fact she was quickly growing up was the catalyst for making the decision, for resolving the dilemma. She applied for two passes to visit her daughter.

The day finally arrived and Alice dressed her granddaughter in her most gorgeous dress and cardigan; she looked as pretty as a picture. Quite by chance, the morning Alice had chosen for her visitors' passes was a glorious one; sunny and warm, with not a cloud in the sky. This was so apt for the day the curse will come to an end, she thought, and left the house, seeming to have not a care in the world. She walked to Ealing Broadway, where a

District Line train was waiting at the station. Not much later, she found herself at Victoria, where she boarded the appropriate train. Alice lost all track of time, but alighted at Maidstone Station, got out her mobile and telephoned for a taxi.

"That'll be ten minutes, my lovely," said a chirpy voice on the other end of the line.

"That's perfect," she replied.

Alice found a spot, a little apart from the other travellers, and turned her face towards the sun. She felt energised by its rays and so was reluctant to move when the taxi pulled up beside her, but she had to.

Perhaps it was the fact Alice was a lady of a certain age, or perhaps it was the fact she was pushing a small sleeping child, but she managed to get through the prison gates into the visiting area with only a minimum of fuss. Beth had fallen asleep in the push-chair, which pleased Alice, who had always felt reluctant to expose an innocent child to Amy's world.

In the waiting room, Amy was sitting patiently, smiling. Alice approached her table and put her finger to her lips, signalling that she thought it better the child be allowed to continue sleeping. The two women stared at each other, unable to express how they felt; everything sounded so trite. They broke the silence by discussing the weather and then moved on to the flood of new words Beth had started to say. Amy, of course, became a little upset, acutely aware that hearing these first utterances would be an experience forever denied to her.

As Alice tired of making conversation, she began to fumble around in her bag. She had ingeniously created a false bottom under which she had hidden three small syringes, filled with poison intended for rats, but probably just as effective with humans. She found them. A feeling of calm came over her, as though she was happy to do what she had to do.

Alice reached over and plunged the first syringe into Amy's arm. There was no reaction; Amy just calmly let it happen. The older woman gazed upon her daughter's serene face and thought how beautiful she looked. But she pushed harder and injected the fluid, before taking the second syringe and bending over to her young grand-daughter.

At that moment, those big blue eyes shot open with a start, and a smile came to her face. The blond curls, the little white baby teeth and the dimples in her cheeks; Alice thought in that instant what a beautiful picture of innocence she was. She pulled back and turned the syringe on herself, injecting its contents into her arm with all her might.

The two women fell forward, as though in an awkward embrace. A prison guard rushed forward, ashen-faced and unsure what to do. Beth, meanwhile, simply stared at the adults around her and chortled. What was this new game of make-believe?

ABOUT THE AUTHOR

Gordon Phillips was a French teacher and lecturer, who discovered writing for fun in retirement. He is currently working on a biography and lives in the beautiful county of Wiltshire.

BLOOD INK

BY SHY'KERIOUS BLANTON

The bell rings calling all students to be in their class-rooms before 8:30. Lucia sat down at her desk, pushing her dark brown hair to the side. Her bifocals pushed her hair back in front of her face. Her face was a palish color. She was a lone wolf all to herself now - after the incident. She sighed.

"Ok students good morning, and how are you?" Her teacher walked in with his black, slicked back hair." She blushed a little. He would always make her laugh. He was her only friend.

"Hey, Mister John, we are all doing well, but I think Lucia is feeling sick and needs you to make her better." The blonde laughed and sat at her desk, next to all the other laughing kids. Lucia felt embarrassed, her face bright red. She was different from them. They were fit and popular, while she was two hundred pounds on the dot. No one wanted to be friends with her.

"Alright, students we do not bully, and I'm married; but for you, Lucia, anything is possible." He smirked and looked at the blackboard. "Today we will be writing a book report. It doesn't have to be a specific book, just one you find in the library. Now that doesn't mean go looking for a Doctor Suess book, Arnold. This report will be due in a week. Anyone who doesn't do so is repeating the 12th grade. Understood?"

"Understand." the class said in unison. Lucia looked behind her to find a bunch of kids staring at her and laughing.

"Let's go to the library class, and find a good book." Lucia got up, grabbed her backpack and ran off earlier than the other students. She entered the library, which seemed to go on for miles and smelled like coffee.

"Hey Lucia, how are you today? Has that Tanya girl been messing with you again." The brown-skinned woman with the tight dress that shaped her body like a doll asked.

"Hey, Mrs. John. Not really, it's just the usual." She nodded shyly.

"Well, guess what? I found this book in a garage sale, and it looks horrific, just your type right?" Mr. John walked in with the other students. He walked around the table and grabbed Mrs. John.

"Hey sexy, you know Lucia here is trying to take your place." He chuckled and kissed her. Lucia grabbed the book and quickly walked away burning with embarrassment.

She walked to a dark corner in the back of the library. sitting in her favorite chair with her favorite light and thinking about life before high school, before her best friend became her worst enemy. "Tanya and Lucia, best friends forever. If someone messes with us, we'll send them to the devil," they would sing while playing hopscotch. What happened? She looked down at the book fascinated with the leather wrapping it.

"Wow. No name. Very weird," she thought to herself. She opened the book and the dark red words shouted out to her - *DO NOT READ*. "Is this blood?" She slowly ran her finger against it, touching it softly. She flipped the page.

"Ouch." The page pricked her finger and the blood twinkled down the paper. Another message appeared on the page.

Now I have your blood, Choose wisely.

She chuckled at the book. "Right."

"Oh, hey Lucia." Jake walked in front of her with a seductive voice.

"Hey Jake, what are you doing over here? Where's Tanya?"

"I just wanted to talk to you. Only if you want me to." He touched her hair and pulled it back.

"I don't like this; you never talk to me, so why now?" Lucia asked. Jake tugged on his dreads.

"I've been meaning to tell you something. I'm not in love with Tanya, I'm in love with you." He leaned in for a kiss. Their lips connected, when Lucia heard giggling. Tanya walked out holding her camera towards them. Five other kids came from the bookshelves with Tanya, laughing and snickering.

"Yo, Jake how she tastes, bro?" A long-haired blonde boy bumped into Jake.

"Dude, she tastes like baloney! Worst dare ever." They all laughed.

"Look, my millions of subscribers, Lucia thought he loved her!" Tanya turned the camera to herself. "Subscribe."

"Tanya, why would you do this? What have I done to you to make you hate me? I understand if you don't like me anymore, but does it take all this," Lucia questioned with tears running down her face.

"You know what you did, so don't play dumb now Bestie. If you think that wasn't bad, something is wrong with you." Lucia stood up and ran off.

"Hey, Lucia, where are you going?" Mr. John called, following her out of the library. Lucia ran into the lady's bathroom and into an empty stall.

"Lucia, talk to me." Mr. John talked from the outside.

"I know why she hates me. We grew up together. I braided her hair while she braided mine. I did one prank. We were kids then. Now we are adults. I wish her out of my life."

"Look I don't know much, but trust me when I say you will get better. Now please come out." She wiped away her tears and came out of the bathroom.

"Thank you, Mr. John. Can I go home?"

"Hmm. Go to the principal's office and check yourself out."

Lucia opened the door to her mother's home. "Mom? I'm home." She walked into the kitchen to find a note there.

"I'll be gone for the month with my new boyfriend. I left you enough money for two months just in case and if your dad comes by, go stay with him." She threw the letter away and picked up the money.

"I wish I could stay with dad! Too bad he's cooped up with work for the past five weeks." She walked into her room and got into her pajamas. "More like cooped up with Sarrah, the assistant stereotype is true."

"The book." She grabbed her book pack and rummaged through it. "Dang it. I must have left it." She lay in her bed and cried to herself to sleep. The loneliness soon fed on her heart.

The alarm went off - midnight on the dot. She turned it off and walked into the bathroom. She opened the bathtub curtain and almost fell - the book sat there waiting for her. Lucia picked up the book. Red liquid began pouring out of it.

"What?" She opened the page she left off on before.

CHOOSE

She confusedly turned to the next page.

Make Tanya Disappear or Make Her Suffer

She closed the book, and dropped it.

"Mom, are you home? This isn't funny." No one answered. She walked into the kitchen. The book sat on the counter.

"No way." She picked it up once again.

"OK, whoever is doing this, I admit you're fast. I'm going to play your game." She opened the book.

"I'll choose, hmm. Make Tanya Suffer." As she closed the book it pricked her again.

"OW! Old book." She went into the tub and relaxed.

Lucia dried her hair after finishing up. When she walked into her bedroom, the book sat on her bed.

"OK, REALLY?" She screamed out to those who were playing tricks on her. She opened the books once again, but something was different. Her choice was circled in red. It was the same substance as the writing at the beginning of the book. She threw the book on the floor, threw herself on the bed, and threw her mind into a fitful sleep.

Boom! Boom! Boom! - the knocking woke her up.

"Open up Police!"

She got up and ran to the door. As it swung open, four cops stood on her porch. Mrs. and Mr. Blade stood crying.

"Yes, can I help you?" she questioned.

"We're here because last night we got a call from Tanya's cell phone. She was screaming, and a voice told us that her suffering would end when she did. That call traced back here. We are bringing you in for questions. Where are you parents?" the cop asked.

"WHAT?! I didn't do anything." Lucia cried.

"Ok ma'am we will figure that out later. Until then, you have the right to remain silent. If you do say anything, what you say can be used against you in a court of law. You have the right to consult with a lawyer and have that lawyer present during any questioning. If you cannot afford a lawyer, one will be appointed for you, if you so desire." The cops put her in handcuffs and walked her to the patrol car.

"If you did anything to my daughter, I'll kill you!" Tanya's mother screamed at Lucia. They put her in the car before Mrs. Blade could finish. Lucia used to think of Mrs. Blade like a mom, before the fall out between the two best friends . She thought back to that moment.

She and Tanya walked together in middle school every day, until they both started crushing on the new boy at school. He soon picked Tanya over her. Lucia didn't appreciate that fact, so she started a rumor.

"Hey guys, guess what? Tanya is pregnant by the new boy." Tanya and the new boy were removed from the school and sent to a reform school by their parents. Lucia started stress eating every day until Tanya came back, but it was never the same.

Lucia woke up in an isolated cell. She couldn't hear anyone but herself.

"Hello? Can I call my dad please? She started crying."

"You get one call." The guard showed her to the phone. She called her father.

"Hey Dad. I'm in jail. Please come get me." She sniffled.

"Oh, hey honey, this is Sarrah. Your dad is busy, and we are in New York. I'm sorry. Bye" The phone hung up. The guard put Lucia back in her cell. She turned around to find the book waiting for her to open.

CHOOSE

Kill Sarrah or Get Out Of Jail.

She couldn't believe her eyes, but again she chose. The book once again pricked her finger. She closed the book, laid down, and slept.

"Hey, Lucia, you're being bailed." The guard shouted.

"By whom." she thought. The guard walked her outside. Waiting for her was Mr. John. She hugged him.

"Thank you."

"What happened is unbelievable. The police found Tanya in a sewage drain cut up and almost bleeding to death. They figured you were innocent." They got in his car.

"Hey. Thank you, I appreciate this. I really do." Lucia said.

"It's no problem. I'm just glad you're okay." He looked into her eyes. Without thinking, her lips connected to his. He jumped back, bumping his head on the window.

"Lucia, no I'm married! We are just friends." She felt embarrassed by it. They didn't speak the whole ride to his home.

"You can sleep in the guest home. Just call if you need anything." He walked her to the small house in the back.

"I'm sorry about that. Please don't say anything," Lucia begged.

"I won't." He walked away. She entered the small home with the book in her hands. She sat on the couch. The book pushed her into opening it again.

CHOOSE

Make Him Love You, But His Wife Dies or Make Your Father Kill Sarrah

She slammed the book down, not knowing what to do. She would never hurt anyone or tell someone to do it. She needed her parents; this wouldn't happen if they were still together.

"Why a divorce?" She heard screaming coming from across the yard.

"What do you mean she kissed you? I'm through with her. She's not sleeping here." Mrs. John came banging on the door. "Open up you brat." Lucia opened the book and answered the question, this time it cut her hand; the blood leaked down the page. She ran and hid. There were a few loud noises, then the banging stopped.

"Lucia, she's gone." Lucia ran outside to find Mr. John clutching a pistol. Mrs. John lay still on the ground.

"What did you do?"

"You did this to me Lucia. I can't live. I love you." He turned the gun on himself.

Rain started pouring, as blood ran down her feet. Lucia grabbed the book and ran. She ran all the way home crying in the rain. She opened the home door and ran to the fireplace. She looked at the book once again and let it go - letting the fire greedily gulp it down. She cried until the sun came up.

She turned the volume up on the television. "Today's news with Jinnie and Tod. Where back again with a tragic story. A teenage girl was found near death in a sewage drain and now two teachers, wife and husband, have been found dead. Evidence shows it was a murder suicide. The victims were Thomas John and Laicey John. That is all we have for now."

Lucia walked into her parents' room and went into the closet, looking for answers. Just as she started looking, she found a note.

"Hank, I love my daughter, but I don't want her. So, please win the case. Bill and I are trying to start a new life with new kids. I know you and Sarrah are expecting, but Lucia can help." She couldn't believe what she was seeing. Then, she found another letter.

"I don't care about you or her. I pay child support! In 2 months she's going to be 18, so she doesn't need me nor you." Lucia couldn't breathe. She started to panic. The room was spinning. She fell to her knees.

"Why?" Lucia woke up in the tub.

"How?" She tried to stand, but she was paralyzed. The book sat next to her. She felt weird and warm, but this didn't feel like water. When she saw the blood, she screamed and kicked with all her might, but the blood pulled her under more and more, until she was drowning.

She woke up in her parents' bed.

"What is happening to me?" The book lay next to her. Lucia had to figure out how to get rid of it. She got up and found her old laptop.

"Demon book, no name, just leather wrapping." She typed in the search. Only one article came up.

"I'm in a prison. I was a young lady about to start college when I found this book. I thought it was just a prank my friends played, until the questions it asked me became scary and real. No one believes me, but if you find the book, do not play its game. It will use your blood and make you choose answers to deadly questions and, when it's finished, it will use your blood for the devil's ink, writing your name and the people you used in hell."

Lucia found an address underneath the article. She packed a bag and packed the book. She got on the bus not knowing where the address would actually lead her, but she had to find out.

She dozed as the bus droned along on its journey. After what seemed like days, she reached her stop. As she exited the bus, she heard a soft voice in the wind.

"Turn around."

A shiver crawled up her spine. She probably should have listened to the warning, but she needed to push on.

Lucia arrived at a big, black, dark house. The grass and flowers were dying, no not dying, completely dead. She walked across the broken driveway and reached the crooked stairs. Every step she took made her feel colder and colder. She knocked. The door creaked open and a tall figure stood before her. It opened the door and walked, almost furiously, into the next room.

"Sit." The old raspy voice directed her as it sat on a couch. Lucia took a seat in an old rocking chair.

"Who are you? I..I'm Lucia." he nervously asked.

"I know who you are. Did you bring my book?"

"What? How did you know? Who are you?"

"I know everything about that book. I know when it's coming back, and I know that you will be the last." The old figure chuckled. Lucia could now see that it was a woman.

"No. I don't want it anymore. I came to ask you," Lucia hesitated, "How can I make it leave?"

"You. You're not going to do anything. It likes you. You look just like her." She pointed to a painting on the wall. "My mother's sister!"

"How would I look like her? Who is she? Does she have a connection to the book?" Lucia gripped the book tightly.

"Yes, I've been waiting for you. Ever since I found that - thing! My mother had just died from self-hatred; killed herself with a rope. I never understood why. I went into the attic to find answers, and found the book. I opened it, but nothing was there. When I started to close it, the damned thing pricked me. I thought my eyes were playing tricks on me, but a whole book had written itself in my blood - like it was ink!"

"The book read: Dear sister I know I haven't been very nice since the dare. Now, I'm in trouble, and it's no fun being looked up here in the attic with no one to play with or talk to. So, I will write some 'would you rather' questions. You pick one, and I will do it, OK?"

"That's how it started," the old woman said. "The first questions were just child's play, but as the sisters got older, the questions became more terrible. My aunt started asking my mom who she would rather kill, my grandfather or my grandmother, so my mother stopped talking to her. My aunt started sneaking out of the attic and writing things on the walls and mirrors. My mom had enough, and she finally moved out. The next year, my grandparents told my mother that her sister killed herself. My mom blamed herself for not being there for her. They all knew that my aunt had mental issues, but they left my mother alone to deal with it by herself. Back in those days, therapy for a woman was locking them up. My mom eventually had me and named me after my aunt, Jane. Ten years later she killed herself, leaving my father and I alone. If your parents are still here, kid, love them."

"Yeah, I would if I could," Lucia replied. "My parents basically abandoned me. I just need to know how to rid myself of this book."

"You need to finish the blood sacrifice. Kill five people you love, then you can pass the book to someone else - or you kill yourself." The old lady grinned. "Choose wisely."

"Wait, if those are the choices, how did you get rid of the book?" Lucia asked. "You're here so..."

"I never loved after my parents left, so what can I say?" The woman stood, "being alive just wasn't me."

"What do you me-." Before she could finish, the woman disappeared. An old newspaper lay on the couch.

The headline read: **Young woman sets house on fire, killing herself. Mystery book found - could be worth a fortune.**

"I was talking to a ghost?" She dropped to her knees.

"I'm all alone and my only friend is dead. What do I do?" The book opened.

Choose

Kill Your Parents or Kill Yourself

She slammed the book closed.

"Jane, the original owner of this book, come out! I'm calling you out!" The silence answered her. The book opened again.

Choose

They don't love you. Why chase after them? My family did the same. I can show myself to you, but after that, you must make your choice or I will take your life as well as theirs. Do you want to see me?" the book questioned.

"Yes." Lucia saw a little girl.

"Jane?"

"I'm the original Jane, before my sister gave my name away," she said.

"Why did you choose me of all people?" Lucia asked her.

"You were the odd one out, like me. We are so alike. My parents disliked me, and I had to show your parent's truth too."

"What do you mean?"

"Those letters you found were written by me, not your parents. I did that for you, so we can be together - sisters. They didn't write those things, but I promise that's how they felt." The little girl grabbed Lucia's hand.

"What, those were fake? How would you know how my parents felt if you never met them!" She snatched her hand away.

"You were desperate for love from your teacher, but I'm the only one you need. I rid you of him. I love you sister."

"I'm not your sister, I loved my family, you took them away!" She threw the book.

"If you loved them so much, why did you kill your mom before school? Then, you wrote yourself that letter."

"I would never." her eyes widened.

"Whose blood did you think you were soaking in? Then you sliced your best friend and threw her down a sewage drain, when your dad came to check on you, you buried him alive with his newly-wedded wife. Look under your nails." Lucia stared at the dirt under her nails.

"When you kissed your teacher, and you noticed he didn't like it, you murdered him and his wife. I admit I was the one giving you the choices, but you made them. You did all the hard work for me. All I need is you now. Your blood shall finish my book. I shall publish it in the depths of hell." Jane giggled.

"No, you're lying. I didn't kill anyone. You just told me you would kill them if I didn't." The television suddenly switched on.

"We are still looking for 17-year-old Lucia Sandra," the news anchor read. "She is wanted for murder. A reward of seventy thousand dollars has been offered. She is believed to have murdered her parents, her stepmother, and two teachers - Thomas John and Laicey John. It is also reported that she attacked her classmate and former best friend. If you have any information on Lucia's whereabouts, please contact the police immediately. We have an interview with her former best friend."

Tanya's face was on the screen. "I know that we weren't on good terms anymore because of what she did to me, but I never thought it would get this bad. If I could change things I would, but please, Lucia, please turn yourself in." The television switched off.

Lucia couldn't process what was happening. "How do I know you're telling the truth this time, huh? You lied about the letters and everything else! So now you want to be truthful?"

"I can't control people." Jane said. "I can control what they see, and everything you saw today was fake, but they don't know that. In about two hours your phone will be traced to this location, and the police will come and collect you. You will be put on trial for murder and given the death sentence. I can prevent this. I know I have lied, but I'm not lying about you and your parents, you die twice. Once here and again when you go to hell. I can make your parents go to hell, too."

"So, what about the book?" Lucia's hands were shaking. "Was it real?"

"Very real - everything you did was because of the book. It holds my demonic powers. I **am** the book! You thought you were making a different choice every time, but it was all the same. Join me." She held her hand out. "There is no other option."

This was the only possibility for Lucia now. She grabbed the little girl's hand. Jane touched the wall and started a fire. Soon, the whole home was burning with Lucia in it. When the firefighters finally extinguished the blaze, they found a leather book laying atop the ashes.

"Guys how did this book survive this." The firefighter picked up the book.

"I don't know, but I'll give it to my daughter. She like the creepy ones." They laughed, not knowing what they would release.

ABOUT THE AUTHOR

I am a writer who like to write horror and fantasy stories.
My favorite stories are the ones with the most complicated
plot twist.

KINDRED ROOTS

BY EDDIE COLLINS III

My eyes opened to the popcorn ceiling. The minute hand chased the second hand, failing to realize it would never keep up. I took a deep breath and exhaled slowly. My lips quivered before parting.

"Ah." Still here. A soprano trapped inside a tenor.

I did the exercises, I followed the instructions! Deep breaths, A, E, I, O, U! Applied pressure to my larynx, humming, reading that poem with loud music blasting in my ears...and yet, she haunts me.

Puberphonia is what they call her. Functional falsetto; I can't afford treatment because I don't work, not because I'm lazy, but I can't raise my voice above a whisper. I scrunch my nose as I scroll through a virtual world, scoffing at my peers, living lives I can only fabricate while walking Mimi.

The bunk bed creaked as I shifted my feet to the floor. A loud thud sent tremors between my toes.

"Nana?" only a muffled groan from the floor. I rushed to the basement and found her with a box on top of her. Nana hid her gaze behind her lank hair. I stood her to her feet and helped her up the squeaky stairs. She took a seat at the table.

"Nana." The same woman that could hear a pin drop leaned forward to hear me. "What were you doing down there? Why didn't you call me?"

"Didn't want to be a bother!" she dusted the black from her nightgown. "You help enough. Wanted to go through that box of books, not be under them." Nana said before letting out a brief chuckle.

I went down to the basement to retrieve the box of books. I wiped the black off my feet onto my pants legs before entering the kitchen. Nana and I went through the box and sorted through picture books, obituaries, and my father's old college books.

One book made my flesh crawl. It appeared to be covered in roots; vascular, like a man on steroids.

"What's this?" I asked. Nana put on her glasses.

"Great grandmother was a gypsy, witch or sum. Ma never let us touch it. Garbage pile it goes."

"Can I have it?" I asked.

"If you'd like." Nana's thumbs chased one another as she looked down at her lap. Her bottom lip was like a stuck drawbridge until I asked what was on her mind.

"Chance, I know you have a...problem, but I don't want it to be your excuse not to live." My momentum slowed as I sorted through the books. "Let me help you. Get this treatment in India, or whatever."

"No, Nana. I have to do this on my own."

"At least let me help you start a business."

"Nana-"

"I think losing your parents may have caused trauma-"

"Nana!" I placed my hand on hers. "I'll figure it out." She shook her head and told me she hoped I did before she died.

I kissed Nana on her gravitated jaw and thanked her for the book.

Crickets and katydids performed they're chaotic symphony as the summer breeze filled the room. The TV's lights bounced off the walls until something captivated my attention. A show about a powerless boy who dreamed of becoming a hero in a world filled with power. As expected, his wish is granted through perseverance, power he fought so desperately to attain.

Rubbish. That's not how reality works. You're dealt a hand in life, with the option to fold or put on a poker face. There is no reshuffle.

I turned off the TV and reclined in my chair. A thud against the window startled me, causing me to fall. A bird had fallen victim to the power of Windex.

I squinted at the red smear. Through the reflection, I saw something propped on my pillow. The book I got from Nana. The book I believed to be in the living room where I left it. I grabbed it and sat on the edge of my bed.

When I opened the book, the pages were blank. No index, numbers, dedication. As I flipped through the book with my thumb, I felt a searing pain, perhaps the worst paper cut I'd ever experienced. The Book hit the wall as I jumped in circles. I sucked the copper-flavored red until the pain subsided.

After a bit of first aid, I retrieved the book from the floor. How much blood did I lose? The blood seeped into the blank page and began to take shape. Symbols? No, words.

Offer received, red as cherry. Eat the fowl, to sing like a canary. The house finch lay motionless on the window sill. I tossed the book across the room. Blood pounded in my ears, throat dry as sand, and I could hardly move.

Nana's concern for me downstairs sobered me up. I composed myself and knocked on the floor to let her know that I was alright.

All night, I paced the room. The book didn't move, but was in my line of sight at every waking moment. After mustering up the courage, I took up the book again. The words were still there, with the stained ink now a shade of brown.

My feet dragged as I walked over to the window, cracked the screen, and grabbed the little bird. The shivers in my body wouldn't stop, but I had nothing to lose. I tossed my head back. It felt as if I'd taken a chunk out of Nana's memory foam.

Expeditiously, I chased the winged creature down with water, coughing and gagging. With every cough, I felt a vibration in my throat, a thunder in my chest, and breath passed through my mouth like silk. Goggle-eyed, I spoke.

"Ah." I quickly covered my mouth when I heard the base. It worked! Freedom at last! I could live a normal life, embrace my masculinity, and help Nana!

When I looked at the book, the words were gone. Instead, there seemed to be an image of a woman's ear. At that moment, I vowed to never take up the book again.

Finally, I obtained my deepest desire, but after having the pitch of a woman for twenty-three years, transitioning proved to be challenging. Nana got used to my voice after a while, wondering who stole my phone, calling the police, thinking someone broke into the house, but she was happy for me.

Granted, I had everything I desired, but I had no idea where to begin on this new journey. Nana was one of the only people who knew what I sounded like. So, to everyone else, my bass would be no surprise.

Hailey was the girl across the street. When I moved in with Nana, I'd always watch her play alone in the yard, or read on the porch. I'd get weak in the knees at the mention of her name. She had ginger hair, radiant as the sun, and a taste for fashion.

Things were different. There wasn't a voice in the back of my head saying she'd mock me or laugh at my voice. I took a deep breath and headed out the door with Mimi. There she was, sitting on the swing, a cup of coffee in one hand and a book in the other.

I let Mimi off the leash and put on an Oscar-worthy performance as I chased her up to Hailey's steps. With Mimi in arms, I was met by a sunny smile and emerald eyes.

"S-sorry about that." I said.

"It's okay. Chance, right?" she asked. I nodded. " Funny, you've been here for like, eleven years?"

"This fall."

"And we've never spoken till now." I apologized. Hailey asked if Mimi were friendly. I walked the shih Tzu up to the swing and allowed her to pet Mimi.

As I started to talk, Hailey frowned. She sniffed her hand after petting the dog. She'd just had a bath; I guess I didn't do that good of a job.

"So, I was thinking..." I said. Hailey's eyes danced around before she covered her nose with her book. "Maybe we can get to know each other, hang out?" she shut her eyes tight and muffled under the book that she'd love to, but she had a jealous-type boyfriend.

Of course she did. I told her I understood and headed down the driveway. After returning from my walk, Nana was taking her usual plethora of pills at the kitchen island. When I announced myself, she rested her fingers on her nose and welcomed me home.

"Nana...does my breath stink?" I asked. She blew.

"Ever since your voice changed, maybe we should see a doctor." A bead of sweat trickled down my spine, my armpits grew cold. That's why Hailey...

No matter how much I brushed, the smell wouldn't subside. Chewing an entire pack of gum made it bearable. Now I could move on to phase two, making money.

After a few weeks of applying, I managed to land a job at a shipping center. The labor was intensive, but the payout was worth it. I was able to help Nana with bills, fix up the house, and keep the fridge full.

Nana would wait up for me every night. The more I was away, the more drastic changes I noticed in her, pale in the face, chapped lips, and no motivation to do anything but watch her soap operas. When I'd offer to take her to the doctor, she'd always perk up and decline, assuring me it was just old age.

One evening after work, I hit Mimi with the front door as I entered. She ran to the opposite side of the room and cowered under the TV stand. The air was putrid. She must've gone in the house and felt guilty.

"Hi, Nana." Nothing, she laid motionless in the loveseat with her head cocked to the side.

I covered my nose as I approached her. She had defecated on herself.

"Ugh! Come on Nana! You had an accident!" I shook her vigorously by the shoulders, nothing. I put my ear to her chest and only heard my short-lived breaths.

I screamed and turned in every direction. Someone! I had to call someone! They'd understand me on the phone clearly now because of ...the book.

I rushed up the stairs, slashed my hand with a blade, and slammed it on the empty page. The page soaked up the blood like a sponge.

"Save my Nana! PLEASE!" the blood slowly formed into words that read, *A gift of air, a task of sorts. Give a piece of limb, and I shall revive the corpse.*

My eyebrows drew together and I rested my hand on my furrowed forehead as my jaw hung to my lap. I took several steps back until my heel met with my bed frame. I sank into the worn out mattress and stared at the blank wall.

"How much?" I asked. The blood began to shift on the page. It read, *A piece for peace. A finger, lobe, or toe. Harden your heart, or Nana must go.*

Every swallow felt like GERD as I made my way into the garage. I turned on the shop lights and dragged myself to the work bench. My hands trembled as I reached for the saw. Giant bread knife in hands, I rested my fingers on the workbench.

The teeth of the blade rested on my hand. I screamed to the top of my lungs, but there was no momentum. Coward! I threw the blade across the garage. Mimi stood in the door frame trembling as if fresh out of ice.

"It doesn't have to be me." I said. A salty tear raced down the corner of my mouth. I snatched the shears off the wall. Mimi ran in terror as I darted after her. Cornered, she shook under the kitchen island. My pursuit came to a halt as urine trickled to the floor.

"What am I doing?" the shears fell to my side. "I have to accept it, I can't hurt..." I looked over at my deceased grandmother and down at the sheers. With staggered breaths, I marched over to the cold body and took her hand in mine. I wheezed as I shut my eyes tight and rested her pinky between the rusted blades.

Crunching followed by gushing. Teeth exposed, my mouth drew back. My lower eyelids were tense and drawn. I could feel it in my hand; cold and wet. Without looking, I ran up the stairs and slammed it onto the blank page.

Slowly, I opened the book. There it was, the image of Nana's pinky. It slowly faded away, and the image of the woman's ear reappeared accompanied by half of her face.

Coughing and wheezing echoed up the stairs. I ran, falling in the process. There she was, standing. She turned to me with rosy cheeks.

"Stay there, Chance. I had an-" I held her tight. Telling her how I thought I lost her. When I grabbed her hands, all digits were accounted for.

Was I dreaming? No, couldn't have. Mimi was still shaken up. She refused to approach me or Nana. I took the next few days off work to monitor Nana. Normal. In fact, better than ever. She started going on walks, tending to the flower beds, interacting with strangers, even going on a date with Mr. Jefferson.

The only downside was Mimi. Since Nana cheated death, Mimi couldn't stand to be near her. She now resided in my room, followed me everywhere I went, and would growl and snap at Nana if she got too close.

I concluded that with every blessing the book granted, there was a drawback, like Mimi, or my breath. High risk equals high reward. The only confusing thing about the book was the half image of the woman. Who was she?

Telling Nana about the book would be a mistake, telling her she died would be a crime. I pried the floor boards under my bed up and hid the book there. Last time, no more.

With my wishes granted, I had the power to accomplish anything I put my mind to.

However, the book was displeased. I was tormented by round-the-clock whispers that grew stronger when I laid down. So much so, I'd rest my back against my headrest and watch the sun rise.

The lack of rest affected my performance at work. I went from employee of the month to filling out job applications. My health started to decline, bills began to pile, and I had constant hallucinations of a woman standing in the corner of my room.

Enough was enough! I pushed my bed to the side of the room and removed the floorboards. The whispers stopped. There it was, just how I left it. I took the book in hand and slowly pried it open.

"Chance?" I closed the book and turned to my door frame. "Hanging out with the girlies, need anything?" Mimi growled as Nana bounced and danced in the doorway. She was happy. Always, happy. I'd grind my teeth at the sight.

"I'm fine." I said. As she started to walk away, I stopped her. "Actually, do you have any old photos of you from when you lived in Louisiana?"

"In the basement." She blew a kiss and waved goodbye.

After an hour of going through dusty boxes, I found it. A scrapbook filled with black and white images of Nana's childhood. As I flipped through the images, a picture of a woman stood out to me. A woman by the name of Bohemia. Dressed in ancient garbs with beads around her neck. The date was faded.

I took the image from the scrapbook, carefully folded it in half, and aligned it with the half-image from the book. A perfect match.

With heavy eyes, I ran my thumb across the edge of the page. When I pressed my bloody thumb on the blank page, it seeped in.

"This you?" I asked. The blood shifted and spelled out *yes*. "What do you want?" *To bring you joy.* "By taking everything away from me? Keeping me awake throughout the night?" *If you don't want to go insane, you must finish the game.*

Just one more final request and I'd be finished with this curse forever. I chewed my flaky lips. I shut my eyes tight before releasing a thick cough.

"I want to be the most famous, and wealthiest actor in the world. No drawbacks, problems, or technicalities; just a good life. What will you have me do?"

The ink blood swirled rapidly before filling the page. The book read, *Bring the soul, who made your life a curse. Bury him with the seed, beneath the earth. His soul shall provide nutrients, and sprout a tree. Within a year's time, Nana must eat its fruit, then, and only then, shall you be...FREE!*

The book slammed and shut tight. The veins in my arms bulged as I desperately tried to open it. I gave up. After hours of reviewing what the book said; I figured it out. The seed was the book. The book would sprout into this tree that would bear fruit, but not without nutrients.

It didn't take long to figure out the soul in question. The soul who brought this life upon me. Balomin Holder, the man responsible for my parents death. He gunned them down eleven years ago. They were caught in the crossfire as he defended his car from a burglar with an automatic rifle. He was released on a technicality. His soul would sprout this tree...it had to.

He served as a youth pastor at a church downtown. Sunday, I convinced Nana that I needed prayer. Prayer for opportunities to land a new job. Nana agreed.

We sat in the back of the congregation, like fish out of water, as people worshiped and prayed. Towards the end of the service. The pastor opened the altar for prayer. Nana nudged me. I walked to the altar and made my request known. The pastor frowned as he rested his palm on my head.

"Young man, there is a demon that haunts your soul, I bind it in the name of Jesus!" he gripped my hand and prayed as another man rested his hand on my back. Through my peripheral vision, I saw him. Holder, reiterating the pastor's words.

After service, the pastor recommended I join the youth program and mentor under Holder. The book was already in motion.

I spent weeks with the man who killed my parents. Not only learning about God, but Holder's habits. Where he worked, what he ate, his hobbies. A part of me wanted to spare him, but a stronger force wanted me to end his pitiful existence.

One night after Bible study, I had Holder drop me off at home. When I told him Nana wouldn't be home for a while, he asked if he could come in. I welcomed him inside and offered him a seat. The same seat Nana defecated in. I offered him tea. He smiled, saying he would love a cool glass. I locked Mimi away in another room. After pouring the tea, I stirred antifreeze in one of the cups. The kitchen knife took shelter under my long-sleeve before I walked the beverages over to the coffee table.

"What did you want to talk about?" I asked. I handed Holder his tea and sat in the chair opposite to him. He took big gulps of the ice tea and sat it down on the coffee table instead of the coaster. He leaned forward.

"The bible."

"Go on." I said.

"You know, I feel like there are areas of...misinterpretation."

"Like?" Holder snapped his finger as if his thoughts would come running.

"Sodom and Gomorrah. If God eradicated the gays..." he reached for my knee. "Then why are they still amongst us?" Holder frowned and shook his head. I stood to my feet and rested my hand on his shoulder.

"I feel the same." I said. When he smiled, I plunged the steel through his ribs and twisted the blade like a key to a lock.

When the body grew stiff, I wrapped the heavy man in the rug like a pig in a blanket. Prior, I spent days digging an eight foot hole in the yard. The body made a large thud as it fell into the earth. I threw the book inside and spent the rest of the night filling the hole.

I fidgeted with things in the backyard for days, trying to make the excavated dirt as inconspicuous as possible. Just when I thought I was losing my mind, that the entire ordeal was a figment of my imagination; a small sprout broke the surface of the earth.

Within an hour, I got a call from an agency, extending me the opportunity to be in a car commercial. I nailed it, and from there, the opportunities kept rolling in.

Commercial after commercial. From background character, to supporting cast, to lead roles. Stand alone TV shows and films came next. My name was up there with the likes of them.

Nana and I walked red carpets, moved into a mansion, and took luxurious trips to some of the most beautiful places in the world. I even proposed to Hailey. I'd accomplished all my dreams in the span of a year.

One night, I tossed and turned in a thirty-thousand dollar bed designed for optimal comfort. I kept hearing faint whispers about, "the fruit".

I jolted out the bed. That's right! It had been a year! Nana had to eat the blood-red fruit in order for this to be over. Nana was confused as to why we were heading back to our old house in Michigan, but she said she trusted me.

The private jet landed by nightfall. Our driver took us to the house. There it was. You could see it from the front yard.

A gnarly looking tree with jagged branches that resembled spider legs covered in vines. Nana and I walked through the house and into the backyard. One singular fruit hung from the tree as it emitted a red aura. I plucked the fruit and walked it over to Nana.

"Here Nana. Eat this fruit, and we'll never have to worry again." She looked down at the fruit and back up to me.

"Haven't steered me wrong yet." She smiled before taking a nibble. Her eyes bucked, pupils dilated before she finished the fruit like a starving dog.

"Nana..." she licked her hand clean when she finished. She suddenly grew stiff, and stared forward.

"Nana! NANA TALK TO ME!" A tear of blood raced down her cheek as she gradually turned white as snow.

Nana's skin hardened, leaving her like a Greek statue. I fell to my knees.

"What've I..." the statue started to crack. As the pieces fell to the ground, it revealed youthful skin. Bohemia stood before me with her arms stretched wide.

"Ah." She said before looking to me. "Thank you blood relative. Centuries, trapped in the dark." She looked around. "My, have things changed. Anyways, see you around kid."

I grabbed her ankle as I sobbed.

"Wh-where's Nana?" I asked.

"D-dead. Thanks to you of course. With your blood and her body, I live once more." She patted my head before opening the back door.

"You said we'd live a happy life."

"I said YOU, not her. I can only look to the future, I never had any control over your destiny. I only needed your blood and a piece of flesh." She kneeled to my eye level. "Don't be so down. Now that your blood courses through the book, you too have the gift of immortality. Ta-ta." Bohemia skipped inside of the house, leaving me lying in what remained of Nana.

ABOUT THE AUTHOR

Eddie Collins III was born and raised in Memphis, TN. In a city known for its reputation for violence and crime, his parents saw an avenue for him through his vivid imagination and love for animals.

When he discovered he could paint images of his imagination for others to see on paper, he fell in love with the art of writing.

ECHOES OF VOLITION

BY CHRIS R

Of course you have free will, you have no choice but to have it.

We begin in a coastal town, where the most eventful thing to happen is the "Name Day Dare". It is almost a custom of the town's youth to spend the night in an abandoned structure on their sixteenth birthday. Oftentimes these young people have boisterous parties in the woods along the shoreline before sending off their slightly drunken guest of honor. There are plenty of abandoned structures in and on the outskirts of town. Closest and safest, are the houses that have been flooded and ruined, burned and never rebuilt, that are enveloped in residential areas. However Motel 86', located half a mile from Aislin's Point (a popular cliff jumping site), is not only the largest structure, but the most popular place to spend the night.

Juke Welton's parents were not the only ones who opposed the dare. However, the Weltons knew they couldn't withhold the Name Day Dare from their son. Juke, as he very well knew, was the first person to complete the dare in three years. He was an ambitious boy; Smart and fit. So, no one was particularly worried about his safety on the night of. For the year leading up to his sixteenth birthday, he boasted about how he had a room reserved for himself at Motel 86'.

The morning after his sixteenth birthday, Juke wandered into town, covered in blood and grime, muttering about decisions. It was not Motel 86' where he chose to sleep the previous night. There were many reasons given by friends who attended his dare party as to why he changed his mind: *He was too drunk to know what he was thinking, He was too excited, He was pressured into it.* He made the choice to instead spend the night in the lighthouse. The tower stands solemn, visible from Aislin's Point, but nearly impossible to get to. Large, jagged rocks block any path from being created, and high tide completely covers the peninsula. It was this choice to spend the night in the lighthouse, that would completely alter the course of the lives in this coastal town.

Five years later, Emcilia Mann is fifteen. It's March, the morning of her sixteenth birthday, and early spring is beginning to seep into town. This morning, the town is adorned with fog and twinkling dew drops on the grass. It's an innocent morning like this, that Emcy races down to the shoreline below Aislin's Point.

With her bag slung over her shoulder and her mind on her destination, she hardly notices the signs of life stirring awake around her. A car starts and Mr. and Mrs. Welton pull out of their drive, heading for the highway. Birds chirp in the treetops as Emcy reaches the sparse woods separating the town from the sea. The birdsong penetrates the mist and overlaps with the lull of water licking the shore.

The shore of Aislin's Cove is littered with water-beaten stones, polished with the waves of the sea. These beautiful specimens of nature are what Emcy has come for. After a moment of rest, she's scouring the ground for the best-looking rocks. She picks out seaglass among the pebbles, adding them to her bag. A dark green stone glints in the sunlight. Emcy adds it to the bag. Something shiny catches her eye from far up on the cliff of Aislin's Point. Letting the glimmering object lead the way, Emcy follows a deer path through the trees and emerges at the top of the point. The object stuck in the ground on the cliff is still reflecting the sun like a shard of a disco ball.

A shard of a disco ball isn't that far from the truth. Somebody, sometime, stuck a fragment of a mirror into the ground. The shard of the mirror is cracked, creating diamonds of reflections. Emcy's amber eyes stare at multiple diamond-shaped faces, studying her freckled, rosaceous cheeks in each reflection.

Suddenly, a gust of wind nearly knocks the mirror shard out of Emcy's hand. As she looks up, her eyes land on the lighthouse. It's boarded up, and has been for years. No one dared go near it after what happened the last time. Emcy remembers the terror Juke brought. Every shop was broken into, almost every house, and sometimes you were unlucky enough to be attacked on the street. People said he was looking for something, but nothing was ever taken. Family pets went missing and showed up gutted on doorsteps. The local police were called, but Juke went missing every time they were milling about. Emcy suspects he was hiding in the lighthouse. The chaos went on for months until finally something catastrophic happened. Emcy's guardian and sister, Gamine, was murdered. No one knows how, as she was perfectly healthy, and there was not even a scratch on her body. She just stopped living. Even though there's no evidence to tie the death to Juke, he tried to take his life that same evening and failed. That was proof enough for Emcy.

The State finally made a decision. It wasn't until Juke Welton was shipped off to an institution, that the neighbors could relax. Though everyone pretended it never happened, the town and the people inside were never really the same.

Emcy was never really the same.

After a moment gazing upon the lighthouse, Emcy sighs, stashes the mirror shard in her bag and turns to move down the bluff. But then, like a whisper, the wind carries a voice. ...*Em*...

She had to have imagined it, but the gooseflesh on her skin doesn't disappear when the wind stops. That voice...

It sounds like Gamine.

Emcy rushes off to the school house, where everyone is already inside. Everyone except a tall, lanky boy called Spliff, who's leaning against the side of the building, an unlit cigarette hanging out of the corner of his mouth.

Emcy beelines to Spliff, who doesn't seem to notice her striding up to him. She plucks the unlit cigarette from his mouth and puts it in her own.

Spliff notices her then. "Hey-- Oh, it's you." He forces a small smile.

"What're you doing out here not smoking?" Emcy digs a lighter out of her pocket and holds it out for Spliff to take. He holds up his own.

"Already got mine."

"Then really, what's on your mind?"

Spliff sighs, takes the cig back from Emcy and lights it. After a long drag, he responds. "Juke's coming home today."

"I thought not until next month?" Emcy's heart skips.

"Mom got a call from the hospital, says he's had good behavior." Another drag. This was rare for Spliff, this type of conversation. He doesn't talk about his brother, especially not around Emcy. He feels too guilty. Everyone in town knows he's a Welton, a villain. Every teacher he's ever had has always kept an unnecessarily close eye on him, as if the younger will follow the older. Why would he bother to talk about his own story? Everyone else is doing a fine job of making it up for him.

Spliff stares into the trees behind the schoolhouse, where the lighthouse rests just beyond. "I heard someone in the lighthouse this morning." Emcy says.

Spliff turns, whatever fog clouded his mind suddenly clears. They speak at the same time. "Why were you--"

"Don't think I'm crazy--"

Spliff pauses. "You go first." Another drag.

Emcy takes a breath, unexpectedly anxious. Is she being insensitive for bringing it up? Today of all days? "Something's going on at the lighthouse and I want to stop it."

Spliff tips his head back against the side of the school-house, blowing smoke through his nose. "No one is stupid enough to go back there."

"I might be. But only if you'll come with me."

"Em--"

"Before you think I'm totally out of my mind, I just want to be sure whoever went in there is okay."

"Right. Nothing to do with your long-standing, intense obsession about the place."

"Save your sarcasm asshole. I'm not going to do anything without you. It was just weird this morning. It was like the tower was... staring back."

Spliff crushes the cigarette into the ground with his foot and offers a small, nervous laugh. "And you're sure you're not just reading into the lore a little too much?"

"Meet me at Aislin's Point tonight and you'll see what I mean. Deal?"

Spliff sighs, "Deal."

The evening of Emcy's sixteenth birthday is a warm one. She inhales the night air, calming her nerves. Emcy is perched on top of Aislin's Point, watching the water lap at the shore of the cove beneath her. A soft breeze plays with the loose ends of her braided hair as she waits for Spliff. The clouds have turned a soft shade of orange when he finally emerges from the woods sporting an overnight bag on his shoulders.

Emcy tugs him over to the cliff edge and points to the lighthouse.

He takes a moment to stare, lighting a cigarette as he does. "It just seems like the ol', eerie-as-hell lighthouse to me."

"Maybe." Emcy sighs, looking for signs of mystery. There are so many questions about the past that desperately want to be answered.

Suddenly, a gust of wind blows against Emcy's face. The cigarette is knocked out of Spliff's grasp. He follows with a curse, but Emcy is focused on another sound that the wind brought.

Em...

Emcy jumps to her feet. "Did you hear that?"

Spliff is busy searching the ground for his lost smoke. "Hear what?"

"Listen."

The wind blows again, softer now, and with it a softer voice.

...choose me.

Spliff has gone pale-green, and for a moment Emcy thinks he might be sick. "That sounds like..." But he doesn't finish. He doesn't need to. It's Gamine.

"Is that weird enough for you?" Emcy interprets Spliff's silence as agreement. "I think the lighthouse and your brother are connected. It can't be a coincidence that your brother comes home the same day I start hearing voices from the lighthouse."

"You sound crazy."

Emcy can't help but give a nervous laugh. "You heard it too. Now, are you coming with me?" She shrugs her bag higher up on her shoulder.

Spliff tightens his grip on his own. "Yes." He answers firmly.

"Are you sure?" She lifts her head off his shoulder and shifts to properly face him. With a stiff nod, the pair head down to the shore.

At the base of the peninsula, the tower stretches into the sky, casting deep shadows onto the beach. Low tide allows the pair to climb over the rocks, still slick with water. Cool wind whistles through the lighthouse's cracked bricks. There's something sinister in the very foundation. Emcy can feel it, and still she finds herself drawn to it.

Spliff slides his hand into the crevice of Emcy's elbow as they reach the boarded door. With a couple of heavy kicks from both of them, the rotted boards give way, revealing a small circular room. In it rests a bedframe with no mattress, a shelf mounted on the wall, a staircase, and a cracked mirror.

Spliff releases an audible sigh. "I don't know what I was working myself up for. A near-empty room isn't so bad." He busies himself searching through his bag for a flashlight as the light begins to disappear with the setting sun.

Emcy wanders to the shelf, where a leather journal sits upright, seemingly untouched by the litter and dust around it.

"Who knows," She says, caressing the binding of the lonely book. "Maybe there are demons in the walls."

"Not funny." Spliff says, ignoring his increasing blood pressure. "I can't find my flashlight. I swear to god I brought it though, it's the one with the engraving on it."

"You mean the one you ruined with a knife. Let's hope I have one." Emcy begins rummaging through her own bag. Her hand pushes through the rocks and gems, a balled up sweater, and catches on the mirror shard from Aislin's Point. Emcy quickly retrieves her bleeding hand, and her flashlight.

"Shit." Emcy presses her bleeding thumb to her lips.

"You okay?" Spliff asks.

"Yeah, fine. Just, the stupid glass." Emcy clicks on the flashlight, illuminating the room and all the dust floating in the air.

"Why do you have glass in your bag?"

"Doesn't matter. Ugh, of course I don't have bandaids." The cut on her thumb drips down her arm. Emcy uses the hem of her shirt to clean it up. "What I'm really interested in is this book." She retrieves it from the shelf. On the front is a purple gem embedded in the leather. "You with shiny things. I thought this was a ghost hunt."

"Just look at it."

Spliff picks up the journal and flips through it. "Empty."

"With no dust." Emcy takes the journal back, bloody prints transferring to the blank paper. The blood fades into the page and is replaced with swirling ink.

You have heard my voice and found my field. Do you desire monotonous regularity or do you possess the curiosity for the truth revealed?

"I don't like this." Spliff says, reaching to take the book from Emcy.

She moves it away from his reach, studying the words. "Do you think..." "I *think* that this feels like a contract. One I don't wanna sign."

"I want the truth. What if this leads us there?" As the words are spoken, the choices on the page disappear. She wonders if she's imagining it, but the book becomes warmer. The leather relaxes, and Emcy thinks it must be the heat from her hands.

It must be.

"What happened?" Spliff strides over to get a better look over Emcy's shoulder. "I think I... chose." Emcy waits for the next swirl of choices, but they never come. She flips through the pages with her non-injured hand. Why did they appear in the first place? Her injured thumb throbs against the pressure of the book's spine. She switches hands and presses her bloody thumb into the page.

"What're you--" Spliff begins to object, but falters when a new set of choices appear on the page.

Friend and foe wear the same face. Is it pain or pleasure that you embrace?

"Don't choose pain." Spliff says quickly.

"Well, I'm already in pain--" Suddenly a scream erupts from Emcy as she drops the book to the ground. She grabs her hand as her body explodes with burning pain. Blood begins to flow from her wound again, dripping onto the stone floor.

Tears prick Emcy's eyes when suddenly, the pain ceases. She straightens up to face a panicked Spliff searching through his bag for something to help. Her face is hot, her arms trembling and voice shaking when she speaks. "I hated that."

"Are you okay? I might have something--" Spliff presents a small roll of gauze.

"I'm okay, it doesn't hurt anymore." She sighs. "Looks like I need to be more careful about what I say."

"Why didn't it happen when I said pain first?"

Emcy retrieves the book. "Maybe it's because my blood was on the paper." "So it's a fucked up voodoo doll?

Great." Spliff gathers himself from the floor. "Do you think Juke found this book?"

Understanding hangs in the air around them. Whatever happened to Juke, whatever happened to the town all those years ago, the book was there.

After some convincing, Emcy places the leather book back on the shelf. For hours, neither speaks. Spliff stares at the shelf with his knees curled into his chest. The book stares back, as if forming thoughts of its own. The night air creeps into the circular room, chilling the stone beneath where they rest. Emcy squirms in her sleep, unable to lay comfortably with her dreams.

Blood and ink flow like violent waterfalls. Choices to make. Running down spiraling stairs towards the red sea, only to be pulled under the waves. A voice calls out to her. Gamine. A whisper of saving grace. The book sits there beneath the raging tide, glowing with warmth. A rope slithers around her neck to free her from the darkness of the depths, only to yank her awake.

Emcy snaps her eyes open at sunrise to find Spliff has not moved more than a couple inches from his book-watching spot. If it weren't for the lines on his face, obviously made from his jacket sleeves, she would have assumed he hadn't slept. Emcy rubs her eyes, clearing the fast fading dream from her mind.

She yawns and stands up to stretch. Without thinking, she crosses the room and slips the book into her bag. The purple gem glows more intensely now.

"Woah woah, what're you doing?" Spliff jumps to his feet.

A low hum, like a pur, fills the air around Emcy. "I need to know the truth." She says automatically.

Spliff considers Emcy for a moment. And as the pair step out into the morning sun, he understands that something in his friend is changed.

This morning, Juke Welton stands at the corner, staring into the windows of the shop he attempted to rob years earlier in a desperate rampage. He wonders if the key is still here somewhere... His doctors advise him not to think too hard about his past. He doesn't think of the break-in with much remorse anymore, as he's spent years feeling guilty over the damage caused. But the windows are fixed, and the walls are patched now. Juke learned with the help of his doctors, that you have to choose to let things go. He knows that you always have to choose.

In the distance, he can hear the crunch of shoes on gravel and the voice of his brother. Juke follows the sound, and intercepts the pair at the end of the street.

Spliff quickly swallows the previous conversation. "Juke, what're you doing here?" Juke studies Emcy with his sunken eyes. He inhales sharply. "Put it back."

Emcy meets his gaze. Her hand rests inside her bag, on the binding of the book. Of *her* book.

"Juke, let's get you home." Spliff starts to move towards him, reaching for his arm. Juke backs away. His eyes are wide, fearful and alert. "The door..."

"What do you mean?" Emcy reveals the book. "What door?"

In an instant, Juke crosses the distance between them and snatches the journal from her hands. Emcy, who was holding on tighter than she realized, is yanked to the ground. Juke throws the book down and unsheathes a knife from his waist. Spliff, seeing the knife, dives for Juke. The two barrel into the ground, grappling for each other. With her heart pounding in her ears, Emcy recovers and reaches out for the journal. It lays open on the ground, so close, when Juke's knife slices her arm. She recoils as the blade plunges into the pages. Suddenly, with an eruption of force, the fighters are thrown backwards into the gravel.

For a moment, dust hangs in the air. Spliff sits up gasping for breath. Emcy brushes gravel from her hair and pinches her shallow cut. Juke is unmoving. Alive, but unmoving. "What... the fuck..." Spliff sputters.

"The book can't be destroyed." As she says it, Emcy knows it to be true. Relief floods over her.

"We have to get Juke home." Spliff is already up on his feet, throwing his brother's arm over his shoulder. "Help please?"

Emcy gathers herself and goes to retrieve the book. That's when she notices the ink displayed on the page.

Uncover the past and see it's run, risking the death of one, or leave the future unprecedented for anyone?

Ignoring the choices for now, Emcy rushes to help Spliff. Together, they carry Juke home. All is silent except for a low hum in Emcy's ear. It's at this moment that she's sure the book has chosen her.

Juke is laid safely down on the couch in the front room of the house. Spliff immediately disappears to the kitchen. Emcy can hear the sound of cupboards opening and closing, the clink of glasses and running water.

Emcy opens her book, flipping to the page displaying the choices. She looks from the page to Juke, and back at the page. She's angry. Angry at Juke for trying to destroy the book and ruin her mission of uncovering the truth of what happened all those years ago. The truth of what happened to Gamine. Emcy digs out a pen. She scribbles on the page.

Gamine? What if I don't choose?

Her writing fades into the paper and is replaced by new swirls of ink.

**Fear is pain arriving from the anticipation of evil.
But what is evil but inaction?**

As she reads, the words fade.

Juke begins to stir.

The hum grows louder.

She considers the choices on the page. Who will be sacrificed, Emcy can't predict. She must know the truth. From down the hall, she can hear Spliff's footsteps coming back. Emcy quickly stashes the book. He holds a glass of water in his hand.

Spliff lays his hand on Juke's shoulder and gently shakes him. "Time to wake up, dude." But Juke doesn't stir.

Spliff shakes again with more force.

Juke doesn't stir.

"Juke!" Spliff yells in his ear. He leans down closer to his brother's face, listening to his lips. There's no sound. No breath. No pulse. No life. The water glass falls, shattering the silence. "Oh my god." Spliff speeds through every curse he knows, shaking his brother, desperate to wake him up.

Emcy stands up and begins to back away. Did she do this? Did she choose this? Did she mean to?

As if sensing Emcy's thoughts, Spliff turns on her. His eyes are red and wide. "The book did something." He accuses.

Emcy does nothing but shake her head.

The hum grows louder.

"Give me the book!" Spliff is yelling now, advancing on his friend.

Emcy backs away, heading for the door. "I didn't..." She says quietly.

"Was this you?" Spliff pauses in shock and disbelief. "WAS THIS YOU?" He screams. She can't answer. She isn't sure. Her words are all tangled up in her throat. Everything but an apology chokes her, threatening to pull her under. So she runs. She runs out of the door and down the drive. Her feet thump against the ground in time with her heart. She runs all the way until she reaches Ailsin's Point. It isn't until her feet have stopped that she realizes where they've taken her.

Emcy stumbles to the top of the cliff, her breath catching in her throat as if an invisible rope is wrapped around her neck. She places the book on the ground and sits next to it, hugging herself around the middle and swaying back and forth.

"It's fine." She tells herself and wipes tears from her eyes.

Emcy grabs her pen and opens to a blank page.

What do I do?

The ink absorbs into the page, but no response appears.

Emcy retrieves the glass shard from her bag. It seems impossible that less than twenty four hours ago she was pocketing this piece. The glass slices into her arm with ease, allowing a fresh line of blood to form. Droplet by droplet, it stains the page.

The hum grows louder. And this time, she lets herself embrace it. It wraps around her, subduing her guilt and shame. Almost numbly, she gazes at the new ink.

The sun will set and the future will cease to be, or reset the clock and find the door to which you have the key.

Emcy looks up at the sun. It's almost midday. She knows she can't waste time. The book has chosen her, she cannot disappoint. Not like Juke. She jumps to her feet. The door. Juke never found it. She remembers the break-ins and the fear of being jumped while walking alone in the street. Emcy is sure he was looking for the key. The key that she now somehow possesses. Emcy gazes over the cliff edge at the shore below. Aislin's Cove is full of mysteries, but not home to any door. Juke has already searched every shop in town, and while she could retrace his steps, the pit in her stomach tells her that she'll be as unsuccessful as he was. Her eyes search the horizon and come to rest on the lighthouse.

Of course.

Suddenly, it seems so clear. *The door is inside the light-house!*

By the time the tide allows Emcy to safely make her way to the tower, the sun hangs low in the sky.

"I better be right." Emcy mutters under her breath as she climbs over the slick stones. The diminishing sunlight doesn't penetrate the semi-familiar circular room. The empty bed frame and decaying shelves cast even more sinister shadows than before. The gloom is darker, the silence somehow louder. The mirror is gone.

Emcy reaches into her bag and gathers the mirror shard in her hand. She grips it hard, feeling the edges dig into her palm. She needs to focus. She's running out of time. The hum grows louder.

The door is here somewhere. She just has to find the mirror.

Emcy tip toes up the spiral staircase leading up to the top of the tower. She passes another circular room that has nothing in it, most likely picked through by young people long ago. She passes another with peeling wallpaper and frayed carpet. Finally, after what feels like hours, she reaches what has to be the last room before the top. In this room, she finds what she's searching for.

She spots a cracked mirror in a room piled with junk.

The upper right corner of the mirror is missing, leaving only the backing frame exposed. As Emcy approaches,

climbing over boating equipment and other rubbish, she
hears a familiar voice. Gamine.

Fix me...Find me...

A mysterious purple light slowly fills the circular room,
bathing everything in a deeper shadow than before. The
lull surrounding Emcy swallows her discernment whole.
Her palms sweat, and her chest swells with tension. However, captivated by the glow from the mirror, she places the
book in the center of the room. She takes care to make sure
it is open to a blank page. It's what it wants. Emcy is sure.

The hum grows louder.

Emcy cautiously steps closer to the mirror and watches
as her grisly reflection comes into frame. Her eyes have
sunken into her freckled cheeks. Her dirty hair hangs out
of her braid in knotted clumps. Her blood-stained shirt
hangs loosely off her body, seeming to be baggier now

than when she put it on yesterday morning. Emcy
touches her hollow cheeks, wondering if this is what Juke
felt. She hugs her shoulders, wondering if she'll ever hug
Spliff again. The voice whispers, sounding as though it
were coming from Emcy's own head. Is it? She can't be
sure.

I have answers...

Answers. Yes. Gamine. That's what Emcy has been after
all this time. Emcy places the mirror shard in the empty
space of the frame. The broken piece clicks into place as if
it were magnetic. Suddenly, the room erupts into swirls of

purple light, and the clutter begins to swirl in the air, as if it were made of feathers. The mirror no longer shows Emcy's reflection, but rather a ghastly entity covered in thin black veils. The entity reaches a cracked, bony hand out to Emcy, right through the mirror, and clutches her arm.

Emcy shrieks and falls backwards, ripping herself from the grasp. The lull that envelops her body is gone, and for the first time all day, she realizes how tired she is, how fragile she feels.

This is not how this was supposed to go. It was supposed to be Gamine. The betrayal in Emcy's heart overwhelms her. She searches the room with her eyes, finding a flare gun. She lunges for it as the entity begins pulling itself out of the mirror. A numbing, overwhelming calm fills the space, creeping into Emcy's head, filling it with fluff. If she gives in, she won't feel herself wither away to nothingness, feeding the entity beyond the mirror. She aims the gun and fires.

With a deafening bang, the room fills with a blinding light. For one moment, all is quiet, then the next, Emcy is rolling over, trying to brush broken glass from her mangled clothes and sliced skin. She wanders over to the shattered frame, trying to shake the ringing in her ears.

Adrenaline begins to dissipate as she stares at the mess in front of her. Thousands of tiny bleeding Emcilias stare back at her from the pieces scattered across the ground. "It's over." She whispers.

In the darkness behind her something sinister slithers.

Emcy sinks to the floor in relief. Tears swell in her eyes, but only two fall before a coarse necklace slides over her head. A rope, malevolent in its very being, has hooked itself around a support beam and wrenches Emcy towards the ceiling. She begins to squirm, but it's too late. Her adrenaline is gone, limbs turned to jelly. There's no fighting back.

Emcilia Mann hangs, swaying lightly, in the top most room of the lighthouse, gasping for air but receiving none. Blood trickles down her ravaged arms, dripping from her fingertips onto the floor. The book lays open beneath her, receiving the crimson gifts.

Deep within the pages, ink begins to swirl.

ABOUT THE AUTHOR

Whatever you do, don't go into Chris R's google docs. You will only find pieces of unfinished stories and half built worlds that only leave you wanting more. It pains Chris as much as the next writer to have so many old stories from middle school rotting away in storage on your laptop when they hold so much potential.

Chris is currently twenty-one, and has been creating stories since before they could write on paper (just ask their grandmother, the former scribe). When they were eleven, they finished their first novel, and were rejected from seven agencies. Of course they were. They were eleven with no previous professional writing experience. Ten years later, Chris is still working on the novel, and in the meantime trying to build up their writing resume in other ways. They want nothing from their writing except for at least one person to enjoy it.

Outside of writing, Chris coaches competitive gymnastics for a living, and enjoys watching their fair share of anime and bad horror movies. Chris longs deeply for a cat, but unfortunately is not allowed to own one because of their grumpy landlords (Both of them are wonderful people).

Chris also understands that they are really bad at writing about themselves, and they are much better at writing fiction.

TO LIVE AND LET DIE

BY AARAN THAKORE

It happened again. The words. They appeared out of nowhere. Thin air like they say.

And then I was there. Another time.

The ocean. It's thrashing waves. The boat. It's aching limbs. The people. Their cries within.

Blood. The chance to relive. To live or let die. Try or let die.

Because that's the choice. That comes in the neatly-bound leather book. To turn back the clock. Or to choose to not.

It started about a week after. The blank pages of a notebook suddenly finding the words to fill themselves. At first it was just the once. Then once a month. But now it's happening almost every day. The same choice. Everyday. The same five words. To go or to stay.

But they never remain for long. Dissolving. Like salt in water. Writing on paper. The ink of my blood too soon runs dry and with them the words and the chance of saving a life. I know it sounds stupid. Blood hitting paper and a time portal it does create. I learnt that the first time I told anyone about it. They thought I was joking, and I didn't know what to say. So, it became my little secret. A bloody little secret.

It's been almost a year, yet it still feels as if it were yesterday.

He was four. A lifetime still to live. He didn't know how to swim. It's my fault. *I* didn't teach him. *I* should have taught him. But I didn't. Karma is well and truly a bitch.

The words, they just appear. And carry me back there. To the boat. Overcrowded, flailing limbs. The jumps. Splashes. Ripples of bodies hitting water. The screams. The cries. The deadly silence. And then the choice. To live or let die.

It was never meant to be like this. When we left Syria, we were full of hope, a promise of a better land. One of plenty, wealth and so much more. It'd be different, they said. Don't believe the stories, they said. It's safe and so put your fears to bed. And we believed them. Or pretended to. I was always scared but didn't want to break my wife's heart. Not when it was her last wish. To take her son and go. Because we are a war-torn people. Refugees. People no longer safe at the only place we've ever called home. People killed, taken, forced to flee. People who love and dream to be free. And so, we believed.

Look. There it is again. The book. The letters. Can't you see? Out of nowhere. Quick! Grab the knife. Just a little blood, just a drop. No. Deep, too deep. Squeeze it onto the book. There - see? The letters appearing out of the white desert sand. The words. To live or let die. I close my eyes and allow my finger to trace the letters I choose.

To live. Always to live.

And then I'm there, back in the boat, the water lapping and gently hitting the sides.

"Baba.' I turn around, and I see him. Those gorgeous brown eyes, those caterpillar-thick eyebrows furrowed in concentration. Baba. My son.

'Baba, I'm hot.' He takes his brown jacket that I insisted he put on and with a cheeky smile, plonks it on my legs. 'I'm too hot.'

I pick the jacket up, the material rough in my hands, and put it in the bag by my feet.

He looks at me and I go to touch him, stretching out my hand, but as soon as I near, he disappears. I look around, and just moments later, he's there again. Now on the opposite side of the boat. Crying.

I know how this goes. I look up. The sky's turned. Once red, now a moody grey. The sea's rough. Rain falling, filling the boat.

'We're filling with water," someone shouts, and people start standing up in a clamour. They block my view, and he disappears once more. A second too long. And then he's there again. Flailing in the water. I know what to do. I've rehearsed this too many times to count. I lunge into the rolling blue beneath. Let its cold arms embrace me. Taste the salt in my mouth. And swim. As fast as I can. As strong as I can. Arms. Legs. Heart pounding in my chest. Following my son and his floating head. The one there, barely visible above the waves. I ignore the calls from the boat. The warnings I've gone too far. I can reach him. I will reach him. I can do it this time. I swim, ignoring the burning of my skin. My son gets smaller, a mere dot on the horizon. Every stroke I move, he moves three more. But I won't give up. I can't, not again. And I still have hope, until I lift my hand from the water for one more time and see that the once blue water has turned a bloody red. The red of his blood.

I let him down. Again. And everything goes black.

By the time I regain consciousness, the pool of blood on the floor has already dried, the specks of red a polka dot design on the otherwise dull, beige floor. My trousers feel crisp and rough, like heavy leather against my skin. I hope the stains will come out. These trousers were the last gift I ever got from my wife. I can't replace them but don't want to have to answer any questions either. I look around the room I have called home for the last eleven months. I search for the book, but already know what I will find. It's gone. And all I can do is wait for it to reappear.

It has never happened at night before. But it has today. It took me a minute to make out the silhouette. I check my clock. Still three o'clock. It is cold. I couldn't sleep. I was up thinking. Thinking about how I would have to change tactics. I couldn't keep trying to swim. It's impossible to save him like that. I would have to get the whole boat to turn around and search for him. Yes, we would have enough power, I am sure of it. And he is just a kid. They would have to understand. And just while I was thinking, as I was coming up with a plan, the book appeared. It has never happened at night before. No matter, it has now. And I know what I must do.

Blood. Letters. Words. A choice. To live or let die. To live. Always to live.

It is warm. The sun's golden rays, soothing on my skin. I look around. The ocean's calm. Tame. Soft. I hear chatter, Arabic words strolling to my ear. Someone's hungry. Some-

one's thirsty. Someone is asking somebody else for money. We are all tired. We all ignore him.

My son is sitting, not next to me, but no more than an arm's length away and so I decide to let him be. There is nothing I can do. He will end up in the water no matter what I do. The only thing I can change is what happens after. Keeping one eye on him, sitting idly looking out at the blue expanse that surrounds him, blissfully unaware of what the next few minutes hold, I get up and haggle myself through the boatful of people, pushing hot irritated skin closer to other hot irritated skin. I ignore the yelps of pain from a child as I step on his hand, and the shouts of his mother and the dirty looks. I don't care that I push a mother, breastfeeding her child, into her neighbour, so that the pushing force of my hands and the pulling force of the child's lips rip the barrier of dry skin around her nipple, tearing to reveal a little drop of blood. I don't care whose hair I pull or which enemies I make. These people, they already have their fate.

Once at the stern of the boat, I find the self-designated driver at the helm. He was twenty, young to carry the responsibility of nearly double the amount of lives, but the only one of us to have ever had experience with boats. The smugglers said he would be best to steer, and we didn't know any better to say no. As I approach, he looks at me in a way that should make me feel sorry for what I'm about to say but doesn't.

'You're going to die.'

He looks at me but avoids my eyes. I recognise that look. A look of fear, of confusion, of loss. I say it again. He still doesn't look at me. Shame, guilt, despair. Neither of us blinks. He looks nervously to his right hand on the boat's tiller, and I can see his grip tighten and his knuckles go white. He shakes his head, returning to face forward, but still doesn't say anything. I repeat it once more. You're going to die. And then, only then, does he say a word.

'Majnun.' Crazy. Almost too quiet to hear, and yet now I have heard it, it's all that is ringing in my ear. You're crazy, you're crazy, you're crazy. I'm going crazy. I feel a heat rising in me, and it's not from the sun. I misread him. That look on his face. He isn't afraid. He's smug, the tightening of his grip on the tiller a reminder that it is he who has the power. I look back. My son's still there. But I don't know for how much longer. I grab the man, practically a boy, by the collar, and lean down so that our faces are nearly touching. The others start to look and move away, not, I presume, just to give me space. I smile. He looks scared now.

'You're going to die soon. And you deserve to. But before you do, you need to let me take over the boat.' He looks at me, wide eyed and mouth open, and I can see the confusion behind his eyes. I feel guilty because he is just a kid, and so I loosen my grip and let him fall back to his seat. He doesn't deserve an explanation, but I give it to him anyway. 'You need to help me save my child.'

It's only then, when I say those words, that I see his face. The smile. His hand clutching the knife. I have no time to think and kick him on his shins. He falls. So does the knife. Its silver blade hitting the orange fabric of the inflatable boat. It takes a minute but when the boat starts filling with water, I know it's too late. Panic sets in. People are shouting and screaming, desperately flicking water out with cupped hands. No, no, no, no.... it's not meant to go like this. He wasn't meant to have a knife. The boat is not meant to go down like this. It isn't meant to happen like this.

I want to scream, let out the frustration inside, but I know I haven't the time. I look back to the place where, just moments before, I left my son. He's not there. I scan the surroundings. No, he's not on the boat. I think but no thought comes. I jump in the ocean, and I begin to swim. The water's warm. I feel hot. I can see him, there, in the water, two strokes away.

I swim, but deep down I fear what I will have to expect. But I try not to think of this as I pound with my legs. He's there, I'm getting closer. Closer to him. I reach out my hand and let out a sigh of relief when I feel him against my skin.

I look down to talk to him, his head barely above the water's surface. He looks up at me.

'Baba, why did you do that?

'Jump in?' I say, 'Isn't it obvious – I had to save you.' It's his turn to look down and he shakes his head.

I reach out to touch him again, but this time all I feel is a rough fabric against my skin. Empty. Floating alone. It's the jacket, brown and leather. No! He's not meant to have this. This isn't how it happened. This isn't how it goes.

I look up and then I see it. The boat. It's gone. I know I've failed. Another time. Again.

I wake up with a jolt. Skin raw, face hot. My heart hammering against my chest, trying to break out. Light seeps into the room from the edge of the blinds. Though the sun has already risen, the blinds have kept the room dark, and I can only guess for how many hours I've been out. Instinctively, my hands go to my arms. They feel wet and sticky, like glue trying but failing to stick. I can't see, but I know that I'm still bleeding. Fumbling about in the dark I head to the bathroom and turn on the light. Though I know what to expect, the sight still shocks me. I check the clock - 5:00 pm. Chloe will be here in an hour. I better start cleaning.

I hadn't quite finished cleaning by the time Chloe came. She saw the streaks of red, but she didn't say anything. I've always liked her for that. She understands, and not all of them do. She knows that I have to save my son. I can't give up, not when I'm so close.

To live or let die. Always to live.

'Here, take this.' I look to my side, to my son, brown coat dangling from his outstretched hand and smile as I take it from him and shove it down beneath my feet.

'What,' he says, seeing me smiling.

'Nothing. I'm just glad you're taking it off.' He makes this face as if to say 'Are you feeling okay?' but doesn't say anything and begins to fiddle with the bottom of his fiery red t-shirt. We both allow ourselves to sit in silence, listening to the sounds of the sea and the hushed whispers of the other people. After a few moments, when he has moved seats and is now talking quietly with another boy his age, I get up. Quietly stepping over a lady breastfeeding her child so as to not awaken the baby asleep on her nipple, I make my way through the crowd of people to the back of the boat. No aggression, no anger, this time has to be different.

'Excuse me brother,' I say to the man at the tiller, 'I need your help.' I wait for him to say something, but he just nods so I continue. 'Are you able to help me save my son?'

He lets out a sigh before replying. 'Brother, please, let me be.' Right, why did I ever think this would be that easy. He continues to avoid looking at me, instead straining his neck to see around me, so I move to the side, as much as I can given the cramped boat, to clear his view. He gives me another small nod in recognition. Like I said, this time was going to be different.

I don't say anything for a moment, and he continues to steer the boat, knuckles whitening ever so slightly as his grip tightens to move the helm a little to the left before relaxing once more to move it back to its original position, I ask the lady by my feet if I can sit, and she moves a little to make *space for me. Looking back to my son, I can still make out the top of his wind-spread brown hair, leaning down close to the boy next to him, in deep conversation. I have time, but not much.*

But I wasn't expecting what would happen next.

While I was still thinking about a way to address the issue with the driver of the boat, he surprised me and broke the silence first.

We're too heavy.' Three words that change everything. No one reacts, and I pray I imagined it. 'We're too heavy.' This time louder. Everyone hears. There's no denying it. We're all too heavy.

I shake my head, and feel the adrenaline start to course through my veins. No – this can't be happening. I don't remember this. How could I not remember this?

'We're too heavy!' People are shouting, and now everything has changed. Grey clouds invade the once blue sky, and it starts to rain. People get on their feet, absentmindedly knocking into each other in their rush, and start flinging their lives' possessions off the boat, the only things they have ever known, falling into the ocean like worthless rubbish. It's like a switch has been flicked. A button pressed. It's all so sudden, and it's caught my breath.

I don't understand. It was all happening so quickly. Bags, books, money, anything without life thrown into the sea, entire livelihoods, hopes, possessions and dreams. Children are crying. The boat sways from all the commotion. It starts to fill with water, now reaching our ankles. The dinghy sways too much to the left and someone shouts. I hear the sound of a body hitting the water while others yell. I look up to check but my son's still there. This time has got to be different.

I turn to my side, to the young man steering the boat, and that's when I see it, the fury in his eyes. He gets up and, somehow, I know, even before he starts to walk, directly towards my son, before he starts to shove his way through the crowd, before his dirty hands grab his red t-shirt, before he pushes him over his seat, before the red begins to be engulfed by the blue, blue sea. He pushes my son.

I shout and he looks back at me and smiles. I feel a fire growing inside of me and my fists long for the impact of his skin. I charge through the crowd until my hands find his neck, wrapping themselves around it and squeezing with all their strength. He doesn't fight back, but just looks at me and smiles. I hate him. I hate this person. I have never hated someone so much. I squeeze with all my might, until I feel I can't breathe, until my knuckles go white, and my fury subsides. Until I feel numb, dead and hollow inside. Until my anger's released, my frustration at life.

This time was supposed to be different. I guess that was a lie.

I'm awoken with a jolt, sweaty hands smacking my face. The light is bright, too bright, and I try to close my eyes but the person smacks me again and so I keep them open wide. I'm hot and tired, my mouth begging for a drink. But I don't ask for one. I don't say anything.

'Abbud.' It's Chloe. She looks worried. 'You passed out.'

'I was close,' I say. 'So, so close'.

'You passed out,' she says again.

'He was there. We were almost there...'

'Abbud, you're not hearing me. You passed out,' she is practically screaming. I look around. And then I see it. The blood all over the floor. The defib in the corner, the worry in her eyes. It all happened so quickly.

My back feels sore, and I notice I'm sitting on the floor, my upper body leaning against the hard brick wall. Chloe's scrubbing something off my skin. She's wearing gloves. Covered in my red blood.

'Abbud. What have you done?' I don't know what to say so I don't say anything.

Chloe's eyes gleam with a shine from the light and it doesn't take me long to look away. There's another woman at the back of the room taking pictures of pools of blood on the floor. She's wearing gloves and an apron, with the word 'Police' plastered on the back, tutting very quietly with every snap of her camera. I look at Chloe and she knows what I am thinking.

'I'm sorry. I had to call them. The hospital, they...' she stops, her own words choking her up and I realise I was wrong. The shine in her eyes isn't from the light, but from tears. From all the pain I have caused her inside. I want to close my eyes but don't. It's the least I could do. If I went, I don't think she'd ever forgive herself.

'Hey, Abbud, you need to stay with me,' she says, noticing I'm flagging. 'The ambulance is on its way.' I do as she says. She needs me. I know that. I can tell. I can't let another person down.

'I'm sorry,' I say, in a voice that sounds like a stranger's to my own ears.

'No, no, no, you don't need to be sorry,' she squeezes my arm ever so slightly to comfort me. 'Don't you ever apologise.' She looks at me in that way that tells me she will never be angry at me. That tells me she is always going to be there to support me, even when everybody else has already left. 'I was just in shock. I came in, Abbud, and I've never seen you like that. You weren't just gone like you normally are, you weren't responding to anything, I didn't know what to do, I panicked, Abbud, I panicked, you scared me, I panicked, I thought you were gone, I panicked.' It's my turn to comfort her now and I let her catch her breath.

'Here. Take this,' she hands me three white pills which I swallow with just as many gulps. 'I can't give you more, because you lost too much blood.' I nod. I understand. She's doing everything she can.

You see, the journey from Syria cost a year's wages and much more. My wife, my child, my health, my entire life. Chloe from the hospital comes twice a week. Helps me clean if I'm in too much pain to move. Gives me my medicine. A tablet. Sometimes two. Most of the time more. For when it's bad. Really bad. If it wasn't for her, I'd probably have died. Forgotten. Left to decay like a rotten piece of fruit. But she always comes, without fail. She cleans the blood. She doesn't ask questions. She doesn't try to probe and with her I don't get defensive.

She knows the book that appears. The choice that it brings. She looks at me, not with pity but love and compassion in her eyes. But she doesn't know the truth. She knows the labels - psychosis, schizophrenia - but not the can of worms they mask on the inside.

'When you finally came round, I stepped out to get your meds, and all I heard was shouting. I rushed back in, and the policewoman was grappling you, saying you were strangling yourself Abbud,' Chloe hesitates before going on, barely above a whisper. 'You were strangling yourself.' *You were strangling yourself.*

I don't say anything because there is nothing to say. Those words tell me enough. It's all come rushing back and now everything is clear. Within one heartbeat, I am right back there.

It isn't hot. It isn't cold. It's calm. The calm before the storm.

'Ya ghali, my precious one, here, take the jacket off, it will make you uncomfortable.'

Kabir, my son, looks at me and shakes his head. I don't ask why. I already know. The jacket, leather and dark brown, unsuitable for what will be the most dangerous trip of both our lives, was the last present his mother, my wife, ever gave him. Before she got shot, when visiting the local market trying to prepare for a journey that she would never even go on. Ever since that day, he has never taken that jacket off.

'Kabir, please, take it off. It's ok, I'll keep it safe.' He looks at me intently and I don't know whether it's due to the genuine pain in my eyes or his recent aversion to any sort of conflict, but he complies, and much to my surprise, hands me the leather jacket that I pack safely away in our only bag.

We spend a few minutes in silence. Both of us killing time. Both in anticipation of very different things. When the weather begins to change, I already know what is about to begin.

It happens so fast. The waves. They rise. The raindrops. They fall. The people. They crumble.

People topple over each other. Limbs grabbing onto one another. Bodies, rising and sinking with the flow of each wave. Rising, sinking, rising, sinking. Someone shouts. We're too heavy. And everything gets louder. More people crying, screaming, praying to a God they have never believed in. Mother's clinging on to children, brothers desperately clutching their sisters. And then the bodies begin to fall. Toppled over in the commotion, they drop into the water. We're too heavy.

People start to jump off voluntarily into the ocean. They wish to save them. Aiming to try and release the burden of the load. In all the fuss Kabir falls over, his red top lost to a sea of blue. I jump in, ignoring the salt as it burns my skin. I move. Like I've never moved before. Until my muscles beg, plead for a break. My legs pound, my arms beat. Until I get to him, and I can feel relief. But now, I look back. The boat's not stopped. It has continued to move away and now I have two of us to save. My heart aches and all I can do is swim. Blindly swim and follow the sound of the waves.

But the waves, they overwhelm me. Massive giants overturning me. The boat is moving even further away. My son, spluttering, his hand in mine, barely able to move without all my strength. He's heavy. The water dragging him down. My heart stops beating. Because I know. Here is the choice. I can't do both.

One fatal action that I will have to live with for life. We weren't both going to live and so I had to decide. I opened my hand, felt his slip away from mine. And I swam to the boat. Alone. Because I chose to survive.

'Abbud. You can't keep punishing yourself.' The hook of Chloe's voice reels me back to reality. I don't say anything. Because words have escaped me. I had a choice – to save me or my child. I chose the former and I don't think I will ever be fine. I don't say anything but instead I shout. A pure, guttural, primal scream. A release of everything I've ever buried beneath. The release of pain. The pain that scores me like the scars on my arms. The pain that tortures me, whenever I get to take another breath. I hate myself. I hate myself so much. I have never ever hated someone so much.

I let it all out. The anger. The torment. The torture. Unleash the demon, the dragon to be slain. I touch my face and feel tears fall down their sides. I close my eyes and let my body sway to the movement of the waves.

The book, it's still there. It hasn't disappeared.

'Look,' I shout. 'Look at that.'

Chloe doesn't look. She doesn't need to. She says there's nothing there. The book, I shout and lunge to try to shove it to the floor.

The book. It doesn't move. It lies there. Open. No choice. Just a decision. And the only thing I can do is try and live with that decision.

The choice I made almost a year ago, I realise now, will never, ever, go. The book. It will remain forever. Whether I like it or not, it will never change. It won't close or disappear. But that doesn't mean I need to always hold it so dear.

Those five words – they will always be there.

Those five words. Those ones I fear.

You killed your own son.

The five words only I will ever hear.

ABOUT THE AUTHOR

Aaran Thakore, student and avid writer, lives in London with his family, drawing upon his own experiences to highlight the lives of marginalised communities throughout the world. As an undergraduate geography student with a particular interest in human rights and refugee crises, some of his best writing achievements include works based on the struggles of those forcibly removed from their home. Through his submissions, and successes, in various competitions, as well as through the writing of his first novel, he hopes to one day help bring about a change through his words and help those disadvantaged by their past experiences.☐

PARADOX

BY K. L. VINCENT

A book lies in a crate. That crate, recently delivered to the residence of Émile Bouvier, sits in a library amongst other rare tomes. It waits to be admired, to be opened, and perhaps read. Émile has no intention of doing these things, at least not the latter. So, the book seeks another before it is sealed away.

***

Demi and her house guests scuttled one by one like rats down the shaft. She trailed Antoine with the sinking black-stone feeling this adventure was a stupid, bull-headed idea. After a round of her father's best absinthe – the legit stuff – markedly followed by the champagne bottle they guzzled like Evian water, Cristine had dared Demi to steal the new gem in her father's collection. And because Demi thought it would be 'fun', she did. It might even warrant some attention from Dad if he ever found out.

She clenched the leatherbound book securely to her chest, praying she wouldn't lose it. Her father had paid zillions for it.

Dear Old Dad never cared for what she got up to as long as she steered clear and kept her cocaine-sniffing nose out of his library. He was a collector, always searching for the most invaluable books money could buy. Money was not the problem in her family. They were dripping in it. Dad used it to sanctify his obsession with the rare and extraordinary, and Demi used it...well, she used it to have fun.

But this trekking into the city's underground tunnels was a step too far for her idea of a good time. She blamed her negligent father. The one thing they had in common was their absence in present life. Dad had a beguilement for the macabre, lost in his antiquities that occupied their Parisian mansion. He had purchased it right above the well-known catacombs for that very same reason.

She couldn't give a damn where she slept. In fact, it thrilled her in some perverse aspect to sleep over the dead – as long as she could party her nights away.

Her ex-girlfriend couldn't handle it, though – couldn't handle *her*.

"Go to therapy, Dem, and get over your Daddy issues." Demi remembered her girlfriend's parting words as if it were this morning. They ran like an echo in her head. "You're so layered in other people's shit you never stop to look at your own, and you're going to lose yourself in it."

The words rang true. But she didn't listen. She didn't want to.

Now, she lugged around a bigger problem: this god-awful book of her father's. It clung to her, digging its buckles into her chest as she scooted down the tunnel while Antoine kicked dirt into her face.

She flexed her bandaged hand over the book straps. Its buckles poked at her dressing.

The tunnels widened, and they could stand, albeit hunched.

Of course, Demi couldn't go back on a dare. That wasn't in her nature. Not when it gave her a secret excuse to see what new relic her father had purchased. But part of her wished she hadn't gone through with it.

The priceless book had arrived the night before, sealed and packaged in a crate. She had overheard some correspondence – a phone call – some wack story about a book possessed by a demon. Like demons existed.

The dried blood on her hand stuck to the gauze dressing, and it itched. She wanted to scratch it off but it would only start bleeding again, and she didn't want to give the book anymore of her blood.

Paradoxically, the letter opener had cut her palm – not the book's sharp buckles. A small knife Dad used to break the wax on his mail. It rested on his vacant desk and was the first thing she thought of to open the crate in her inebriated state. That and Cristine, who'd accidentally bumped her while she wrenched off the wooden slats. The knife slipped.

Her two house guests – not friends, Demi didn't have friends – had gathered around. Blood welled from her fist and dripped onto the contents within. The precious book splattered with red. She rushed to wipe it clean, but something unnerving happened.

It moved.

Buckles and straps flung open, and the book convulsed like a rat with seizures. Either a demon actually possessed the book, or Demi and her house guests were truly thrashed.

Words inked themselves onto the open page:

You have come for fun,
But choices must be made.

A sacrifice for light to night,
and your commitment to play.
Make the choice aloud,
and live another day.

Antoine balked at the message. "This is insane, Demi. What's your Dad into? Voodoo?"

He wasn't far off.

Cristine peered in. "I think you have to choose."

"You're the one who dared me to open it. Why don't you choose?"

"You bled on it and made it do all that –" She waved her hand.

"Guys, it's doing something again." Antoine pointed at the new words as if a ghost held a quill to the paper doused in blood red ink.

The one who bequeathed the blood must make the choice:
Stay inside and find death to those that reside,
Step outside, but there will be nowhere to hide,
or go beneath, and no harm to those who trail will be applied.
Choose now, or the book will if you cannot decide.

"I don't want to die." Cristine gave a small whimper.

"Me neither. Quick, Demi, pick one." Antoine shoved her shoulder.

The world tilted slightly. No more absinthe for Demi in the future and whatever else she took.

"What if this is all bogus?" She wished it was. But as she said the words, new ones appeared on the page. Numbers counted down from ten. On nine, something akin to a knife twisted in her gut. Both Cristine and Antoine folded over, screaming.

Eight.

"Choose, Demi!"

Her head pounded.

Seven.

Pain sliced up into her chest.

Another yell from the others. Black spotted her vision.

So she went with the one that sounded the least ominous. "Beneath! We'll go beneath!"

The pain stopped. Her head cleared.

Her mansion was built above a secret entrance into tunnels that twisted and turned for kilometers under the city. Though the entrance was not frequented – a trap door in the wine cellar – it brought an interest to the house, an allure other mansions did not possess.

That was how Demi found her nose chock full of dust and limestone, unfortunately having no mind-altering effects, her arm laced around her middle to keep the book steady, and a metropolis pressing above her.

She squinted into Antoine's cellphone light. "Can you shine that in the other direction?"

They had entered a part in the tunnels that opened out, and she could finally stand upright.

"How much battery do you have, Antoine?" Cristine's voice came from behind, her own light glaring.

"Fifty percent. You guys?"

Demi lit up her screen. "Ten." She was terrible at charging it.

"I have eighty." Cristine shut her light off and tucked her phone into her jeans' pocket. "Might as well save one. There's no service down here."

Demi switched hers into airplane mode. "We'll use mine after yours dies."

Antoine gave her a wide-eyed stare. "How long are we planning to stay down here?"

Ill-prepared, all they had brought were their cellphones and a bottle of wine Cristine had nabbed from the cellar.

Oh, and the book.

"Until that threat goes away."

"You're not seriously considering opening it again, are you?"

Demi shrugged. "Have any better ideas?" She didn't need to protest further. The book sprung from her hands and landed open with a clunk. Powdered rock gathered in a plume around it.

If you wish to leave in one piece,
Find the Historian with the key,

The Painter who distorts reality,
And two Dwellers from below,
But be careful who you trust, don't be slow,
For one will give a fatal blow,
Another tells only lies,
One more will be your demise,
The last gives you what you truly wish,
Though in the end, you may vanish.

"Excellent choices..." Antoine mumbled.

Demi snapped a picture with her phone. "The words disappeared last time."

"Good thinking."

"What if we don't find these people?"

"We'll vanish?" Demi couldn't puzzle out the meaning of the last line.

As if the book heard them, the rhyme melted into the paper, and new words inked the page:

Good luck finding your way out.

A rumble erupted from the path they came, and small rocks crumbled onto Demi's head. She snatched the book. "We need to move."

More rocks fell from the ceiling. When her house guests didn't budge, she pushed. "Like now."

Their feet finally picked up speed, and they ran down the tunnel as the path behind them caved in. Tripping and stumbling over the uneven stone floor, they only slowed when the sounds of crashing walls ceased. Dust motes floated in Antoine's beam of light.

Cristine began to shake. "We are going to be lost down here forever." Her breaths puffed out short and choked.

Demi grabbed her shoulder. "Breathe."

Cristine coughed as she inhaled more dust.

"We won't. We just need to find these people." Demi tapped the picture on her screen. Her battery read nine percent. "There are other exits."

"How do you know?"

"Tons of people come down here. Seems logical."

"But the book said we can't leave until we find those people."

It didn't technically say that. It said that one of the people would give them what they truly wished, but it also seemed like it didn't want them to leave. That cave-in made it obvious. How long would it take Dad this time to notice she was gone? She had disappeared two weeks before without a word from him. Would he realize she was missing after a day or two?

"Oh god, oh god. We're going to die down here." Cristine cradled her head.

"Shh. You hear that?" Antoine held up his phone, light beaming.

A tinny clink jingled from where the tunnel forked into three different paths.

"It's coming from that tunnel." He pointed to the left one.

Demi tentatively wrapped her arm around Cristine. "Come on."

They walked toward the sound.

In the phone light, a figure materialized. A man veiled in the same dusting of white limestone as themselves, only where they were lightly-sifted, dust covered him from head to toe.

A key ring clinked at his belt. He turned as if he hadn't seen them.

Antoine rushed forward. "Hey! Hey!"

The being twisted back and blinked. "Oh, I am sorry. I thought you couldn't see me."

Okay, weird. He was clearly visible with the cellphone light. But Demi wanted to take advantage of the opportunity and not mull it over. "Are you a Historian?"

The man scrunched his brow, and dust cracked. "I guess I am a kind of historian of these parts."

Hope sparked in Demi's chest. They had found the first one on the list.

"It looks like you've been down here for a long time."

"I have."

"Do you live in the tunnels?" He might count for one of the Dwellers as well.

"Some say I do, but live? I'd say no. Phil's the name."

Demi expected him to extend a hand, but his arms stayed by his side.

"We are looking for a painter and some people who dwell in the catacombs. Have you come across anyone else?"

"I've seen many by those descriptions. Are you sure you don't want the path out? I know a way. It leads to the courtyard of an old hospital on Boulevard de Port-Royal. Though, come to think of it, it may be closed..."

Antoine and Cristine looked about to take the offer, but the book trembled in Demi's hands. "No, no." She spoke before they could. As much as she wanted to find an exit, they had to find these people first. "Have you seen a painter or anyone living here recently?"

"I can take you to a place where many paintings reside. You might find what you are looking for there." His keys jingled, not waiting for their answer, and they followed.

"These old mines have a fascinating history."

"Yeah, like dead bodies," Antoine said. He grumbled while skirting around what looked like a femur on the floor.

"Not all parts. But if you'd like to go to the section that holds the bones, I'd be happy to take you there. They're piled up to the ceiling."

"No!" All three of them said in unison.

"Pity. Some famous ones. Racine is my favorite. Positive there's an exit there, too."

"We just need to find the painter, but uh, thanks for offering."

He raised his shoulders and continued. "Murders took place in these tunnels. A young girl killed her siblings right before the revolution; fights broke out among miners, communards killed monarchists, deaths caused by disputes between adventurers...." He glanced back at them.

"Lovely." Demi tried to redirect his conversation. "You said the place has paintings. Was it always a gallery?"

"No, it was the basement of an old bar."

"Is there an exit?" Cristine's voice pitched up.

"There was one, but it's been sealed."

The group turned around a bend, ducking under another partially collapsed wall, and then entered a space bedecked in color. The walls, floor to ceiling, had been sprayed, marked, drawn, and painted. Classical frescos of naked figures and imitations of famous artworks met yin-yang signs and swirls of psychedelic graphics.

Another light flickered in the corner, not the same bright cast of Antoine's but a natural flame. A woman wrapped in vibrant fabrics, paint splatters, and old jeans sat cross-legged on the floor. Brushes extended from her fingers, grazing the stone wall with a bold red.

At that precise moment, the room dimmed, and only the candle flame's round glow was visible.

"Shit." Antoine clicked frantically. "My phone died." He shoved it into his jacket.

Demi bit her cheek, trying to distract herself from the worry. "Cristine, we can use your light when we need it. But try not to let it die, like this dumb-ass."

"Hey. I'd like to see you use yours. You have what, one percent?" He leaned over to take a look at her screen.

"Five. But we need it for the book's message."

"Where did Phil go?" Cristine turned in a circle. The Historian had vanished.

"I have more candles if you need a light." A sultry voice arose from the artist in the corner. She still fixed her face on her work. It looked as if her fingers had brushes secured to the tips.

"Um, we're oka –"

Cristine rushed toward her. "I'll take one."

The artist stopped brushing and bent to her rucksack, equally splattered in paint. She held out her right hand and revealed three red candle stubs of different sizes. "You'll have to light it yourself. I don't want to burn these." The artist revealed her left hand, which she had been painting with. Her fingers weren't just secured brushes; they *were* brushes.

Cristine leaped back. Antoine caught her before she stumbled over a rock.

"You have-your fingers are –"

"What's wrong with my fingers?" The artist looked at them as if she bore regular hands. "If you don't want the lights, I'll put them back."

Demi strode forward. "I'll take them." She took the three candles and lit them on the small flame. A pallet crammed with blues, greens, yellows, reds, pinks, and purples sat next to the candle's blaze.

"Want to try?" The artist dipped her index finger in the bright blue glob and lifted the paint to her lips, smiling. She had a mouth full of overcrowded teeth. "It will take you to places you've never known. This one –" She dipped her thumb in the yellow glob "– will put you into the deepest sleep. Or this one," Her brush-finger came out purple, "to cloud cuckoo."

As much as Demi liked to escape, this was a little much, even for her. She must still be tripping on the stuff they took earlier if she was seeing a person with paintbrushes for fingers. She stepped away, handing the other two candles to Cristine and Antoine.

"Uh, no thanks. I'm actually looking for people living down here. Do you happen to live in these tunnels?" Demi needed the last two and they'd be done with this place.

The artist's eyes rolled backward. Was she too far gone to answer her question? But she said, "Live here? No....but I can take you where you want to go." Her eyes rolled forward again and flicked to the wine bottle in Cristine's hands. "In exchange."

Demi jerked her head, and Cristine cautiously placed the bottle beside the artist.

She licked her middle finger – paintbrush – and immersed it into the red glob. She drew an arch on the wall with a fast, curving motion. "A door to find what you are looking for." She smiled again, flashing those paint-stained teeth.

"It's just a wall with a red arc across it," Antoine said.

Demi moved toward it. "Doesn't hurt to try."

"Hold on to those candles." The artist gestured to the little stub between Demi's index and thumb. "They'll let you pass, and perhaps you'll find your true colors."

"I'm not walking through a wall." Cristine shrunk behind Antoine.

She had a point. It was madness. But Demi was determined to find those two Dwellers. "I'll go first." She gripped the candle, hot red wax dripping onto her hand and bandage, and plunged it through the wall. Demi expected her hand to crack against the stone despite the strange situation. Instead, it disappeared. She wriggled her fingers but felt nothing on the other side.

Cristine inhaled.

Demi pushed her whole body through. It pressed on her form like toothpaste squeezed from the tube. On the other side was....oh, this was too good. She forced her head back. "You guys need to see this."

Antoine and Cristine exchanged looks, but one glance at the smiling artist had them joining Demi on the other side of the arch.

All three of their candle stubs winked out. The wax melted through their fingers.

Music vibrated in Demi's ears, the beat shivering her bones. The air smelled of sweat-slick bodies, alcohol, and effervescent dreams. Figures with neon paint bounced to the beat, booming off the cavern walls. Their limbs radiated like bioluminescent jellyfish under the UV light.

They had stumbled upon an underground rave.

"There are so many people!" Cristine shouted over the din.

"You think they all live down here?"

It was impossible, fantastical, something straight out of a warped fable.

Demi nudged into the throng, Cristine and Antoine close behind. A few people in, knocking against arms and elbows, she attempted a conversation with a face streaked in neon green and blue. "Hey! Do you all live here?"

The figure kept moving to the music as if they didn't hear her.

She tried again, shouting louder. "Do you live here?"

Instead of saying yes or no, they pointed to the raised platform at the center of the dancefloor – an old boxing ring. Two DJs operated the music.

She pulled up the picture with the rhyme. The book did say *two* Dwellers. Her phone was down to two percent. She lowered the light.

Demi turned to Cristine and Antoine to make sure they were behind her. Antoine looked as if he wanted to dance, but Cristine shrugged against him, trying to avoid the other bodies. Demi waved her hand to get their attention, then jabbed her finger at the DJs. She shoved her way toward the platform without waiting for them to reply.

The DJs were rapt in their music, hands on their giant headphones, heads dipping to the beat.

Demi climbed through the ropes. Something peculiar struck her about the DJs. They looked identical. Their focused faces mimicked rats, with whiskered chins and beady eyes. It seemed as if they were warring with their music. The beats bounced back and forth between them, each note throwing punches at the other. The twins were so engrossed in their music battle, they didn't notice her. She stood in the center of the ring and waved her arms, holding the book high. Cristine and Antoine joined her, also attempting to get the DJs' attention.

Finally discerning the trio, they switched something on their mixers and moved toward Demi, small eyes glued on the book. The music dimmed enough for her to get her words out. "Are you two Dwellers?"

The one on the left angled his head. "I suppose we are. Isn't that right, Ned?"

"I would disagree, Nate," the right one said.

"You are or you aren't?" Antoine folded his arms.

"We are."

"We aren't."

Cristine whined.

Demi wanted to chuck the book at them. "Which one?"

"Why do yah want to know?"

"You're not a cop, are yah? Cops have tried to shut us down before."

"We've been good at avoiding 'em."

"Yah lot do have a cop-ish appearance to yah."

"No, we're not cops. Please tell us. We want to get out of here."

"And leave this?" The DJs gestured to the rave.

"Look, just tell us if you guys live here, and we'll leave you to your party." Antoine was losing his patience.

"Tell yah what, if yah lot agree to have some fun –"

"And don't snitch us out to the cops."

"We'll tell yah."

"Deal."

"We live here."

"Well, not here, here."

Demi wanted to give them rat poison at this point. She clenched her teeth into a smile. "But under the city?"

"Yeah," they said.

A huge sigh heaved out of her, and it seemed the book sighed with her.

The DJs turned back to their mixers. "Now yah lot go and have some fun. Yah can hang at the reserved alcove over there. Looks like your friend is a little spooked," Nate said, or was it Ned? He motioned to Cristine, who indeed looked pale, even under the black light. "We'll send some drinks your way."

In the privacy of the alcove, they slummed onto the whittled stone seats. A candle flame pulsed on a table amongst mounds of wax. The music base thudded around them, but the nook muted the crowd.

Cristine looked less perturbed. "Has the book re-opened?"

"Nothing yet." Demi set it on the table, and they all stared. It stayed still.

She unlocked her phone to see the image of the rhyme, but before she could read the words, her phone blacked out. "Damn it. Looks like we're going to have to rely on yours if we get a signal."

Cristine grimaced.

"What? I thought you said you had eighty percent?"

"I kind of lied about that. It's dead."

"What?" Now Antoine looked perturbed. "Why'd you do that?"

"I-I didn't want to worry you guys. I mean, I was already freaking out, and how would it help if we were *all* freaking out, and after I read that article with your dad, Demi, about what the book supposedly does –"

"Wait, wait, hold up. There was an article about this book and my dad?"

"In *Le Monde*. It talked about how Émile Bouvier purchased a book of the dead and all the myths and stuff around it. Oh, you didn't know –"

"No shit, Cristine, do you think I read articles about my dad?" Demi's voice raised.

"I thought you knew."

She knew the bogus crap she'd overheard over the phone call, but nothing more than that. "Is that why you dared me? Did you know it would make us do all of this?"

Cristine cowered.

"Tell me."

"The myth said it curses the person who feeds it blood. I didn't think it would happen to all three of us."

"So you only wanted it to happen to me?" Demi thought back through the haze of their library break-in. Her throat tightened. "And when you bumped me, it was on purpose so I would cut my hand." The space between her brows pinched. "Why?"

"A guy in a long coat...he saw me reading the article, and offered a lot of money."

"You threw me under the bus for money? I could have loaned you more."

Cristine cringed. "He said he'd wipe my debts clean, even the ones I owed you."

"Did he?"

"I got the notification right before my cell died."

Impossible. Then again, this whole venture seemed impossible.

How well did Demi really know Cristine? A coward, she recognized that now. Some girl she met outside the public library who knew where to find the best Vitamin K. And Antoine...how had she met him? She couldn't remember. Language studies, or another club? Was he out to get her like Cristine? Her temper roiled. She turned to him. "Did you know?"

"Dem, I don't read *Le Monde*." He held up his hands.

"Did you know Cristine was a lying piece of –"

"Okay, let's all chill." Antoine moved between them before Demi could grab Cristine's hair. "Where are those drinks?"

As he said this, a neon figure walked up with a dark bottle and some pre-poured shot glasses on a tray. "The DJs sent these over."

"Thank the devil." Antoine took the bottle and glasses, eyeing Demi.

"The bottle's mine."

"Geesh, okay." He passed it to her.

Demi wanted to get lost again. Maybe in this crowd. Maybe at the bottom of this bottle. She was starting to like these guys and care for their banter. She thought that after she helped get them out, maybe they'd appreciate her. Someone in this godforsaken world had to. But they weren't cursed by this book. She was. The book had lied, too. This was far from fun. She guzzled the content, and it burned like acid.

Antoine gagged and put his glass down. "This tastes like gasoline."

Cristine spat hers out, still looking humiliated.

Demi took another swig, forcing it to stay in her stomach.

The air shifted. Instead of sweat and heat, it clung like a moldy rag. "You guys smell that?" The mildew bloomed in Demi's nose.

"Motor fluid?" Antoine pushed his glass to the end of the table.

She took another swig.

The lights and neon figures blurred with every bottle tilt. Good. That's how she liked it. Demi squinted her eyes, trying to focus on the crowd. Their faces seemed...skeletal.

The book flew open. A new rhyme inked its page:

You have found nearly all,
It is your turn to give the final call,
Choose a path before you now,
And it will be your final bow,

One will take you back to your little empire,
all will be as before.
The other will give you what you alone desire,
to even out the score.

Demi should choose the first one. They had to get out of these tunnels, all three of them. But what was the point of opening the book and giving it her blood in the first place? Cristine and Antoine hadn't sacrificed a thing. She was sick of losing herself in other peoples' problems.

Demi took another swig and stared at the dancefloor, seeing the dead dance, dance, and dance.

She raised the bottle to her acquaintances. "Good luck finding a way out. Give me what I desire."

"Demi, I'm sorry –"

"What, no!"

But too late. The words began to spiral. They whirled into a circle, becoming a black hole on the page – something pulled at the tips of her fingers, her nose, her face, all of herself.

"What the fuck." Antoine jumped from the table.

Cristine shrieked.

Demi felt herself stretch. A weightlessness overtook her.

In one more breath, the book's cover slammed, buckles snapping shut.

***

Émile Bouvier is a self-made man. He originates from a long line of herders in the southeast of France. When he was twelve years old, he decided he would not shepherd sheep for the rest of his life. He was meant for grander things, powerful things, objects that carried knowledge — books. It became his life's ambition.

He had some blips along the way to amassing his prestigious library, an affair in his youth. It saddled him with that child. She is a waste of a life. He does his duty, feeds and gives her what she requires. But she will never compare to what he collects.

She has gone off again, doubtlessly, squandering more of his fortune.

He holds the ancient book in his hands. Émile thought it had been stolen for good. Until that scruffy boy appeared on his doorstep, returning the priceless leather-bound. The scoundrel looked as if he'd seen a ghost. Émile will not press charges, of course not. It was careless of him to leave the book unguarded. He will not let it happen again.

Émile places the book in the heart of the glass case, a unique display to admire his rare find daily. "Right where you ought to be."

ABOUT THE AUTHOR

K. L. Vincent is a neurodivergent writer, aspiring to include this aspect within her writing. Originally from California, she graduated with a degree in Theater Design and Anthropology from UCLA. Later, she received her master's degree in Anthropology and Occupational Therapy in the UK. In her fiction, she often draws on experiences through life and her passion for history, travel, and culture. Recently, she has been a multi-winner, finalist, and honorable mention recipient of Globe Soup's writing contests. She continues to pen stories whenever possible and currently lives in France with her partner and daughter.□

NOBODY SAW ME

BY SONIA PATRICIA GOLT

In the middle of the hospital chaos there was only one thing on the nurse's mind. He was feeling the pressure from the evil book he found a few days ago. He had been hiding it from everyone. He was pragmatic among his colleagues, so nobody would notice his anxiety. After finding

the unfortunate book, which still sat on his desk, poor
Ferdinand could not focus. He tried asking around to see
if any of his colleagues had left a book on his desk a few days
before, but no one knew what he was talking about. Nobody paid any attention to his inquiry either. Ferdinand,
however, could only but listen to his conscience since the
book had appeared. He recalled what had happened and
why he was so intrigued after opening the impressive cover. Regrettably, the pages were blank. It did not seem to
be a journal, as the cover was more adequate for a crime
novel. The dagger with the blood dripping from it was too
daunting to be anything else.

"What is this book about? Why is it on my desk?" He
thought.

The morning was busy at the hospital. It was always
extremely laborious at the recovery ward. He did not like
working there, but he was on duty this week. The hours
were long, the workload immense, but in a way he did like
to be kept on his toes. There was always something new
to do, with many patients constantly needing his help, so
there was little time to linger on his thoughts, especially
now since he had recently been promoted to senior staff
nurse. His aim was to prove to all the others that he could
cope with the new position that entailed longer hours.

Ferdi, as he was called at work, could hear someone
calling him, it was an urgent call.

"Ferdi, quick! I need you to cleanse this fissure before Dr. Brown arrives for his daily rounds...Please hurry," another senior staff nurse said this, while trying to move the patient herself, but finding it difficult. "I need your help here." She sounded agitated. In his new position he knew he had to work closely with her as a team. Ferdinand already knew he was an efficient part of the ward where everyone expected him to respond quickly and with aplomb to any situation. Today, he had to hide his anxiety well, he did not want anyone to notice there was something out of sorts with him. He must work as usual to avoid being questioned.

The day continued very much on the same basis, with him running around helping patients. It was a constant mad rush. By the evening he was exhausted and ready to go home.

On that particular evening he was unable to fall asleep, remembering the strange-looking book.

He remembered picking it up on his short break, trying to work out what the book might be for, but he had no time to open it as he was required to be elsewhere. There was another emergency on the way. He had seen a stretcher coming towards him, and knew he was needed. But as he rushed out of the room, he noticed the book was still in his hand. All he could do now was put it on the stretcher and help move the patient.

Once the doctor arrived Ferdinand was free to go elsewhere, but he would not leave without the book as he needed to put it away first, to be able to check it out another day. The moment he placed it in the drawer the book's hard cover flapped, frightening him out of his wits. The front page was now open. Blood was smeared all over it, and a message had appeared on the adjacent page. *"That woman has been in a car accident, it was her fault, she was drunk and crashed against a tree, killing her 2-year-old son...she needs to pay for this. You Ferdinand have been chosen to carry out this assignment."*

He was stunned and confused, looking around like a mad man to see who could have written this message. He was being coerced into doing something totally unacceptable. Suddenly another message came up. *"Ferdinand, don't let us down, justice is paramount. Remember, you are the chosen one."*

He tried to erase what was appearing in the book, but no matter which pen he used, he could not scratch any of the words out; actually still more appeared. It was a complete nightmare.

"You only have to carry out our orders, you cannot get in touch with us, just do what we ask you to do, nothing will happen to you if you carry them out. Go and make sure that woman does not survive, don't tell anyone, we have ears all over the place."

Ferdinand was frightened and determined not to follow the book's orders, "This must be some sort of sick joke" he thought, and he was about to put the book away when he saw, yet again, another message. *"We know you are frightened and confused but you have the means to do as we say, she deserves to die, so do it or you will regret it."*

He put the book away nervously, stuck it into his drawer, locked it and walked back to the ward in haste. He felt as if other eyes were following him, but, looking around, he saw no one. He continued with his routine throughout the day but was not fully present. He could do most things with his eyes closed, as they were similar and repetitive. His intentions had always been to help others feel better and at peace within the hospital, so how was he going to do what the book coerced him to do! Suddenly, he found himself in the emergency room where the woman in question was being attended to. He did not know how he had gotten there, and, as soon as the nurse and doctor left the room, he did not hesitate to pull the breathing plastic tubing off, briskly walking away to return to the other ward. He was in such a state, he felt dizzy and shaky and could hardly remember what it was he had done. Suddenly awakening from the stupefaction phase he found himself in, he could hear noises coming from the room next door. Someone shouted, "She is gone!"

- 2 -

The next day no one mentioned the said incident, probably because patients had pulled their tubing away on various occasions before, causing certain accidents. It was difficult to decipher how this happened, as they were obfuscated moments. There was not enough staff to keep twenty-four-hour surveillance. It was just accepted as very unfortunate.

Ferdinand was becoming paranoid because of what was happening to him. His walks around the hospital were now fearful. He was always looking behind him, thinking someone was following. It took him many days to start feeling more at ease after the incident. He couldn't always put away the thoughts of the woman who had killed her son in a car accident, but he did not ponder on how he had ended her life. He pushed those thoughts away along with the messages in the book and continued his work in the same manner as before.

Ferdinand had, prior to the book appearing, a very uncomplicated life. His work took up most of his daily life. He had a meticulous routine, going straight home after work and shopping for food on his way there. On weekends he took brisk walks to keep himself fit and, once a week, visited his mum at the old people's home just an hour away from his own place. His mother had been paralyzed from the waist down for over four years, so he had been forced to put her in a care home. He was a good son and frequently visited her, taking flowers or cakes, and calling to let her know when he could not go.

A few weeks had passed since the writings in the book. He had not gone near the drawer, and had attempted to forget the book, after all it was locked away for no one else to see. However, one day when he was on duty in the intensive care unit, a new patient was admitted. He had been treated for a valve replacement, a big operation, which had been performed just three days before. The man was in his late eighties and having difficulty breathing as his oxygen levels were very low. Ferdinand took him in hand and made him as comfortable as possible, ensuring he was recovering from the cardiac surgery in a peaceful environment. It was thanks to the postoperative care that the recovery had been uncomplicated. Ferdinand left his colleagues to deal with the man's medication on that day, as other patients in the ICU needed his attention.

The day went by with no strange incidents occurring; he felt calmer. Late in the evening nurse Margot came by looking for a special instrument to help change another patient's dressing. The patient was bleeding a lot, and Margot needed that specific piece of equipment to staunch the bleeding.

"Ferdi, can I borrow your magic tweezers? I urgently need them." She said this, knowing Ferdi would know what she was on about. Fun talk amongst the nursing staff was to call some of the medical tools fictitious nicknames. Ferdinand gave her the key to his drawer, so she could get them herself while he checked another patient's wound.

Margot opened the drawer quickly to look for the instrument she needed and briefly touched Ferdinand's book, moving it aside. Picking up the instrument, she rushed back to finish stitching up the patient's wound and put on a new dressing. Ferdinand had already applied ointment, but Margot needed to finish off the cleansing and put on a new bandage.

"Ferdi, don't forget your key, it is on the side table, and thanks for letting me use your personal magic tweezers," she said smiling, "They have done the trick!"

The pace slowed down nearer the end of Ferdinand's shift. Nevertheless, he was very tired, and he decided it might be a good idea to take a short nap in the staff room before driving home. Nobody waited for him at home. He lived alone after his divorce, so he could arrive at any time.

The comfortable reclining chair in the staff room was where he cuddled up with a blanket and fell asleep. The clock struck 3:00 am, when suddenly he woke up to the rustling of paper. Looking around to see who was there and listening again to a flutter coming from the cabinet where he kept his things, he remembered the key fob in his pocket and opened his drawer. He had not been using this drawer much, fearful of the book. He preferred to put his things away in another cabinet since then. He listened

- the book was rustling its pages. He did not dare look but felt compelled to do so. Watching a smudge of blood on one page he discovered a new message. He was stunned by what was being written. He read it as it appeared, it told him to go to bed number twelve in the ICU and give the patient an extra dose of morphine, a deadly dose. Ferdinand remembered the senior staff nurse had used his key earlier on, and that on that bed lay her patient, not his. The famous Mr. Glover. Famous for his grumpy attitude towards all since his arrival. This man had severe kidney failure, therefore, needing dialysis and morphine for his pain. On top of all this, the open wound on his arm was infected, which is what Margot had been sterilizing and dressing. Still Mr. Glover kept complaining incessantly.

Ferdinand was aghast after reading the recent message. He refused to follow it. Unfortunately he could not go home now, too late for that. He would be on duty in two hours, therefore, too little time to drive home and back. He thought it best to rest at the hospital and drive home after his morning duty. The pages moved again before he had time to close the drawer and another message appeared. '*Ferdinand do not think you can postpone this, go and give number twelve that extra dose of morphine, it will be your salvation. That man needs to be punished for his severe courtroom verdict on the poor man he accused, most especially as he knew the man was innocent. He has to suffer for this unscrupulous act to cover one of his own.*"

Ferdinand knew the possible consequences of an overdose of morphine. He was really afraid, as well as disturbed, by the message. He knew, if the patient did not die at once, he would have problems breathing through lack of oxygen therefore dying a slower death. His gut encouraged him to disregard this cruel message, but they were still sending instructions via the book, and he could not stop reading them. The pages were once again forcing him to act without wanting to; they seemed to have a strange hypnotic power over him. He walked towards bed number twelve, wanting to stop himself but not able to. Who were these interlocutors who sent the messages? How come he could not seem to disregard them? The power they had over him was massive, leaving him with an uneasy feeling he could not decipher.

On his way down the corridor he met one of the ward sisters who was looking for someone to help her move a patient. He followed her. After the effort of moving the disabled patient from the wheelchair to the bed, Ferdinand found he had no urge to follow the book's instructions anymore, so he continued with his daily rituals, disregarding the messages altogether. Finishing the day's work, and absolutely shattered by then, he went home to try and sleep, but it was impossible to put the book out of his mind. He again felt anxious and extremely stressed. He needed to get away from the hospital and the book;

he would have to have time off before he had a mental breakdown.

- **3** -

Ferdinand had at long last managed to get a few days away from work, for medical reasons. He was suffering from stress and anxiety, and he had requested a week off to go to a seaside resort, the ideal place to rest and recuperate in the sun. He had flown to Faro, in Portugal, for a complete change. He had not really been abroad much, however, seeing his mother was doing well, he splashed out, luckily finding a cheap flight for just £99. It was not the best time of the year to go to a beach resort, but it was the cheapest time to travel there. April temperatures in Portugal were higher than in the UK, meaning there would be spells for him to absorb the sun during his five days away. The travel agent had confirmed sunshine and he longed for this to happen.

On his arrival at the airport, he noticed the hotel bus waiting for him. There were a few other passengers traveling on the same flight from London who waited for the same bus. He did not talk to anyone, boarded the bus, and sat as far back as possible, ensuring he sat near a window to get a glimpse of the town when they drove by. John, the travel agent, had not lied. The sun was actually out. It immediately uplifted his mood. Forgetting all his past worries, the trip seemed sublime. The place had a lot of history. He had read it was a rebuilt city, after a devastating earthquake which had shattered a great part of it. It dated from post-quake rebuilding, a treat for sore eyes. They passed a few incredibly beautiful buildings, and some dazzling architecture, mostly churches, probably from the sixteenth or eighteenth century. Soon he was mesmerized with the view of a bright-coloured Atlantic coast. The beaches they passed were long, with miles of sand. He was glad he had booked a small hotel near the beach itself, because he really wanted to relax. He might even attempt a long walk on the beach during his stay. That type of exercise suited him well.

The bus stopped a few times before they arrived at his hotel in Ilha de Faro. A quaint little façade greeted him. Picking up his suitcase, he noticed another passenger also getting off the bus, probably staying at the same hotel. The moment they walked up to the entrance, the man greeted him with a brief nod. Ferdinand nodded back and headed for the front desk.

After checking in, he settled in his room overlooking the sea. Sitting by the window watching the tide and the horizon was enough for now. He was too tired to go down to dinner, but had bought a sandwich and a drink at the airport, and that would be all he needed. He did not want to move away from the window as the scenery was superb. The incredible orange sunset changed within seconds and looked like a painting on a canvas, one he would not want to miss. The phone rang, making him jump out of his skin. His anxiety came back to him almost instantaneously, and he had to work on his breathing to calm down again.

"Hi, Gregory, is everything alright?" he asked anxiously, seeing the number from his mother's retirement home.

"Never you worry, all is good. Your mother has been asking me to call you all afternoon to see if you have arrived. I will pass the phone over to her now. Enjoy your holiday!"

"Hello Mum, how nice to hear you... yes mum, yes, the flight was okay. Are you doing well yourself?" he asked, listening to his mother explaining every detail of her day. Then he explained where he was, and emphasized the incredible beauty of the nearby beach and how he was looking forward to walking the area the following day.

"Yes mother, I will call you in a few days' time to give you another update. Do take care...Love you too." When he finished talking, he realized he was too tired to go out and soon fell asleep .

Breakfast in bed was not something Ferdinand had ever done. Today was a first for him. He enjoyed the luxury of a typical Portuguese breakfast with a cake called 'Pastel nata' or something similar. He couldn't remember what the waiter had said when he delivered his room service.

What was more important was how it tasted, absolutely delicious; a flaky puff pastry filled with vanilla custard that melted in his mouth. He was thankful there were three to go with his coffee, they were so delicious that he did not leave a single crumb. Replenished after the meal, he needed exercise, so he wandered out into the sunny streets nearby, knowing a post-meal stroll could reduce the gastrointestinal problems which he seemed to be having.

Everywhere he passed, there were people standing by doorways. Men were playing board games on small wooden tables outside their front doors, and women embroidered cushions and tablecloths to their heart's content. Every time he passed someone he heard 'bom dia'. In no time, he had learnt this Portuguese word to add to a few he already knew. When venturing into the pretty narrow streets away from the main thorough-way, he heard footsteps behind him, but every time he looked back the road seemed empty. All he saw were shadows of people entering doorways he had passed, people going home to stay away from the hot afternoon sun.

By the time he came back, he had soaked in a lot of sun, drank a lot of vinho Mateus, and heard the story of how this incredible Portuguese wine had been one of Elizabeth II's favorites.

He went straight upstairs to his bedroom, showered, changed, and got into bed for what he hoped would be a peaceful night. Unfortunately, he woke up on several occasions, having difficulty falling asleep again. He stretched, feeling uneasy. The mattress was not as comfortable as the one at home. At some level of consciousness, he heard a door creak and close, but he was too tired to make anything out of it.

He woke up rather late, got dressed and went down to breakfast. It had been a broken night. He had a terrible headache, so ordered coffee, hoping it would make him feel better. He heard a strange male voice behind him bidding him good morning. Turning around he saw it was the same man who had traveled on the bus with him from the airport.

"Good morning, are you addressing me?" he asked.

"Yes, I believe your name is Ferdinand, correct?" The man saw Ferdinand's startled face and immediately said, "I overheard the receptionist call you by your name yesterday, or at least asking you if that was your name, so she could write it down in the hotel's registration form. I am Mark Abbott, staying here for a few days away from family turmoil."

"Oh dear, I am doing something similar. Would you care to join me for breakfast so I can turn my head round again? It is rather painful looking backwards," said Ferdinand with a twisted smile.

Mark moved to the other table and had the waiter bring over his coffee cup. The men soon started chatting about some of their attempts at getting away from family, but without really saying much, nevertheless maintaining a conversation of sorts. Things moved on to work, and Mark seemed keen to find out exactly what Ferdinand did, asking a variety of questions that Ferdi was happy to answer.

"Well, it is my profession. I have a knack for it. I really enjoy what I do. Needless to say, it is stressful, especially these last few weeks. Something cropped up out of the blue and distorted my concentration for a while, but I have already dealt with that, so all seems better now I think."

"Yes, I suppose a break is something we all need from time to time, especially if you are at loggerheads with your own mind about maybe having to do things under force, things you probably have never done before and do not wish to do again. Things that take you out of your comfort zone. Is that what you mean?"

Ferdinand looked at Mark suspiciously, thinking he had hit the nail on the head, but realized it was probably just a coincidence. Still he did not like the way the conversation was going and, the man's voice sounded so artificial, very strange, as if put on! Ferdinand decided not to reply to any more personal questions, as Mark seemed to be prying. He moved on to talk about the fabulous food instead. Mark did not stay long after that and left without saying anything else, just a mere goodbye.

Ferdinand felt anxious again, wondering whether he should stay on one more day or return home. He decided on the latter. Thus, returning home within twenty-four hours after feeling terribly uneasy from the conversation. He felt he had to run away. Why his intuition told him he had to get away, he could not fathom, but there seemed to be something sadistic about the man who had made him terribly uncomfortable.

- 4 -

On his return to the hospital, he entered the staff room, reluctant to be near the evil book. He had pushed thoughts of it to the back of his mind on a few occasions while away, but today he felt the urge to look at it again, to see if the messages had been erased or if they were still untouched. Cautiously, so no one saw him open the drawer and subsequently the book, he took it out carefully and gasped, a resounding gasp which echoed everywhere in the middle of the quiet surroundings. The book was in motion, or the pen maybe. Writing started to appear. "*I saw you in Portugal. We met because I am following you everywhere you go. My instructions are to kill you if you do not abide by our last message immediately. Your destiny has been written, you cannot change it. I know who you are, and even though you think you know who I am, you are totally wrong. I am not describable. You will never find me. Nobody will ever find me, because not even you know what I really look like. I am the one who generates the contents of your book, all in the name of justice. My human superiors are the superpower that gives the orders to eradicate humans who have been cruel to others. Yes, Ferdinand, I am just a robot made to look human - yet not human at all - I have no feelings, no regrets, no false pretenses. I am devoid of any emotions so I only carry out my orders, as should you!"*

Ferdinand re-read the message; it troubled him so much. His heartbeat was getting faster and faster, he was over-whelmed, paranoid, and desperately looking out for this robot.

"No Ferdinand, do not look for me, just read the last message we gave you. Do what it says if you wish to save yourself. You are in the arms of death right now. Better to read on and act on it. Tomorrow there will be a surprise for everyone, even you!"

Nurse Margot entered the staff room, screwed her fore-head looking at Ferdi curiously. "Are you feeling alright? You look as if you've seen a ghost. Surely your holiday break can't have been that bad dear Ferdi, what's wrong?"

"Hi Margo, I am still not my usual self, but feeling much better. Just wondering how to sort out a few pending things. You've caught me in deep thought, sorry. I am now ready to take on my work schedule. I see you have been pretty busy here and need all the help you can get. Are any of the patients I left behind still around so I can check them out?"

"Only two. Sweet Miss Daisy and grumpy Mr. Glover!" she said with a smile, walking away rather hurriedly.

Ferdinand closed the door behind her and read the message he had seen before leaving for Portugal - the one that induced the anxious depressive days, the one he was adamant not to carry out as things were becoming surrealistic, complicated, even more unclear. He'd better find Mr. Glover and check where Grumpy slept, but first he should re-read the message carefully, in case he decided to do the unspeakable act.

"Ferdinand, go and give number twelve that extra dose of morphine. It will be your salvation. That man needs to be punished for his severe courtroom verdict on the poor man he convicted, especially since he knew the man was innocent. He has to suffer for this unscrupulous act that was just to cover one of his own."

On his walk to the ward to check out bed number twelve, he met a few of his colleagues who wanted to linger and speak, but he kept them at bay, excusing himself saying there important things he had to attend to. Then, he hastily walked away from anyone he met along the corridors. In his rush to get away, he bumped into Dr. Savage, who dropped most of his papers all over the floor. Ferdinand helped the doctor pick them up and was lucky enough to see the name Glover on one of the forms. He noted that the patient had been moved.

"At least I now know where I am heading," he murmured to himself, turning to the left rapidly and veering towards the other direction.

The corridors, by now, had been dimmed to help everyone settle for bedtime. He moved more cautiously now, not rushing, but still vigilant. On arriving at the ward, he looked around for any sign of nurses checking the patients, but none seemed to be around. Patients were trying to doze off now. It took him a bit longer than he expected to see Grumpy. He was snoring to his heart's content. This was undoubtedly the perfect moment to find the morphine and get the dose sorted. Once he had it, he retraced his steps back to the ward, having to hide between the curtains as he heard voices coming nearer. He stiffened as he held the full dose in a hypodermic, which would be noticed by anyone in the profession. Lucky for him the voices passed by and continued onwards. Ferdinand's heart beat so fast he thought he would not be able to do this tonight. He breathed slowly to calm his shaking, because he knew the clearer

his mind was, the quicker the whole procedure would be over. Suddenly he found himself beside the bed, not knowing how he had gotten there. Mr. Glover still slept. Ferdinand injected the morphine into a vein, feeling slightly dizzy. He still managed to mutter soothing words. "Sleep forever more Mr. Glover!"

The following day the nurses found Ferdi lying on the floor beside Mr. Glover's bed; they had both died of a morphine overdose. The murderer killed them both in exactly the same way. No one could fathom how it had happened, and no one would ever find out either. The book had disappeared, and the only thing left within the ward was the laughter of a robot that nobody could hear.

ABOUT THE AUTHOR

Sonia Golt's career in journalism opened out opportunities to write a series of books of short stories, poetry, romance and even a children's book written together with her 8 year old granddaughter. Proceeds from most of these publications have been donated to cancer charities in the Bahamas and Gibraltar where she has resided. Sonia is a cancer survivor herself and the Founder of "The Bosom Buddies Cancer Trust" since (2006) Currently she is the Chairperson of the trust.□

She obtained a British Empire Medal several years ago based on her charitable entrepreneurship.

OPTIONS

BY FABIAN HENRY

The air was humid. Lovis was sweating heavily, although his way was full of shade coming from the thick forest around and above him. The climate wasn't tropical in the slightest but, given the weather, Lovis felt like he was on a short trip straight into the jungle. The heavy backpack wasn't helping. It only added to the amount of sweat running down his face, forcing him to blink as much as the car of a senior citizen who forgot to turn off their turn signal about twenty kilometers ago.

The heavy backpack was pulling him down. Also wearing him down. If not for fear that the others would mock him, he would have asked for a break over an hour ago. The young man knew he was the one odd out, and the others eyed him suspiciously already. They thought of him as a nuisance to their work, so he decided it was best to try and push through.

Everyone besides him had reason to be here. This was an expedition to a ruin that was believed to once have been a sacred location. It had just been discovered recently, almost fresh one might say, so it was only logical to send scientists of different sorts, experts in their fields, to inspect the place and hopefully confirm the theories that existed for years but lacked the final grain of proof.

But Lovis was no expert. Not yet at least. He was still in the midst of his university life. He was *absolutely not* an expert in any field that would explain why he was a part of this group, but Lovis was part of an influential family. They were rich; they donated money all year around. Lovis knew about this fact. He still felt guilty at times for it, but not today, because he was actually excited that the money had helped him be here. It would have been impossible otherwise. Although he had to admit, it wasn't the first time money opened doors for him. It must sound arrogant to say, but he was glad he had the option. Did it help that he knew about his privilege, and also that he was just interested enough to have picked the field, but by far not invested enough to be here because he was some sort of prodigy?

Every other person on this expedition knew that Lovis was here because of money, and they probably also thought that Lovis might just be bored. The classic rich who bummed their way into serious, important business without being suited for it. Maybe they weren't even wrong about that part, though, Lovis wanted to learn. He was excited to see what was waiting for him, at least as much as the others were.

For hours, they walked through the thick forest, mostly uphill, until Lovis saw the first walls of the ruins. Well ... it didn't look like a ruin. For a building abandoned for hundreds of years and hidden from everyone, it was in surprisingly good condition. Only a few walls had collapsed, and the roof seemed fine. Sadly, all the windows were broken. Only tiny parts were in the frames still, indicating colorful glass that once had been there. Lovis was disappointed. He bet the pictures the glass had once held in a silent manner, would have been breathtakingly beautiful. It would suit the environment if it had been. Now, they would never know. All that was left were half-ruins.

"We go in groups," said a tall, blonde woman who had walked in the front. She was the head of this exploration. He had forgotten her name, like most of the others. Lovis doubted any of the other members would remember his name, either. "That way we can clear the place much faster." A flood of names followed, all divided in different groups.

Lovis was joined by two ladies, who looked so similar that they were probably related, as well as a much older man. Even though no one had asked, he constantly talked about his research and how much any find would change the course of his work. Lovis didn't really understand much of it, but he nodded obediently every now and then. He didn't bother to ask questions, though. He wouldn't have known what to ask and, even if he had, there wasn't a single second available to butt-in to this monologue anyways.

The small group made their way deeper into the building. Lovis tried to remember all the paths that went from the main hallway, attempting to create a floorplan in his mind. It was surprisingly hard. Lots of crossways, paths leading somewhere else, and hallways that were so long, he couldn't make out where they were heading. It was dark and not easy at all.

As much as Lovis had hoped for overwhelming views, he remained disappointed. It was mainly cold stone walls without any details or interesting structures. That was, until they made it into a big room - a huge room, actually. Lovis wouldn't dare to say it was the main library, but it was possible. The walls were lined with bookcases made from dark, red wood and filled with hundreds of books of different sizes. A few had fallen over, others were in horrible shape, and some looked like they were just seconds away from falling apart. Between them were rolls and single sheets of paper.

"Exactly what we were looking for?" said one of the women. Her name was Tamara, and she was with her cousin, Andi – the other lady in the group. Lovis had been right about them being related. Both worked for the local institute of history. They focused on local folklore and regional myths.

"Really?" Lovis asked.

"This place was used as a library as well as a hotspot for predictions."

"More like hear-sayings?"

"Both. Some had scientific basis", Tamara earned skeptical looks from Lovis and the old man – whose name Lovis still didn't know. "If you believe the writings. Some were just rumors."

Lovis nodded but couldn't help the cocky smile. He didn't really believe in those *scientific basis*. Anyone could say that.

"The place is said to be the birthplace of a god as well."

Lovis frowned, "What god?"

"The phoenix."

"The what?"

The old man loudly huffed.

"A god based on the star sign. The lore says a human died here under unknown circumstances, and was granted godhood."

"Which basically leveled this place up to holy status." Andi added.

"All of this lacks any logical basis.", the old man scoffed.

Andi rolled her eyes. "And yet, here we stand. In a place, hidden for hundreds of years, rumored to be holy and dedicated to one specific god."

"A god who has been unimportant and meaningless since the last couple hundred years." The man's voice echoed off the high ceiling and throughout the room. Lovis felt incredibly small under that great expanse. His head lolled back as he looked up. There was some color still left on the ceiling - a mix of blues with simple dots. It could have been a night sky.

"We are not here for gods that may – or may not – have existed. We want to explore this place, create floor plans, and secure any literature and written knowledge for future preservation. THAT is our job."

"So what do we do?" Lovis asked.

"Mostly, all of you check this room and its contents. List all the books, scrolls, notes, everything you find that falls into this category. If you find anything that seems of extraordinary value, you take it with you. The rest will follow over the next few days."

Lovis nodded. So far so good; so easy to understand. The group scattered.

Lovis didn't expect to find much. Yeah, a lot of books were stored here and, as far as he could tell from the hours of looking around - holding books in his hands, checking for mold, water stains, or any other damage - rarely anything was of worth. It was just old books about ordinary things. So maybe, it had been just a regular library, if it had been one at all.

He looked behind him. The others were still scattered across the room. None of them had had a heureka situation; no one had screamed in excitement; no one had a great find. So none of their names would make it into history books as something more than a side note – if they were even that lucky.

The walls will move.

"What?" Lovis asked.

The others ignored him. Lovis frowned. How come they talked and then ignored when he reacted to them. He was irritated.

They don't know.

Lovis' eyes wandered. The voice again. Neither the cousins, nor the old man had moved towards the group in particular, they seemed focused on their task. As far as Lovis could see, none of them had moved their lips. So ... they couldn't have talked, could they?

"Shit," he whispered under his breath. It sounded so loud and panicky. Was he losing his mind? Was something in the air - the mold? Was it affecting him?

He looked straight ahead, staring at the bookcase in front of him and... the book in his hands. It must have been just repetition by now: picking up a book, turning it in his hands, checking some random pages, and then putting it back again. This book though. It was different. Yes, it was insane to say this about a book. But Lovis would swear on his own life - this book was warm. Warm like he himself felt warm, how any person felt warm, how any animal or pet felt warm. It felt alive. And ... Lovis swallowed hard. A shiver ran down his spine. Suddenly, he felt cold, which made the book feel even... warmer. Frozen, he stared with huge eyes and held the book.

It had a heartbeat.

It really had a heartbeat. It was hard to feel, fast and soft. Like a little animal. A bunny maybe. But, nonetheless, it was alive.

It was a book.

It was alive.

Lovis clearly was going insane, because there was no other solution to this.

The book was a greenish color. It could be just mold, but it didn't feel like that. Lovis mentally erased that option. The pages were in bad shape at the outer edges. They

looked wet, had dark stains and spots, and apparently
some bugs and critters had eaten good chunks of it.

Move.

He ignored it and opened the book. There was text,
chapters, and little notes. It looked like a regular book.
But the thing... Lovis stopped short. He couldn't read
it. It wasn't just a foreign language. If you see one you
can still recognise it as some sort of language, your brain
understands. But here, he didn't. It was random signs and
no known letters. The combination was so random and
weird, Lovis just couldn't make out some order that would
explain any grammar behind it.

His head started swimming. He wanted to understand
so badly, and he wasn't sure if it was because he wanted to feel success in solving this problem, or if this book
was really pulling him in. Sucking him in like a vacuum
cleaner made out of paper, the power was so immense.
Mesmerised, Lovis couldn't look away. Like a fly, he was
caught in a spider's web.

Run.

The voice echoed clearly in his head. Lovis blinked. Even
if he wanted to, his muscles didn't work anymore. Lovis
was frozen in place. The seriousness and authority in the
voice made him shiver. Was it fear? Anxiety? It filled his
body.

Run now or find out what is waiting for you.

As if strings were cut, Lovis fell forward, his body suddenly reacting again. Loudly, he gasped for air. The voice repeated over and over in his mind and, as he was told, Lovis ran. He held tightly to the book and made it to the closest exit. Behind him, he heard surprised voices calling after him. Questions, then screams of panic and more steps. There was something - something dangerous! He had to keep running as fast as he could. He had to get out!

Lovis ran left, then right. He went back the way they came before and then stopped dead in his tracks. A solid wall was in front of him. There was no path. But this wasn't the right way? Yes, Lovis was one hundred percent certain. He would give his hand; That's how certain he was of it.

"The walls move?" Lovis whispered in confusion.

Go back, first left and then always right.

Lovis hesitated. The voice had been right once, and he didn't know any better. What else could he trust? So, he obeyed. He did just as he was told. Lovis didn't discover another dead end but, at the same time, he didn't exactly know where he was anymore. Behind him, he still heard steps. There was a sound like stone rubbing against stone, as if the walls were shoving their way around.

"What now?" he screamed loudly. He really expected to receive an answer this time. He waited.

And then... an answer came.

Keep running. Go down whenever you can or let the walls sense you.

He wasn't sure what this meant initially, but with blind trust, as if he really had any other options, Lovis started running again. He ran until he met a wall, then he looked around and tried finding any indication of a path leading down. Stairs, he saw stairs, and uneven paths. He processed every little hint in the message and hoped he was making the right decision. Still, he heard the steps behind him - but no voices - just loud steps and heavy breathing. Lovis wasn't sure if it was other group members or not. Why didn't they ask for help or for him to wait? They were just always behind him - looming - waiting to get hold of him.

Deeper and deeper he went. He began to fear that he was running into his own grave. He was not sure why the book would want him to die down here, but it immediately unlocked a deep, strong fear inside of him. His breath was heavy. The slight slope pulled him down, kept him going, like a rolling marble, unable to stop. What felt like hours must have been just a few minutes. He was filled with the agonizing fear of being watched by walls, of the steps behind, of his own breath being too loud and causing all of the things before, until he bolted straight into a small room. It was nothing more than a chamber, basically, windowless and cold. The thick, stone walls radiated a freezing energy, making Lovis shiver instantly. Behind him was a heavy door, broken from its frame, but Lovis could move it over to hide behind it.

Close the door. You have to, or it gets you.

Lovis leaned against the door with all his strength. It was a struggle, but he got it moving. He was breathing heavily, huffing and groaning. He saw someone running up the hallway. Lovis didn't know the name, but he could recall the face. They were part of the bigger group, the ones who had gone to other parts of the building. Lovis slowed down. The other person had seen him, and was running straight at him. If Lovis would just wait a little...

Wait for them, and you will die.

Lovis jerked. That... was so radical, and just couldn't be right. They were just a few meters away, nothing was behind them. Lovis himself was safe already. How could he possibly die? Lovis narrowed his eyes and slowed. He could wait. Just a little longer.

Keep going this slow and die. It's you or them.

"How?"

The walls know they can't stay open. If you wait to save them, then this will not be your safe space anymore, but your grave. You get to decide.

That sounded so absurd. None of this made any sense. The book was still trapped between his chest and upper arm, radiating an overwhelming wave of danger - intense and urgent. The feeling pressed into Lovis, filling every fiber of his body. He tensed. Panicking, Lovis' eyes darted around the room. He was sweating. If he would just wait a little longer. The other person could make it for sure. And the walls... walls couldn't hear or know anything. They were walls!

They don't have to spy on other rooms anymore. You can find your end here or somewhere else.

The feeling was growing, numbing his arms. Suddenly, the fear was so overwhelming that he couldn't move. His mind was racing, thoughts stopped being rational, they made no sense, they were all over the place. Lovis was thinking about everything - and nothing - all at once. He had to do something. Before he knew better, Lovis was pushing on again.

"No! No, no, wait for me!" the person cried out.

The voice echoed through Lovis' head. It scared him. Tears filled his eyes. He wanted to wait, wanted to help, but he was scared. The book's words seemed so real - he had to believe - he couldn't not believe!

So, Lovis kept pushing. There were only two options and, from what he knew, this was the only one that was keeping him alive. Lovis definitely wanted to live.

And, with that thought, Lovis pushed the door shut.

***

The darkness felt different now.

Weeks, maybe months, after being stuck inside that small room, hearing the desperate screams from outside and the scratching against the stone he had placed there to protect himself, Lovis couldn't sleep. Once it was dark, his fear rose and left Lovis in a state of constant panic. It made it impossible to sleep or even rest for more than a minute or two.

Needless to say, Lovis was not his old self anymore. Everyone noticed. Everyone worried about him. Lovis didn't care. Since he had been discovered and brought home, the only survivor, everything felt different. He still couldn't fully grasp it.

Life was different. He was different. Everything felt strange. Lovis couldn't connect with his family anymore. They didn't understand, and he just couldn't explain. He had come home an alien, lonely and separated, even when he was with others. It was so strange. Lovis hated it, but he had no idea how to tackle it - so he withdrew. He isolated himself, thinking he could fix it all. If he couldn't come up with something, then who could?

All the while, Lovis walked up and down along the walls, like an animal in a cage, not giving the walls a chance for a second to close in and overpower him - not again. One might think Lovis was lonely, but he wasn't. There was always that one voice with him, everywhere, all the time. The book. It was the only voice he heard, and he wanted to listen to it all the time. It was louder than anything else in his mind, and he wanted to keep it that way. It whispered to him during the day and made comments when he held it in his arms. He heard it when he fell asleep at night, the book snug under his pillow, because he feared someone might take it from him. This wasn't his idea. The book told Lovis to do it. It told him that it harbored important knowledge, hidden knowledge, and others wanted to take it and own it. It told Lovis to trust no one, not even his own family. At first, he didn't believe. But now, he wasn't so certain anymore. He listened to this day and night, and slowly they were ingrained in his brain. Like deep lines that had altered his thinking for good.

They will take me.

"But why?" Lovis blinked up at the dark ceiling - and the darkness stared back. His eyes were dry; they burned as he stared into the inky blackness. Lovis was tired. He enjoyed his talks with the book. Somehow, they made his brain tingle. He felt fresh, like a whole new world had opened up to him, and suddenly he felt a hunger only the book could satisfy - if it chose to. Lack of sleep was taking a toll on Lovis. Making decisions, forming thoughts, and just living life aside from the book and the whispers was becoming increasingly difficult.

My pages hold wisdom. Knowledge. They want it.

"But, they wouldn't steal from me," Lovis replied. They were family, after all.

Greed reveals the worst in people.

Lovis pressed his lips into a thin line. That at least, wasn't wrong.

They will just take me, or you can hand me over.

"I don't wanna do that," Lovis said, shaking his head.

Of course not, but then they will come and take me by force.

Lovis bit his lower lip. His brows knitted. It sounded suddenly possible that his family might storm the room, kick open the door, and forcefully take the book! His eyes darted around. He could try and hide the book somewhere. In the closet or maybe... under the bed? In with his clothes or maybe with other books if he only got rid of the revealing cover? Or behind...

Waste time hiding me, or be faster than them.

"Faster?"

You have to be fast, or I will be theirs.

Lovis was ready to ask for more information, to protest, but his breath was cut off. Lights flickered behind his eyes, and colors flashed brightly in his brain, ripping away any ability to form a thought. His mind was not his own. He saw images of the door flying open, family members storming in with ugly faces as they beat Lovis down, ripping the book from his hands and making sure he could never get it back. Beating him until he laid in a puddle of blood, barely recognisable as his former self.

Lovis took a sharp breath, then his mind cleared again.

You leave and hide, or you wait for them to come.

Again, he saw another flash of scenes and possibilities equally bloody and gruesome. None were the result Lovis wanted. He didn't want to admit it, but the book might have a point. Maybe it was right. He had to protect it. It was his. He had found it, and it had chosen him. Lovis made it out alive while everyone else died in the ruins, because of the help from the book. That had to be a sign!

First, he hid the book. He moved the furniture so that the bed and drawer and dresser formed a small island in the room. Then, he ripped the floorboards out. He placed the book underneath and pushed the dresser on top of it. He started to rip other floorboards out so the spot where the book was hidden would not stand out to anyone searching. Then, Lovis opened the door and listened. The hallway was silent. No footsteps - not yet. They hadn't come - yet.

Lovis' mind was racing, and slowly he formed a plan.

His heart pounded. His hands hurt and burned. Who would have thought that strangling someone could leave such strains on one's hands? Lovis looked down at himself, hands shaking and weak. His vision was swimming. Suddenly, he heard a loud, high-pitched scream, full of fear, echoing inside his head. Lovis pressed his eyes shut. He shook his head, trying to get rid of the wail. It hurt his ears and sent a shiver down his spine. He thought he could feel a wide, grotesque, smile spread across his face. A choking giggle rolled from his lips. Again, he shook his head, then the scream was gone. His eyes fluttered open. Blood was splattered on his clothes. A slight chuckle escaped Lovis again. Oh no, now he would have to figure out how to fix that. The chuckle grew into a full-on laugh. Did he sound hysterical?

They had tried to take the book and who was laughing now? Literally. Lovis had been faster than them. Fuck them. Fuck them for wanting the book. But now, they couldn't have it - because they were laying on the floor - stomachs gutted open, heads beaten in. Their eyes were empty and glassy, never able to read even one page of the book - ever. Lovis knew it wasn't necessary now, but he cut their hands off - just to be sure. Without hands they couldn't turn pages, right? Lovis laughed again.

For a second, he heard the screams again and the questions and the begging. He heard their footsteps when a few tried to run from him. But Lovis had found them all and caught them and taught them a lesson. He kept them from stealing the book.

Every step made a wet, sucking sound as Lovis walked across the blood-soaked boards as he made his way back to where he hid the book. It called to him, wanting to be read and used and to reveal all its secrets. The book finally belonged to Lovis - and Lovis alone.

All he had to do was go back and get it out.

Just walk through those flames that hungrily ate through the house. It was so hot - incredibly hot - around

Lovis. His fingers smelled like matches. His clothing reeked of gas. The smell of corpses burning mixed with wood and gas was all around. It should all burn to the ground, and take it all. All he had to do was return to the book. He just had to pick it up.

And not burn.

ABOUT THE AUTHOR

Fabian Henry was born as the first child of two in Wadgassen, Germany, in 1993. Since his school years writing and reading had been a huge part of his free time. During his high school years he started working on his first novel, publishing it just before graduation. Since then he continues writing novels and short stories and managed to secure his place in competitions and anthologies.□

IT'S ALL ABOUT THE BOOK

BY LILY FINCH

He carefully watched Janice, the lady he observed conversing with the baker at Georgie's Bakery one day after following her for two weeks after the art show, where she outbid him on not only one piece of art, but two.

Yes, she'll do. Imagine Miss Perfect giving candies to the kids and handing out teddy bears for sick kids who have to stay overnight in the hospital. She makes me ill. And now she's attending the biggest suave art show in San Jose, where two New York Soho Art Scene artists are releasing their new art pieces. She would undoubtedly bid on one or two to make the artists happy, because she can do so with her money. Bitch! Agh, but your seemingly flawless tapestry of life is why I chose you to be saddled with The Book.

Still, he had since followed her and seen her in the bakery numerous times, constantly evading Janice's view.

I can't believe this. Praying? Before eating her breakfast. Oh, honey, that takes the cake. Additionally, consider donning a rosary ring, applying a thin layer since it resembles a newlywed's wedding ring's adornment. Again, I chose you, Janice, for The Book.

You wear the latest fashions in every outfit, with matching jewelry, purses, and shoes. You flaunt your wealth in ways that aggravate me and others, no doubt. There you have it, Janice. I want to make you choose between the most unbearable choices a human should ever face, because you have an otherwise seemingly perfect life. And you need to know what it means to be aggravated.

Blending in with the other morning commuters on their way to work in my pin-striped pleated pants, matching suit coat, vest, crisp collared shirt, polka dot tie, and pocket-watch was easy. My puff matched my tie, and I screamed success when people looked at me. My black shoes were polished and shined. I knew I had to boldly slip the book into your open tote while you were engrossed in grading law papers.

I moved to stand before you and took advantage of the train's movement to feign an exaggerated loss of balance. The flower in my lapel pin pricked your hand, causing it to bleed.

Many other passengers, preoccupied with their phones or work, noticed I was about to leave the train. But you had to make a scene—it must be the lawyer in you, or maybe the professor—that's debatable.

"Ouch! Hey, what do you think you're doing, Mister? What did you poke me with anyway?" You yelled out loud.

"Me? Poke you? With something? I'm sorry, Miss, but I merely lost my balance. If your statement is true, I can only think it's where my flower is pinned to my lapel. I do apologize. May I buy you a coffee when you get off the train for your trouble this morning?"

"That won't be necessary, thank you. Sorry for blasting you. I was concentrating on work stuff. It's just a pinprick. I'll look in my bag for a wipe. No problem."

"Very well, then. Have a great rest of your day!"

I left you, exiting the train at the next stop, knowing that you must've found The Book by then.

I knew you only had two stops to go, but finding the book covered in old shelf paper cut to size was a touch of class that I knew you couldn't resist. I knew you would know it wasn't yours immediately. I hoped your curiosity would compel you to open the Book, and perhaps some tiny drops of your blood would fall onto one of the pages.

***

A *patisserie* is a splendid spot for individuals to gain a split-second view of the corporate world versus the retired folks who frequent the place early in the morning. Their lives are so ingrained in the corporate culture that they can no longer sleep despite being retired. Workers who stand in line call them out. It's a riot. I get there early and grab a back table each morning, except when I drop the book into your bag on the commuter train.

You arrive ten minutes before Alfred places your orders, and by the time you get the order, Alfred has already walked in and sat down.

Your praying over your food annoys me, that and your damn ring. You take a bite and a sip of coffee. You tell Alfred, "I have tickets to an art exhibition at the San Jose Culture Gallery on Fifth if you are interested," initiating a conversation. "I know it's not everyone's cuppa tea, but I am a fun date." Your whimsical approach to life has Alfred focused on you. You are the most captivating person in the *patisserie*; nobody else, except me, cares about your discussion.

Your arrangement with Alfred as your long-standing "plus one" for events makes me vomit. Your business of sharing a key to each other's apartments for emergency purposes but keeping your private lives to yourselves is admirable. Your morning routine of meeting at the *patisserie* without fail to make one another smile, regardless of what else was going on in your lives, makes me think you two are more than just plus ones for each other. Your small talk relying on discussing events around San Jose, day or night, wasn't all you debated now, Janice?

Your agreement to call each other first in an emergency, including family and police, was over the top. Alfred's occupation was a little dubious for your tastes; you knew it involved protecting and keeping elite personnel away from the general public using firearms.

You're oblivious that Alfred keeps tabs on you. His full-time job allows him to follow you while keeping a few hundred other people in the city protected from the general population. He has many employees.

Seeing you board the train alone without Alfred's interference was peculiar. His men were already on the train and watched as I carefully fell on you. Of course, Janice, you were unaware of Alfred's actions and never truly understood why he met you daily in the bakery.

***

But after the blood dropped on the page, you read about the first choice you had to make, and your myriad emotions must have told it all. Horror, disbelief, and fury might sum up your reactions. I only wish I could've watched you go through them all. That would've been awesome!

"Why me?" you screamed aloud as you left the train. "I don't want to do this. I mean, a handicapped person, a child, and a healthy person—that's not fair to make me choose." You moaned and wailed. Please, God, help me.

***

To add insult to injury, Alfred's men saw the interaction between you and me, which became Alfred's new focus, according to him. His men followed but could not catch me, so they let me go.

After you stopped feeling sorry for yourself, you called Alfred after encountering me. A necessity in her eyes. When he failed to answer, you pinged your phone's location to his iPhone, texting, <<*Help, I need help.*>>

Alfred returned your call immediately.

"Are you okay? I'm sending a car. Just get off at the next station; tell me which one, and I'll have a car sent."

He sent me a text to: <<*Get away. She alerted the men .*>> He deleted it and cleared his cache.

"Yes, please. I'd like that. Alfred, I'm just a bit shaken by all of this."

Alfred contacted some of his men, and once they arrived, he found Janice and escorted her to the car. I watched the whole thing.

Once Alfred got you in the car, he told her he would drop you off outside her office. She thanked him and got out downtown since he frequented the place.

***

She opened the book to the first page, and two blood drips fell on it. The words that changed her life appeared. It read.

Three names appear here; another page about each person will be revealed daily. When you decide—and you will choose—who dies out of the three, you will have the most information available to decide whom you choose to die.

Alfred approached the police station, knowing you were inside.

The names were:

1. Cheryl Mason, a paraplegic who enjoys music and live performances, was the first to study alternative solutions to car fuels, like cars that run on water and water components. She hates storms.

2. Gabriel Smith is a 10-year-old boy who enjoys baseball and hotdogs but not pop.

3. Nancy Broomsteader is not real.

The police officer looked at the page in the book and said, "What do you want me to do with this?"

You said, "I don't know. It hasn't happened yet. But I have to choose which one to put to death. I am not involved in the death, just in the choice. I came to ask you to help me keep these three people safe from harm. Someone slipped this book to me. It had nothing written in it until I accidentally dropped my blood on it and these names were revealed."

"Listen, lady. There's no crime, and nothing has happened to any of these people yet, so I can't help you. Sorry. But I'll tell you what I'm going to do. I'll send some units out to each house for a welfare check. Okay? Do you feel better now?"

"Yes, thank you, officer," you said, taking the book from the counter with a sullen look.

***

You had your doubts, I'm sure, about whether the police officer even believed you. He must've concluded that it was nonsensical stuff you told him. Nobody except Alfred and I believed anything you had to say. Alfred and I think alike on this one. You turned to leave the station house, and

Alfred opened the door to enter so that you could step out. You laughed, and he walked you back to your work building. He pressed you for more details about the book, but you were suddenly tight-lipped.

Later the same evening, Alfred and you attended the opening performance of "Tommy." You were engrossed in the music, relishing every second, and avoided the book's subject by dancing and singing. I saw you there and watched your entire sickening performance.

You must have been anxious to know what you would learn about the three people in the book the following day.

Alfred met you at the bakery; it was like a rainstorm with clouds. This time, you discussed nothing but the book.

1. Cheryl's brilliant mind worked in any direction, and she was happy to entertain and embrace the dark and sinister. She took a bag full of kittens and drowned them in a ditch.

2. Gabriel's being a boy became complicated once you read that he watched his mother have sex with men repeatedly throughout his early years.

3. Nancy's information was a little more complex.

She became a more serious contender when you read of Nancy's involvement with the sex trafficking of foreign women and young girls.

Your choice became less and less complicated by the page. You knew you were leaning more towards one over the others. You bid Alfred farewell and went to work.

The following day, you texted Alfred, <<*I can't get out of bed since my head feels like it has a tuba in, and my stomach feels like it swallowed a growling dog. I can't even look at the Book and won't make the meet at the bakery.*>> You slept and slept. When you awoke, you texted Alfred again. <<*My insides are turbulent, and my tongue is thick as double cotton balls. Sorry, Alfred, I may not see you tomorrow at this rate either.*>>

Despite wanting to know what the pages said today, Alfred settled for the sickness excuse and left it at that. She stayed home the following day, too.

The day after that, you were ready to tackle the world. You got up and prepared yourself for work before your regular time. You boarded the train, and while you sat there, you gazed out the window.

You quickly approached the bakery counter, ordered breakfast and a coffee, and sat at your table. You pulled out the book and read the pages you'd missed from the last two days. What you uncovered helped you make your choice all that much easier.

1. Despite her dark side, Cheryl is a composer who music aficionados claim is on par with Beethoven. She also has Tourette's syndrome.

2. Gabriel's news, however, couldn't have been better. He received intense therapy and is a Mensa student who volunteers to help others who've suffered like him.

3. Nancy also deals with the production, distribution, and sale of drugs in major cities across the United States. She donates a lot of money to municipalities for needy children.

There is no event this evening, and Alfred is calling to cancel your morning breakfast date. You go about your daily rituals, and when you return from work, you try to guess what you will learn next about each of the three people in the book.

But a fire alarm pulled in your building, sent you wandering half asleep out into the cold rain to stand with the other 185 residents for two hours before the Fire Department could figure it out.

The following day, you slept through your alarm and didn't wake until noon. Alfred had sent numerous texts and gave up around ten o'clock. According to the doorman, everyone else in the building was also late for their appointments. There was no contact between Janice and Alfred. But Alfred and I texted back and forth for a bit. The day was over, and the information remained unseen in the book.

It was the day you dreaded—the day you had to choose who would die. Cheryl, Gabriel, and Nancy had all been whirling around in your head for the last four days, and the new information you read about them today will only help you move closer to your choice; you were sure you were prepared to choose.

1. Cheryl has killed four people and stolen from unsuspecting marks since she was 18 years old.

2. Gabriel's Mensa brain was used to set up elaborate murders of some kids in foster care under his charge, and he had an affair with his eighth-grade teacher.

3. Nancy had never killed anyone and had donated baby blankets to prenatal units for premature babies.

What you read today has yet to secure an opinion or choice. There was a blank page at the end; you stared at it long and hard. On it, you wrote your choice. You placed the book in your bag and hopped on the train. You got off downtown and headed to the police station.

You found the same officer at the same counter and plunked the same book down before him.

"See! Doubting Thomas; Here's the book. My choice is on the last page. I'm curious if there's time to get to the other two—if not all three-? But maybe, if you hurry!" You stared at him and studied his eyes as you looked deeply into them.

The officer saw the writing in the book, wrote down the names, and nodded at you.

"Yes, ma'am, we'll put a car on it, pronto," the officer said.

You turned to leave the station. The police officer yelled at you to return and grab the book. You fell. The officer went around the counter to help you up. When he got to where you were, you disappeared into thin air!

Stunned, the officer returned to his counter; the book had also vanished.

He gasped, saying, "I better send a car to pick up Nancy and Cheryl to ensure their safety."

***

Alfred sat alone in a bakery on the other side of town, as he had done before he met you.

This time, I came in to sit down, asking, "Is this seat taken?" I sat, and after a moment, my eyes met Alfred's. "I apologize for the woman; I understand you had a good impression of her, but how do you believe we performed together?"

"It went perfectly. The woman meant nothing to me. Don't worry about her now. I have another mark. But it means moving bakeries in the morning," Alfred said. He smiled, and we sat quietly. Alfred produced a book with blank pages.

"How did you know she would choose correctly?" I asked.

"Simple. Janice's intelligence won over her heart, as is always true with brainiacs. They're so predictable." Alfred smiled an eerie grin and asked, "Do you want me to be the courier this time?" He had one hand on The Book directly in front of him on the table, halfway between him and me.

ABOUT THE AUTHOR

Lily Finch is a fiction and nonfiction writer who is undergoing rehabilitation from a traumatic brain injury. Among her writings are "The Art of Negotiating With a Big Fish," published on April 2, 2023, on Spillwords.com, and "The Beauty's in the Watching," published on September 20, 2022, with The Literary Yard. On November 9, 2022, "Escape From Morocco" was featured in Half Hour To Kill. On June 2, 2023, in v334—the 30th-anniversary issue of cc&d magazine—on http://scars.tv. Her story was chosen as a finalist for the Globe Soup Open Short Story Competition (2023); it will appear in the forthcoming Wingless Dreamer Publisher anthology Heavenly Harmonies (2024).

PERSONAL PARADISE

BY J. G. MCGRATH

"This is for you," Grandpa Henry said.

He held out a journal. The family birthday party was smaller than the gathering I had had the day before, but there were enough people there that I had to hide my shudder. The cover had the same consistency as the hand that held it, but the book was much darker. When I politely took it from him, the texture was as tough as an overworked callous.

I managed to keep a normal tone. "Is this custom-made?"

Grandpa Henry leaned forward in the chair he had demanded. "This is a family heirloom, going back generations, passed down from father to son. Now, it's yours."

"We have an heirloom?" my mom asked from behind me. "I never heard about this."

Grandpa's face flashed red. "It gets passed down through the *men*. It's for Wade, not *you*."

The other guests made awkward coughs while my dad and sister, Brigitte, glared. I looked to my mom to show I didn't support his words.

"Gee, thanks, Father," Mom muttered, "so glad we've reconnected." She cleared her throat to put on a painfully formal tone. "Thank your grandfather, Wade."

I gave a respectful smile. "Thanks, Grandpa. I'll...get some use out of it."

"Oh, you will," he leaned in close like it was a secret. "The men in our family have gotten a lot out of it... without limit."

He said the last part while leering to the only girl in the room not related to me. Virginia had lived on our block for as long as I could remember. None of that time of being close had made her start dating me, and as she wrapped her hoody around herself like a turtle retreating into its shell, there was little chance of that changing.

Mom and Dad were quick to deal with Grandpa, so I mumbled something respectful to everyone and went to do damage control. Brigitte had already gotten to Virginia, patting her on the back, so I had my work cut out for me to outdo that. Getting closer, I bumped Brigitte aside, knocking the glass from her hand to smash on the floor.

"Jesus," Grandpa Henry said, "maybe if you made your daughter dress properly, she wouldn't be so cold and clumsy."

I had to give another round of sorry looks to the guests along with sorry sounds as the girls picked up the glass. Brigitte bared her crop top like a protest sign until Virginia yelped. Her hand came away from a shard welling with blood.

Brigitte was giving her tissues as I assured her it was okay over more of Grandpa's comments.

Virginia stood. "I think I should just go."

I gave reasons for her to stay, alternate rooms we could go to, and another tissue, but none of it convinced her. She left me holding the used tissue and went to the door with Brigitte's arm around her shoulders. The rest of the party passed in the background while I was stuck to my phone pleading for her to come back. Eventually, the family filed out, and Grandpa was convinced to give up his chair, so I put my phone away long enough to haul all the gifts to my room to be sorted.

Once the cash was in my wallet and the cards were in the trash, all that was left was the book. The feel of it still made me shiver, but I fought through the disgust to look through the pages. They were blank, no family wisdom or, more disappointingly, family bank account numbers.

My phone buzzed. I forgot the book and yanked the phone out so fast everything else in my pocket scattered across my desk. If Virginia was coming over, I could clean up, but otherwise...

My phone had a notification for an update. I sank back into my chair with a moan. The detritus from my pocket covered the desk in front of me. One item cut through my disappointment. At some point, I had shoved Virginia's bloody tissue in my pocket, and now it was soiling my desk.

Fighting my instincts, I picked up the tissue at the edge with the tips of my fingernails. The grip only lasted a few inches, and the tissue dropped onto the open book. I made something between a gag and a scoff and—

Was the blood on the tissue getting less red? My instincts couldn't stop me from leaning in and confirming it was! How was that happening?

Starting from the spot where the tissue touched, red lines spread across the book page. They curved and rounded into—

My instincts finally kicked back in. I flailed to get up, knocking things around my desk and stumbling away. I fell through the door and into the hall... right into Brigitte.

"What the hell, Wade?!" she yelled.

My arm still shook as I pointed back into the room. "The book!"

"Book?"

My hands shook too hard to grab her before she walked in. I could have made a second grab, but that would have brought me dangerously close if she unleashed something.

Brigitte held up the book. "You mean this?"

"There's something inside..." I said.

She flipped through the pages then looked over each one with slow meticulousness. With each turn, her face turned more and more disgusted. I set to sprint away.

"God, this thing feels gross," she said. "Is that what freaked you out? 'Cause I'm not seeing anything written in here."

I stumbled. "What? There were a bunch of lines!"

I forgot my fear and walked to take the book from her. I was ready to point it out, get it through her thick skull so I could be justified in running away... but every page was blank.

I was still checking when Brigitte put a hand on my shoulder. "Just get rid of that thing."

"It would look bad to get rid of it," I said without looking up. "It's from Grandpa."

"And Grandpa is a racist, sexist asshole," she said on her way out of the room. "Just because something has history doesn't mean you have to keep it around, especially if it comes from someone like him."

Then she left. Part of me wanted to go after her and correct her, but I stood still checking the pages.

As I made it back to the first page, I hadn't found anything. I drifted back to my desk to stare in hopes I could pressure the lines into coming back. Even when my eyes started to water, nothing changed.

Blinking my vision back to normal, I spotted something white at the far edge of my desk. Pulling it, the tissue came free from where it had gotten caught between the desk and the wall. Virginia's blood still marred the white of the paper, but the spot was smaller and browner than red. Hadn't that happened when the tissue touched the book?

An idea hit me, and my arm moved while my mind flinched away. I touched the blood to the front page, and the last hints of red faded from the tissue. The lines stretched out from where the papers touched, curling into letters, then words, then a full text.

To build a personal paradise. For pleasure may come from pain, but the recipient of that pleasure need not be the recipient of that pain.

I read the words again and again. They glittered, red and wet. They looked like...

I checked the tissue. Brown. None of the blood left there could be mistaken for red.

My chest was too tight to let out a scream. I had to show someone! I had to show them... what *I* had done with Virginia's blood.

I slammed the book shut, turned out every light, and closed my door. It was too early to sleep, but I got into bed, covering everything but a small gap to keep watch for witnesses.

Fear kept me up for longer than should have been possible, but at some point, I blinked. When I opened my eyes again, the sun streamed through my window. I shot upright, but the book was still on the desk, unmoved. I opened the cover to see if the evidence was still there.

There was nothing under the cover but blank paper. No sign of the bloody words was left, and when I brushed my fingers across the page, there were no indents.

It had... run out? Part of me relaxed that I didn't have any evidence of... blood magic, but my curiosity was hurt. I still didn't have any answers about what the book was. Even if no one could be horrified that I had it, what was the point of not knowing what I was risking getting caught with?

My eyes landed on the thumbtacks in the container at the corner of my desk. Checking that my door was still tightly closed, I pulled one of the tacks out and jabbed it into my finger before I could flinch. Blood welled, and I touched the spot to the book.

The sting of the cut on paper was overpowered by the feeling of sucking. The book was drinking from my finger like a straw! I ripped my hand away, holding my finger like it might wither away. The tip was still bleeding, but my finger was fine.

The page had no fresh red spot or wet words. It hadn't worked, but why? I gave the book a shake like that would help when it hit me. The words had said something about pleasure and pain not needing to come from the same person.

Virginia's tissue still sat on the desk; the only blood was crusted and brown. Touching it to the book produced the same result as my blood. If I could get fresh blood...

"Wade?" Mom's voice called from downstairs. "Don't you have work today?"

I slapped the book closed again. I had been thinking about getting someone else's blood right in the middle of the house! I didn't have a lock on the door or anything!

I did have a shift at my job that day, the perfect reason to be anywhere else. I was dressed within a minute and had my hand on the doorknob to leave when I looked back at the book. It sat out in the open. Picking it up to find a hiding place, nowhere in my room, in the whole house, felt secure enough. Finally, I put the book into my backpack because keeping it close had to be better.

I was out the door before anyone could ask questions about it. On the walk to the restaurant that underpaid me to clean tables, no one gave me a suspicious look. I got into the employee area and locked the bag in my locker before anyone could suspect anything.

Work was boring and not distracting enough. I did try to take my mind off the book by approaching my manager about increasing my pay.

"It's a corporate thing, Wade," he answered. "I only have so much money to divvy up between all the employees. Gotta keep things fair."

I was going to tell him it *was* fair given the quality of my work, but a scream from the kitchen interrupted me. I followed my manager to keep the conversation going, but I stopped when I saw the scene. One of the cooks had mishandled a knife into his palm, and a puddle of blood was on the counter. My manager was in full worker's-comp-avoidance mode, pushing the cook toward the first aid kit and leaving me with an order to deal with the blood.

Making sure not to touch the puddle, I placed paper towels. There was so much! And... wasn't it a waste? The cook had bled all over the place, and no one was getting anything out of it. Who would care if I made the best of the situation and got some information?

Making sure no one was watching, I took one of the less gruesome paper towels and hid it in my pocket. I went through the motions of cleaning up until another cook stepped in to take my place. It was close enough to my clock-out time, so I ended my shift, grabbed my backpack, and left.

It was too risky to test this at home. The restaurant was in the middle of a shopping center, so I went to sit in front of my favorite clothing store. Foot traffic was slow on a Sunday afternoon, and I waited until I was truly alone to bring out the paper towel and the book. Opening the cover, I touched the blood to the first page. The words spread across the paper.

"Hello?" I whispered.

The words might have been able to appear with blood, but they didn't respond to voices. Was this all it was? Grandpa had said this helped him get everything he wanted.

I turned the page and found more red words.

Greater wealth without the need for greater labor.

I had intended to flip through to see if each page had writing, but that title caught my eye. There was more writing, but the tight symbols didn't form any words I knew except for the last line at the bottom of the page.

If this is needed for your paradise, touch these words and speak your acceptance.

The book was offering me more money? How was it supposed to do that? The same part of my brain that told me no one should see the book told me not to tempt fate. At the same time, what could it hurt? I hadn't gotten the money I had wanted from my manager, so why not ask a creepy blood book?

I put my hand to the page. "I accept?"

I wasn't sure what I had expected, maybe a crack of lightning followed by cash falling into my lap, but I hadn't expected the book to pulse. I jerked my fingers away. Where I had been touching, the words squirmed like muscles in effort, but it ended so quickly I thought it was a trick of the light. Then my phone buzzed. With the hand I had just jerked away, I pulled it out of my pocket.

There was a new message from my manager. "Wade, I gave some more thought to what you said before. Decided you are right. Enjoy the extra cash!"

I had to read it at least twenty times before all the words fit together. He was giving me the raise? Then I noticed another notification, this one from my bank. With everything else going on, I had forgotten today was payday. I clicked to make sure there weren't any problems.

There was nothing wrong. In fact, it was the opposite! I hadn't taken the time to calculate exactly how much I would make from the pay period, but I knew it wasn't this much. I had just gotten at least twice what I normally would have!

Other notifications started to chime on my phone, but I couldn't look away from that number. The book had worked! It hadn't just given me the money; it had somehow manipulated the world so I got it. Now I could point to a legitimate source for the money, something I couldn't have done if cash had just fallen into my lap. No trouble for me!

I finally dragged my eyes away from my bank balance to look at my benefactor. The words still glistened on the paper, and my curiosity couldn't help but look at the next page.

Desired possessions without the need for equal trade.

I mouthed the words to figure them out. It made things cheaper? I checked the shopping center around me. People walked between the different shops, not close enough to get a good look at my benefactor, but none of them went into the shop in front of me. I loved its style, but I couldn't afford more than a belt from it... or I couldn't without help.

There were the same unintelligible lines and invitation to speak under the book's second title.

I didn't hesitate this time. "I accept."

There was a pulse and squirm. I knew not to expect anything flashy and kept my eyes on the shop itself. A worker was already walking behind the front displays and stepped into the window to stick a poster to the glass. It announced that everything in the store was *eighty* percent off.

I was on my feet and didn't sit again until I was home. As I set out my haul, it covered not only my bed but half my floor. It was such an enthralling sight I almost didn't notice my phone ringing.

Grandpa's voice came from the speaker. "Made use of that gift yet?"

I touched a real gold necklace. "It's... incredible, Grandpa. How is this possible?"

"Magic," he whispered. "Incredible magic! Generations of men in our family have used it to get exactly what they want. My father used it to keep the family fortune growing. I made sure your grandmother was always mine."

I paused. "The book did something to Grandma?"

He laughed until he had a coughing fit. "Don't think of it like that! The book did things for me; it's all about pleasure. Where the pain goes... don't worry about that. If you're smart with the book, you can protect you and yours. Things will be fine, and they'll be fine on your terms."

"And... did Grandma know about your terms?"

There was a smile in his voice when Grandpa Henry spoke again. "That wouldn't have been my terms if I did it that way."

I mumbled through the rest of the conversation on autopilot. In all of the excitement, I had forgotten about the pain. Grandma hadn't known about it, but what about the pain from the most recent use of the book? Was there pain this time?

I got my answer when I ended the call. For the first time since my big payday, the other messages attracted my attention. The group chat I had with my coworkers had exploded, and I needed to scroll back through dozens of rants to find the first angry text. After reading it, my heart dropped to my toes.

My coworkers had been underpaid. While I had gotten twice what I had expected, the cooks and the girls on the registers were missing several hours' worth of money. Both groups had complained to the manager, but the cooks had been threatened with immigration authorities, and the girls had gotten messages about corporate policy. Now, both groups were discussing their next move and swearing vengeance on the manager.

If they knew I had gotten more money, what would they do to me?

"Do you think they did something with the money?" I wrote.

Dozens of angry hypotheses filled the chat, but none involved me. My heart crawled back to its rightful place, but my brain was still working. If they kept getting underpaid while I went on shopping sprees, they were bound to find out.

The thought of my shopping brought to mind the pain from that. The pain from the money had gone to my coworkers, but what about my second wish? Searching through the texts, I couldn't find any more incidents. Had it gone to someone else?

I suddenly remembered I was in a house with other people who might see my shopping and blame their misfortune on me. I snatched the book like it might be stolen, got out of my room, closed the door behind me, and... almost ran into my mom.

"Wade!" she scolded. "Don't rush around like... honey, you're pale. Is everything okay?"

"I'm fine," I said, voice cracking.

"Did something happen? I heard you on the phone with someone."

"No, that was just Grandpa Henry. He was checking in."

Mom's face fell. "Oh, him."

I latched on to the not-my-room topic. "Mom, what's up with you and Grandpa?"

Her face went from fallen to stony. "I love your grandfather, and whatever problems we had, we're still family. That... are you buying any of this?"

I shook my head.

She sighed. "We'll need to sit down for this."

I was able to guide her away from my room and into the living room. It took her several false starts before she could get on topic.

"I wasn't lying when I said I love him," she said. "He was never abusive, but... it was like everything had to conform to his will. Your grandma tried to work her own job, and he never liked that. He never stopped her, but when she quit because there was so much sexual harassment in her office, he was *so smug* about it."

"So, Grandma got hurt, and he got what he wanted?" I asked like it was unexpected.

"Exactly. I swore it would be different for me, and I cut all ties with him after college. It worked for a while, and all I heard from him was yelling in the background when I called your grandma. I wouldn't have heard from him at all after she passed, but then your dad had his accident, and it was let your grandfather pay the mortgage or lose the house."

"Grandpa's rich?" I asked.

"Our family has had money for quite a while. Your grandfather made a lot of money shorting stocks, but most of it was passed down to him. That money... Wade, I know this sounds bad, but if you look back at our family history, you'll find we were involved in some horrible things in pursuit of wealth. That includes... the slave trade."

My jaw dropped.

Mom's shoulders sagged. "I know, and your dad and I are working to get out from under your grandfather's thumb and away from his money. The history may be bad, but we don't need to let it define us."

She had more comforting words, but I was too far gone. There wasn't just the risk of being blamed for my payday; I could be connected to slave traders! After I automatically assured Mom I was fine, I found a bag that clung to my body and put the book in to keep it as close as a secret.

I kept my head down for the rest of the day. The clothes went out of sight, and I scanned the group chat for signs of more pain or realizations about me. Their anger stuck to the manager and no other pain came up. That mystery remained, but as I sat in the living room ignoring Brigitte's boring news show about Chinese sweatshops, I started to relax.

The next day brought back the stress and school. I put the book in the bottom of my backpack. I kept an eye on everyone who passed on the street as I walked to school, determined to keep my secret. Then my phone buzzed.

Virginia had texted. "Can we talk before school? Something awesome to tell you!"

I started replying like a psycho. In a minute, I had named where to meet, how soon, and assured I would be there.

Then someone bumped into me. It barely penetrated my excited haze until I felt a tug at my backpack. I spun to catch the culprit, but they had already turned down another street. I reached around to check my backpack. It felt normal, but what if...

The street was too exposed, so I sprinted towards school. My feet slid as I slammed into the bathroom. I was alone other than a classmate at the sinks dealing with a gruesome nosebleed, and he was out of sight when I locked myself in a stall. The zippers protested as I forced open the bag and... found the book.

It took several deep breaths to get my heart under control. Then a smile spread on my face. I still had the book, and I would soon have Virginia.

I left the bathroom and got to the agreed place. She was there, waving me closer.

"Thanks so much for coming," she said, bouncing like she could burst.

"I'd always come for you," I said.

"I could have waited until after school to tell you but..."

Her bouncing had become an excited tremble. She leaned in with a hand cupped around her mouth. I moved my ear to her. The closeness, her breath, and anticipation made my heart pound so hard I was worried she could hear. I waited for what I was due.

"I came out to my parents," she said.

My heart dropped. "What?"

"I know! I was so scared about how they would react, but my girlfriend told me she had my back, and I told them, and they didn't get mad, and..." Her words had become so high-pitched that everything else was a squeal.

My words were stiff. "So, they accepted... that you're a lesbian?"

She still couldn't make words but nodded. After getting a few breaths in, she gave me more details. No matter how much she got herself under control, she never picked up on my pain.

Eventually, the bell stopped the torture. She waved goodbye, and I held it together enough to wave back. My legs were lead, but I got to my classes in a haze. The teachers talked about something, but I didn't hear.

How could she do that to me? I wanted her so much, had wanted her for so long. After being such a good friend to her, she had left me high and dry for some girl! I needed her, deserved her! For so much waiting and so much support, I was due my reward! The world shouldn't be taking her from me; it couldn't! I had to make this right!

And I could... with a little blood...

The last bell rang, and I ran back to the bathroom. The classmate had left the sink, and the porcelain was spotless white. I plunged my hand into the trash, shoving aside used paper towels until I saw red. My bag fell to the floor, forgotten once I got the book. The pages drank the blood, and I flew through the offers until I found the perfect one.

Union without chance of rejection.

"I accept."

This time, I wanted more than a pulse and squirm, crashes of thunder, bolts of lightning, and Virginia running in to throw her arms around my neck. I got none of that. No one ran into the bathroom, leaving me alone with my hand on a bloody book.

I raised the book above my head, ready to throw it against the wall, but that could expose me. I still had the money and clothes even if I hadn't gotten the girl, so I slammed the book back into my bag and slunk in the direction of home. I grumbled the whole way, taking no notice of anyone or anything I passed. That was probably why I bumped into the cop car parked in front of my house.

I blinked at it. Could someone from work have found me out? I ran for the house before anyone could grab me in the yard. Two policemen stood in our living room, hands on hips as they faced down Mom and Brigitte. Mom had her arms around my sister, and Brigitte held her arms around her ripped crop top.

"How the hell is my daughter the one in trouble here?" Mom bit at the question.

The taller policeman was unfazed. "Ma'am, your daughter exposed herself in public."

"I *exposed myself* because a guy *ripped my shirt*!" Brigitte shouted back. "And he ripped my shirt because I wouldn't kiss him!"

The policeman raised a finger to her. "Watch it. We're letting you off *this time*, but the new ordinance is clear: women are not to draw attention with sexual displays."

Mom had a response, but I missed it as my phone buzzed. Virginia was not only messaging but calling. I moved upstairs to get away from the noise and put the phone to my ear.

"Wade?" Virginia bowled over my greeting. "Wade, thank god, I need your help."

I could have laughed at the request after she had denied me, but something told me to wait. "What do you need?"

"Have you heard about the new law?" she asked. "Something about women not making public sex displays or something. Well, it turns out me kissing my girlfriend counts! Some guys assaulted her for it, and the police grabbed *her*!"

"So… you can't be with your girlfriend?"

"No! Or any girl! My parents are freaked out that I might get arrested just for holding hands, and they're threatening to send me away. I keep telling them I can keep out of trouble, but they…" She sniffed. "I hate to ask this, but I need something to assure them I can be safe. Could you act like my boyfriend?"

She had more pleas and apologies for asking so much, but I just smiled. "Of course. I'll do anything to help."

She was ready with thanks, but I assured her it was no problem as I walked into my room and closed the door behind me. The world might be horrible to Virginia, but I would keep her safe, I would *never* be horrible to her. Brigitte might need to stop wearing crop tops, but home would be fine for her, I wouldn't make her feel unsafe.

I brought out the book as I arranged all the details with Virginia. I needed something to make sure I had the control I needed. The words still glistened, so I found the right request.

Power and resources without check or limit.

ABOUT THE AUTHOR

You may have heard of him from his feature on the Two Writers Walk into a Bar podcast or his featured story, That Light, on the upcoming Life is Strange podcast, and now, Jackson McGrath welcomes you to his newest tale. Originally from America, McGrath has lived in (and certainly wasn't chased out of) Vietnam and Spain and has settled in the Netherlands, working as an ESL (English as second language) instructor. While many would consider autism a hindrance to writing, McGrath has used his unconventional mind in conjunction with his worldly travels to construct a unique writing style. □

A GLIMMERING SUNSET

BY MIRIAM TOYAMA

The world was made of an ever-moving sunset, on the edge of a cliff that belonged to a liquid place where nothing stayed the same, but kept dripping and flowing. It was beautiful, he thought. He could stay forever watching the golden turn into orange, and then into red in this impossible sunset. It must be a sunset, he thought. He read about them. People who lived on planets, lovely planets orbiting around a sun, had this. He heard "You could stay forever, Lucas", before waking up in his tiny home on the space station. Life was so unfair.

There was someone at the door. Only one person could wake him up so early - and on his day off! That's what you get for having brothers: pranks, late-night outings, early morning breakfasts, sharing of good and bad news. His brother started touching everything as soon as he entered. His attention was immediately drawn to the object on the table.

"What is this for?" asked Thomas.

"Old tech, you know, to add to the collection. It's called a book."

"What does it do?" he said as he picked it up and shook it.

"It seems to be a device to pass on knowledge, information. That's what the seller said."

"But how?"

"This one is blank, but he said other ones have things written on them, you know, so you can read."

"I don't understand. How do I search for topics? How do I read the news?"

"No no, each book is about a fixed topic, you see? So what is written inside doesn't really change. If you want a different topic you have to get another book. And if you want to read the news, well, I don't know."

"Too complicated! Why do you collect this kind of thing? So boring!!! You're so weird! How can you be so weird and be my brother? But also, what is this covered in? The outside of this book thing is really odd, what is this?"

"Oh, the seller said the book cover is made out of leather."

"What is leather? It feels old and gritty. I don't like it."

"Leather is a dead animal's skill, remember? History class"

"This is made out of dead animals? Why?" he said, dumping the book on the table.

"Come on! Be careful!"

"If it's super old how did you get your hands on it? Did you spend a month's wage on it? How many month's wages? Do I have to pay for your food now?" He poked the book.

"He made me a good deal. This one doesn't have things written, so it's less valuable. And he was restocking, making space for new things! Also, no one else wanted to buy it, so he sold it to me at a discount."

"Of course, no one else wanted it! It's useless and ugly! Who is the seller? Is it that old man in the market district? The one with the little signs that say 'If you break it you buy it'? That keeps following you inside the store, is it that one?"

"Bret is not that bad."

"He kicked me out!"

"You wouldn't stop touching things."

"Gee... How can he be re-stocking? Where did he get a new batch of old stuff from?"

"Antiques, he sells antiques! He has to travel around, curate, and all that stuff. Don't be so annoying, yeah?"

"Whatever, can we go now? I'm hungry."

"I have to run back to the office, it will be real quick. Can you wait?"

"You go by my house then, and I'll take the book thing as a guarantee you'll not just leave me hungry."

He lay down in his bed but couldn't sleep. Sleeping was for when you die, or for when you come back from work too tired to do anything else. You just hit the bed and wake up the next morning. He sat on the table and stared at the book, and it felt familiar, almost comforting. It was just like the times he visited his grandmother, and he would spend hours staring at the ceiling, watching faces come up, and then disappear.

"It's normal," someone told him, "it happens to everybody."

"The brain looks for things it can recognize, patterns, so you see faces in ceilings." His grandmother said she would see animals in clouds when she was little, back when the sky had clouds.

The book only had a few faces, and they stared back at him. It was disconcerting. It had been over an hour, and Lucas hadn't come back yet. Another porridge breakfast, the fantastic life of a bachelor abandoned by his brother.

The book was still on the table. He played with it for a bit, but it did nothing. Such a boring thing, it didn't shine, it didn't do anything. It just stood there, with its many faces looking back at him. Better to spend your money on shiny things. He himself had a collection of shiny and pointy things: knives. That's what his grandmother had told him they were called. She said they were really useful back in the day, to cook, or to just have around. She gave him the first one. He liked to clean the knives, so they would be shinier.

One problem with those shiny, pointy things is that they are often sharp, and sharp things sometimes cut careless people. He'd never seen so much blood. It should be inside his body, not flowing free on his table.

"Shit! He's gonna be so mad! Why is the blood staining this book thing? Why isn't it coming off?" He tried to wipe it off, tried running it through some water. It only made things worse. What a damned thing!

He suddenly felt tired. Despite being mid-morning and, against his personal beliefs, he laid in bed and soon dozed off. He dreamed of a liquid world where the colors of the sky would fade into the ground, and nothing was ever fixed. In this world, he could hear a voice calling, a sweet sound, and he followed it to the edge of a cliff with a sunset that exploded in gold and red. He felt someone beside him, but he couldn't move. He could barely make out the silhouette from the corner of his eye.

"A dream, I've heard about those. Didn't know they'd be so colorful".

"*Not a dream.*"

"Of course, it's a dream. We don't have this."

"*A memory.*"

"Whose memory? I have never seen anything like this to remember."

"*It doesn't matter. It's just a place we can talk. Tell me, if you could have anything, what would it be? Anything in the whole universe?*"

"Hum... it could be anything, right? That's how dreams work? Payback. My brother stood me up. Payback seems appropriate." His mind went blank; he didn't know what he should want.

"*Then it shall be.*"

He woke up covered in sweat, heart beating fast and head pounding. When he was younger, one of his friends said this was how it felt to face a predator. But, how could any of them know? There were no predators to humans. Such a sweet dream, but his skin was crawling. He didn't have much experience with dreams, but he thought they were not real, so he just stopped thinking about it and got ready for work.

Work was hard, one of the last remaining physical work positions on the space station: fixing things. That's what he usually told people: fixing things that the little bots couldn't or wouldn't do right. Usually, people wouldn't ask further than this. The money was good, and he could care for himself and his brother. Today's assignment was in the docking bay. He was leaving when the police showed up at his door.

"It's your brother. His body was found at his desk. We contacted your superior. You have a couple of days off". That's what they said. He felt his knees hitting the floor and the world began to spin.

It was a nightmare. His younger brother was gone. What could he do? He didn't do anything. He didn't tell people. He didn't make arrangements. It was almost nighttime, and he still hadn't managed to leave the house. He paced back and forth, drank more caffeine than he should have, ate too much sugar; he would have drunk alcohol if he had known where to buy it. He finally collapsed with his head lying on the table. Again he saw himself in an ever-changing place, colorful and bright, facing the sunset and unable to look to the sides.

"I don't have time for this," he thought.

"*Oh, but you do. What else could you do with your time?*" Her voice was soft and calm.

"My brother is dead, and that's more important than whatever this is." Tears gathered in his eyes.

"*You asked, and I delivered.*"

"What?" He furrowed his eyebrows.

"*You said he had to pay, so he paid.*" Her voice was like velvet.

"That's not what I meant!" he screamed.

"*Hum, what did you mean, then?*"

"Not this! Bring him back!"

"*Humans are so volatile...*"

"Undo it!"

"*If that is your wish. What will you give me in return?*"

"You messed up! Just bring him back!"

"*Hum... No. You asked, and I delivered it. I know what I want, that corner of your soul where you hide who you truly are. Give me that, and I will change his fate.*" A feeling close to lust could almost be heard in her voice this time.

"Fine! It's all yours! Keep the dark corner of whatever! Just bring him back!"

"*It's a deal. Remember your words, remember them precisely.*"

Another dream. Who knew these dream things were so awful? Who knew they would cause you to wake up in tears? He preferred a time when he didn't have them - when his brother was alive and complaining. But today, well today, he couldn't keep delaying the inevitable, he had things to do.

At the Medical Center, he was immediately greeted by the police, again.

"Can you follow us, please? Your brother's case has had a development." He was taken to a private room at the very end of the medical center. At first sight, it looked like a dead person had forgotten to lie down, and was now strapped to the bed growling and screaming. It was his brother. He looked pale; he looked gone.

"What happened?" He moved toward the bed.

"Don't get too close, he's biting. We don't know what happened. We were hoping you could tell us. Did anything out of the ordinary happen? He was dead and today he is like this." They stopped him from getting too close.

"Not really. Last time I saw him, he said he had to drop by his work. He always eats the same things, and he doesn't do any drugs. He bought a book thing!"

"What is a book thing?"

"It's an old item, he collects old things."

"Can you bring it over?"

They ran several tests on the book but found nothing. It seemed it was just cellulose, some blood, and organic material, nothing really dangerous. Whatever was wrong with his brother, they said, it was not the book's fault. They tested Thomas, as well, and found nothing out of the ordinary. When he was finally sent home, he tossed the book back on the table. The stains were no longer bright red. He opened the book for the first time, and to his

surprise, there were things written on it! It was hard to rea
d.

"What fucking font is this? It's so wobbly. Is this an 'e'?
Why is it reddish-brown?".

He could read parts of it - something about a pact. She
would grant a wish, and the receiver would pay with... with
what? Damned useless thing.

His head was hurting. This time he just lay on the floor
and slipped back into the ever-changing world, the only
dream he had ever had.

"*Long time no see!*"

"This again? I don't even feel rested after this fucking
dream!"

"*Oh, that's because you're not technically sleeping.
You're just wandering around in my place.*"

"Can I wake up, then?"

"*I'm afraid not. I'm here to collect. Also, you can
make another wish. What would you like it to be?*"

"Another wish? You didn't even grant the last one! My
brother is all screwed up, tied to a hospital bed!"

"*Oh, but I did! You said 'bring him back', and I
did.*"

"What did you do? That's not what I wanted! I wanted
him whole! Not this messed up thing!"

"*No matter, I gave you what you said you wanted,
and now, I get what I want. But you can make an-*

other wish. What do you want this time around?" It sounded like she was smiling.

"I... I don't know, what is there to want?" He felt a sharp pain in his chest and saw a bright light.

Once more, he woke up covered in sweat. But this time his heart was quiet. He opened the book once more. The blood stains were fading away, but he thought the writing inside seemed to be filling more space. He still couldn't read everything - something about souls. He was starting to hate this thing.

He took the book with him anyway, and passed by his brother's place. He wanted to grab a couple of his favorite things when he visited him. The house was sealed, and the police were searching it, wearing protective gear. It made it look like the place was contagious.

"Excuse me, this is my brother's place," he said to the officer.

"Wait here, please."

Standing there made him realize how exhausted he was. All these nights filled with colorful dreams were leaving him tired and scared. It felt like days until the officer came back with his superior.

"You're the brother? Can you tell us about his last days before... well, before? Did you notice anything out of the ordinary?"

"Not really. He went to work, then came home. We were supposed to have breakfast. He likes to go to that store that sells old stuff, the one on Market Square. That's what he does most weeks, he works, comes home, we go get something to eat, and he browses for old stuff."

"We'll check the store. Thank you for your help. The medical center is closed to visitors at the moment. That whole section of the station is off-limits. You should go back home or to work. We'll contact you when needed." The officer just turned and walked away.

Thomas still wanted to see his brother, so he headed to the medical center. It seemed the cop was telling the truth; he couldn't get near it. There were so many officers patrolling today. The station had a series of maintenance tunnels, and he worked maintenance.

"The Medical Center probably could use some maintenance," he thought.

He looked for an empty corridor, found the maintenance entrance, and let himself in. He wasn't used to this part of the station and had to follow the maps on the walls. There were so many contingency doors! It took him more time than he wished, but he found an exit just to the side of the Medical Center. He tried to open it, but it wouldn't budge. He could hear people screaming from somewhere. His heart sank.

"Shit, how do I find my brother?" He tried another exit door after exit door. All of them were sealed. Behind each one, he could hear screaming - and smell blood. There was nothing left for him to do, so he went back home. Once inside, he sat on the table and stared at the book for a while. It didn't do anything. He was forced to open it - still the same - some pages were stained and some had writing on them. He still couldn't read it all, just snippets here and there.

He knew he should be feeling something about his brother, but he didn't. He thought he should cry or scream, but he couldn't. He felt nothing. He banged his head on the table a couple of times just to make sure he was awake, and that he had any feelings at all. Maybe he should sleep, find the sunset lady he could never really see. Maybe dreaming would help him cope. He closed his eyes. I took even less time for him to find himself in front of the sunset. He knew she was there, and this time he tried hard to turn his body, his face, toward her. It was in vain, she was always in the corner of his eyes, no matter what he did .

"*Do you have another wish?*" she asked.

"I want to know what this is, I want to know if this is real, if this is making my brother sick. I want to know who you are."

"*So many wishes! Which one do you want to fulfill first? Do you want to know the price?*"

"Why should there be a price for this? It's not a wish, just information!"

"*Hum.. It's information you wish me to share with you. You see, wishes are tricky little things. They can be as little as wishing to wake up and as big as wishing life was different - and humans are filled with all kinds of wishes. Delicious!"*

"So will you answer me?"

"I want your brightest memory, the one that brings a smile to your face when you think of it. Yes! That one, from when you were little and you showed your favorite cartoon to your brother!"

"What the fuck are you? Just why?"

"I am me, and there is no one just like me, or even remotely close to me, in the whole universe - in all of creation, I am unique. I am real, and a memory, and a dream. I just am."

"That answers nothing!"

"Have it your way."

"Tell me your name."

"No."

"Is this real? Are you affecting reality?"

"You are the one affecting reality! I am just here to help."

"What does that mean?"

"It means that what you wanted, what you asked for, has happened."

"I didn't want any of this! The book! Is the book yours? What is it for?"

"The book is yours, it's your contract with me. Is there anything else you wish for? Money? Fame?

Power? Maybe happiness? Otherwise, it's time to pay."

"Pay? You didn't even tell me your name."

"My name wasn't part of the contract. You wanted to know if this was a dream, if this was connected to your brother's 'illness', and you wanted to know who I am. All of those were answered. I have all the time but you don't, so what is it going to be? Another wish? Payment?"

"I... what do you mean I don't have all the time?"

"Well, you are sleeping, but events are unfolding. Would you like to take a look before you make your next wish? I can grant you a glimpse. I'll do it for free, because we're friends."

Still inside the dream, he could see the station. *"As of now the Station is in quarantine. Stay in your quarters, do not go to the streets, do not try to leave the station".* People were running, fighting, and biting each other. The Docking Bay was on fire.

"What happened? I need to find my brother!"

"I think this is what is happening, or will happen? Not sure anymore, it's been years since I've done this. But your brother is kind of safe, to be honest. He's still in that same room, strapped to the bed. He's better off than most of the other people. Remember, we still have one last conversation, OK? I'll collect

what is mine later. But if you want to wake up, well, that's easy." He heard fingers snapping.

He woke up in his place, his face on the table with the book lying beside him. The world seemed quiet.

"Maybe it's just a dream, maybe this has nothing to do with me," but he wasn't sure.

This time he got into his work clothes, grabbed his tools, and headed out. First stop: the Medical Center. Walking and crawling through the tunnels, he found himself getting closer. It seemed to be the same as before, especially the screaming and the smell. How could this be? This time he could open the exit door. He regretted this instantly.

He was met by one of the screaming people, pale skin and colorless eyes, covered in blood. His screams were attracting other zombie-like people. Some of them were missing limbs, some had bite marks. The one in front of him was missing most of its jaw and probably had a broken ankle, but he was close enough to grab Thomas's shoulder.

He fell to the floor under the weight of the thing. He kicked and screamed, then he ran and ran until he reached one of the contingency doors. They were meant for things like fire or water, not raging bleeding people missing body parts. But it worked. Whoever they were, the door held them back.

What should he do? Could he evacuate the station? Could people be saved? Was there even time?

He decided he should check on the places that were burning in his dream. The Market Square was first. Following the tunnels, he found an exit in the middle of a deserted alleyway. It seemed nobody was spitting blood, a good sign, but people were on edge, walking fast and looking back. There were more cops too.

There was tension in the air. The store where his brother bought the book was closed. It looked like it had been closed for days. He asked around to see if anyone knew what happened to the owner. Rumor was, he just closed one day and left, never to be seen again, probably left the station.

People seemed to think something was happening in the Medical Center, but they were not sure what. Some said it was an ill-fated experiment, a new virus, or maybe it was just a prank. Well, whatever was going on, something was definitely amiss, that much he knew. At least the Market Square was still there. There was hope, so maybe the dream was just a dream.

Then, suddenly, he heard it - a desperate scream, followed by even more screaming. He looked back. A crowd was forming. He could barely see what was happening. It looked like a fight. A tall man was holding someone back as others attended to a lady on the floor. She was holding her neck. He had a bad feeling in the pit of his stomach. The smell of blood and decay spread in the air. He could hear more and more screams and moans coming from the alley - no words, just indiscernible screams.

"No... did I do this? Is it my fault? Did I not seal the tunnels correctly?"

"Run! Just run away!" he screamed at everyone.

A slightly mad person, yelling slightly mad things, was nothing new to anyone in the Market Square. No one listened, no one moved, and when the horde of zombie-like creatures emerged from the alley, it was too late. They launched forward into the middle of the crowd. They tore pieces of flesh and tramped people to the floor.

He ran for his life. He heard the sound system announcing they would be closing off the market district. They would be closing off everything, quarantining, and waiting for help. He ran. They all ran, but there was nowhere to go. He ran for home.

"What should I do?" he gasped as he closed the door. "My brother? The people? They should be saved, shouldn't they?" He thinks he should care more, but he doesn't. Wondering what to do, his eyes landed on the book. The blood on the sides was almost gone. "Is it possible? This damn thing did all this? I'll destroy it!".

He tried. Fires were not allowed but he managed to start one using an old thing his grandmother said was used for camping, whatever that was. The flames were beautiful, orange and yellow, they rose and fell, but the book seemed to remain unharmed. He tried to cut the book to pieces, nothing. It seemed as if nothing could destroy it. A wild thought crossed his mind. "Maybe just throw it into space, maybe it will be lost forever and no one will lay eyes on it again. That would be good, wouldn't it? He's not sure."

He decided to head for the Docks. The streets were empty. Everybody was safe and sound - he hoped. His hands were shaking a little, but there was no one else to do the job, so he stepped forward. He walked into the maintenance tunnels once more. He had to take one of the tunnels close to Market Square. He moved as quietly as he could, paying attention to everything. Even though he was expecting it, he jumped and nearly fell when he heard the first scream break the silence. It was like the zombie people could hear him. After the first one, others followed, and the tunnels were flooded with screaming.

"So many! How many have died? Because they can't be considered alive, they might as well be dead."

He reached the docks. His hands trembled with fear as he reached for the door. He opened it anyway. No fire. Relief. It's what he thinks he should feel. Something could be saved. If he could save at least a few people, at least stop it from spreading, then everything would be OK. He stepped out of the door. Nobody was there, as it should be. They were all safe and sound. All the non-dead-like people were safe and sound. Yet he could still hear screams and growling at a distance. How could this be? The Market and the Medical Center should be far enough that he shouldn't be hearing them.

"How do I do this? Should I just put the book in one of the airlocks?" He tried, but he found out that the station wouldn't let him. He punched in his access code. It didn't work. The station sat still in space, closed, waiting for help. "No... what should I do? Manually override the system?"

He had a plan. He would open the inner door, leave the book inside, close the inner door, and open the outer door. If it didn't work, well, he would have to rethink who he was and see if he was the self-sacrificing type. He didn't think he was, but maybe facing death and the possibility of this, whatever this was, maybe he would have a change of heart. He hated that this was life now. He took his tools and started tinkering.

It wasn't long before he managed to open the inner door. Only then did he realize that the screams and growling were louder, and he smelled blood - old blood mixed with fresh blood. The room wasn't empty anymore. He could see them coming. The zombies had already blocked the path where he came in. The only option was to step into the airlock and close the door. They had driven him to a dead end. In just a few seconds, they were piling up at the inner door, banging and screaming. On the other side, there was only space - lonely, cold space. He sat on the floor.

"There's no escape now," he sighed, remembering all the people locked in their homes, remembering his world, remembering his brother - remember that glimmering sunset and waiting for help.

He thinks he should help them; he thinks he should feel sad or scared. He started working on opening the outer door. It shouldn't be too difficult. Death should be quick, and the book would be gone. He was working on the door mechanism when something went wrong, and he started a fire. He tried putting it out, got burned in the process, missed a step and fell on the floor, hitting his head. The last thing he heard was growling and screams.

The sunset was forever gorgeous, the colors dripping and glimmering.

"Do you think you'll be on fire? Humans are pretty flammable. Or maybe you will just run out of air! What do you think will happen first? Hunger, oh no no... you all die of thirst first, right? It's a good thing that you can be here and not feel it. I'm really nice to you! Maybe you're my soft spot."

"Just why?" he sighs.

"Why not? This is what I do, I take, I expand, and conquer."

"You want more people?"

"Of course silly! Did you think you would be enough?"

"But why? You don't need us! Look at this place!"

"Could have, wouldn't have to be honest. This would have always been the outcome when you and your brother bought the book, opened it, and bled on it. There was no other path, you see."

"Let me stay then. It's my last wish. Bring my brother here. Bring him whole." He thinks he should save him.

"I could do that. Are you sure that's what you want?"

"Yes, I'm sure"

He looked to the side and saw his brother, but not the person he used to be, the bright and complaining brother, but now the pale, seeking blood brother locked in the Medical Center.

"What did you do? That's not what I wanted! I want my real brother, not this semi dead thing!"

"Oh, my mistake! You see, they are both your brother, and this is him as a whole. So, in the end, I did give you your brother. And here's the good news - in here none of you can die! Isn't it neat? You can stay together forever!"

ABOUT THE AUTHOR

Míriam Toyama is a Brazilian teacher. She lives with her husband on São Paulo's countryside, and enjoys writing fantasy and horror stories. She also loves to practice martial arts in her spare time. □

THE ELEPHANT IN THE AVOCADO

BY SUSAN IMBS

Late spring sunlight danced with the prisms in the window of the galley kitchen in our student flat at St. Michaelmas College of Magic. The bell in the clock tower struck
8:00. I still had an hour before class.

Over the weekend, I had found a blank journal at a rum-
mage sale. The heavy vellum pages bound in faded leather
had whispered to me of spells and secret sigils when I saw

it lying in a discard pile. Now it waited on the counter, ready to record my cooking creations, in case they turned out well. Cooking and Magic have a lot in common, and I am good at both.

Humming a dance tune, I gathered my avocado from the hanging fruit basket and sliced around its length. As I started to pull the top half away, the pit burst open. The loose half went flying, bouncing on the counter-top. A three-inch-tall white elephant with pink-edged ears hopped from the pit onto my palm. I was so startled my razor-sharp paring knife slipped, nearly taking the tip off my left ring finger. Bright red blood spurted from the slash, splattering all over the counter and the cover of the journal.

The elephant, unperturbed, made a leg, bowing her tiny head. A high soft voice redolent of the Raj spoke. "Greetings, oh daughter of Eve. I am Marissa Ranhel of the Maj Torindae, daughter of Queen Larstinga Ranhel, may she reign long in peace."

I'll admit it. I froze for a moment. I had an avocado, a talking elephant, and a blood-slicked finger on my left hand, a glistening knife in my right, and the cover of my new journal was getting stained with blood. I didn't know how to prioritize the demands.

Except. The cover wasn't staining. The blood was soak-ing in as a beautiful crimson script flowed across the leather. "**The Book**" it wrote. I leaned closer, ignoring avocado and elephant and spurting more blood on the cover.

"**of Choices**" the invisible pen drew, adding an intricate sigil under the two lines of text. The next drop of blood splattered on the cover and pooled, which broke the fascination the book had woven over me. The words faded from the leather; they remained burned in my memory.

"Oh, dear, oh dear," said the little elephant. "That was not expected."

I blinked at her in confusion. My finger started screaming for attention.

"Shit! Sorry! Shiiiiiit!" I yelped as I tossed the knife onto the counter, grabbed Marissa by the scruff of her neck, flicked the avocado near the waiting bowl, and parked the elephant near the olive-green fruit. A dish towel wrapped around my finger kept me from dripping on the wood floor as I raced for the bathroom.

A steady stream of curses and the slamming of a couple of drawers followed as I dug out the required first aid gear. A tense silence descended as I cleaned the wound, realigned the hunk of fingertip, applied pressure and some of my healing energy, and bandaged everything in place.

Returning to the kitchen with the bloodied dish towel, I shoved it in a bowl to soak with some Blood-B-Gone. Shock from pain and blood loss was making me shaky. Food and fluids were going to be required. I turned to the other counter to see what might be salvaged of my breakfast.

I froze. The tiny elephant was levitating the perfect creamy flesh from one half of the avocado into the mixing bowl. The other shell was already deposited in the small garbage bag hanging from a frame hooked on one of the cabinet drawers.

The book's cover had resumed its innocuous brown blankness. Aside from the drop drying on one of its corners, there were no other traces of blood anywhere in the kitchen even though the cut had been deep, slicing back a hunk of fingertip the size of a kidney bean.

It was all too much. I pulled a bottle of Mystic Mango kombucha out of the fridge and sat down on the rug, leaning back against the cabinet that faced my workstation.

Of course, there was a tiny white elephant making guacamole for me.

Of course, I had dragged home a bloodthirsty journal called The Book of Choices.

What else would I expect these days, with graduation exams coming up and all?

I thunked my head gently against the cabinet a few times, then worried the cap off the bottle and drank some of the mango goodness. Eyes closed, I focused on the sweet tingly tartness of the cold drink, grounding myself in the here and now to offset blood loss and rising panic.

"Can't a being sleep around here? Sounded like you were restarting the Third Battle of Mithras Main all by yourself."

I twitched at the deep rumbling voice near my ear. I stubbornly kept eyes and mouth closed. Just what I needed. The wit and wisdom of Harrowfax Hammer-hands, my goblin suitemate. A tiefling named Honor Morlech and a half-elf called Sarwin Miradark completed the roster of our merry little band. Me? I am Becca Merri-weather, human descendant of the dragon Merriweather, foundress of our House centuries ago.

He sniffed deeply. "Smells like you managed to draw first blood. Ow! A fingertip! Dang. That had to hurt."

I heard him head across to stare up at the countertop where Marissa Whatsahoosie had finished mashing the av-ocado by levitating herself into the bowl and doing the elephantine equivalent of a tap dance.

My eyes opened and my voice took on an edge of steel. "Do. Not. Touch. Anything. On. That. Counter."

I knew what the other kids called me, to my face and be-hind my back. *Demented Dragonet. Golden Glitch.* Maybe I have a bit of trouble with my temper sometimes. And my magic is tied to my emotions, so ...

Hamm had witnessed my little flares before and had picked up the splinters of blasted sofas and bookcases af-terwards. He nervously backed towards the kitchen en-trance, hands raised, palms towards me, eager to placate.

"Hey! No worries, yeah? Heard some voices, came down to see if you were alright. Which you are. Or if you needed help. Which you obviously don't."

His hand snagged the first thing it found – a bag of microwave popcorn still in its wrapper. "I'll just take this back to my room for a snack. You give a holler if you need anything, yeah? Ohhhhkay." He backed across the threshold, turned, and bolted for his room.

A prim voice floated down from the countertop. "I say, daughter of Eve, that was hardly sporting of you, now, was it?" The crisp round tones of Received English rolled out of the tiny elephant.

I took another deep swig from my kombucha, wishing there were a stiff jot of dark rum in it, even if it was a quarter past eight on a bright sunny Tuesday.

"No, it wasn't. I had a few other things on my mind. Ya know, a talking elephant that could swim in a teacup and books that drink blood and all." Another slug of mango goodness offered a reason to stop talking for a minute.

"It is customary to wait until graduation to reveal ourselves to our chosen, but when you brought -that- into your home," and she waved her trunk in the direction of the journal, "well, of course we couldn't stand by and watch it all fall apart, now could we?"

I stared at the tiny creature standing on the edge of the counter, feet covered in avocado goo, ears flared out. For a moment I thought I saw her standing there with her hands on her hips, but elephants don't have hands, right?

"We? We who?" I suddenly cracked up. "I know! You and the mouse in your pocket!" It was all too much. I sat there laughing until I cried. I suspect the pain of the sliced digit and the onset of shock may have had something to do with my reaction.

I closed my eyes again.

"This is a dream. I will wake up now. It will be seven thirty, the avocado will be sitting pristinely in the basket waiting for me to turn it into breakfast, and I will be on time to classes for a change."

I cracked one eye open, then the other. Nope. Elephant. Mashed avocado. Bandaged finger. And a weird glow from under the cover of the blood-loving journal.

"Get over here, Miss Rebecca Bandyhort Merriweather. You started this. You awakened the Book with your blood, creating a pact that has only one resolution. It will offer you a choice and consequences. You will fulfill the options given or suffer the penalty. If you refuse, you will not see another sunrise."

I scooted across the floor in response to the command in her voice. The use of my full name pissed me off. A pale wisp of aurum power flickered around me.

"None of that." Marissa was crisp, no nonsense. She flicked her trunk. My rising power snuffed out like a candle.

"Ow!" I had a sudden feeling of empathy for a candle wick. "It's Becca. Just bloody Becca." I hated Rebecca. It always felt like my parents had wished for a lady-like daughter which I would never be.

Rising to my knees put me nose to nose with Miss Marissa Ranhel. That proved to be a bad idea. Up close she was so small I had to cross my eyes to see her, which made the room swim. I grabbed the book and sat back on the floor to examine it.

It still looked like the unused journal I had picked up. Aside from the one dried bit of blood on the cover, the ratty thing was undamaged, unmarked. I tried to scrape the drop off. Nothing doing. I wet my finger and tried to rub it off.

I tilted my head back so I could look up at Marissa.

"Blood pact, huh. That is never a good thing, is it?"

"Not in all my many years, daughter of Eve. That is why I am here. To help you thread the needle and reduce the damage the Book will inflict."

She hopped off the counter, flared her ears and floated to my left shoulder. Her tiny green feet minced down my arm so she could inspect my gauze-wrapped finger. It dawned on me that her feet weren't covered in avocado. They were green. A pretty green, like tree leaves in high summer.

I must be getting loopy.

"This will not do at all," she muttered. I felt an electric current buzz through my hand and into my fingertip. The neatly wrapped bandage blew off, flying across the kitchen to bounce against the facing cabinet.

My finger showed only a thin line pink scar.

"We need to go to a warded work room, Miss Becca. We have much to do and not a great deal of time in which to do it." Her accent was more pronounced now and edged with ice. I sighed. So much for class today.

An hour later we found ourselves in the deepest spell-working cavern on campus, one usually reserved for the graduate students and faculty. Aside from the stone altar in the center of the space and the copper circle laid in the floor near the walls, the only things in the room with us were the items from my spell kit arranged on the altar according to Marissa's precise directions.

Two thick beeswax candles burning on the altar shed a clear soft light and a hint of sweetness. The book and my two ritual knives lay between them. The blue glow of the room wards was clearly visible. Marissa fluttered around me, swooping down to nudge things into proper alignment and circling the candles.

My ebony-handled athame, the double-sided blade with a sharp tip, looked more than ready to feed my blood to the book. That, of course, would never happen. Once a consecrated blade tastes blood it cannot be used for holy purposes. This blade had belonged to my many-times-great-grandmother, handed down through the generations to my mother, who gave it to me when I enrolled at St. Michaelmas. Family lore claimed the handle was carved from a claw that had belonged to the original Merriweather.

The boline is the real working blade of a witch. It is the magical equivalent of a chef's knife, suitable for all purposes from harvesting herbs to slicing placatory bits of liver when your dragonet is fussy. I found mine at a yard sale just before I came to college. The handle was not the traditional ivory; I prefer the feel of maple.

"Open the book, dear. No time like the present." Marissa's voice was a mix of encouragement and requirement.

With a deep, centering breath, I flipped the cover open. There was nothing to see, just faded paisley endpaper.

"Turn one more page. Needs two blank pages facing to work."

Obediently, I turned another leaf. The two creamy pages were empty. Curious, I flipped through all the pages. I could not see a single mark.

I looked at Marissa, who had taken a perch on the edge of one of the candlesticks.

"It's like the cover, isn't it? Nothing shows without blood being spilled."

"Precisely."

Joking, I teased, "I don't suppose I could just pick up some blood sausage from the butcher's? A pint of pigs' blood, maybe?"

I swear she quirked an eyebrow at me.

"Hahhhhhdly. Your blood awakened the pact. Your blood will evoke the challenge. Your blood will end the curse." She drawled the first word in the disdainful tones of the upper class.

My nod was slow as I stared at my left hand.

"Palm? Fingertip? Wrist?" I asked in a shaky voice as I gripped my boline in my right hand. "And which page do I use? The first two in the front?"

"Palm is best. Slice across it quickly and smear it against the two pages. You pick. Each pair of pages has its own challenge, its own choices and consequences."

Calling up my power I started again, turning pages slowly, stilling my mind. My sun-kissed magic shimmered around me as I continued to turn, running a finger down each page.

My intuition flared and I knew. Here. Now.

Without stopping to think, I sliced across my left palm and smeared the welling blood on both pages, saturating them with my life force.

The blood disappeared without a trace. The same crimson script began to scrawl across the left-hand page:

Merriweather men, your time has come.

A reckoning awaits within three suns.

> **Man and boy they share the same**
> **smile and walk and family name.**
> **One will live and one will die**
> **before your bane will draw to nigh.**

My brother or my father? How could I choose between them?

"Mmah-rrissa? Do you sss-sssee tttthis?"

The tiny elephant's shadow crossed the page as she hovered two feet above the evil book. "Keep watching, daughter of Eve. The right-hand side will tell your doom."

The relentless red script burned its way across the facing page.

> **Kill them one, or kill them both,**
> **to do this deed you'll pledge your troth.**
> **The men of Merriweather you will end,**
> **else to darkest Hells your soul we'll send.**

> **An alternate choice you still might make**
> **To save the males from their fate.**
> **Kill two students in their steads.**
> **Leave the corpses, bring the heads.**

This time the ink did not fade. In fact, it seemed to take on a sanguine glow of its own until it burned more brightly than the candles. The words seared into my mind and heart, my vision swam, and the blood pact with the book was sealed.

I must have fainted. When I next opened my eyes, I was staring up at the roughly-hewn ceiling of the cavern. Marissa was standing in the middle of my bloody palm, stroking the cut with her trunk. The flesh was knitting together as she worked her way from webbing to wrist.

"You really didn't need to cut so deep, Becca, dear. Makes my task that much more difficult. You must find the words to complete the pledge, and those words must be very carefully chosen. They may be the only hope your family has to continue. We'll need all the energy we can gather before this day is done."

As I pushed myself carefully upright, the room spun. Fear and anger flared in me. Enough of this. I snarled, "Maybe next time you could be a bit more specific, you poofed-up pachyderm."

The book seemed to be dragging on my magic, trying to drain me. That made me even angrier. The students at school had learned early it was never a good idea to piss me off. Time to teach the damned thing a lesson in manners.

"Stop that, you buggery little book. I gave you your taste of blood. That is all of me you may have for the moment." My magic flared in a nimbus of searing gold power which blazed around the book. The room wards flickered as my rage splashed against them, then strengthened to contain it. Marissa bolted into the air, flying agitated circles around my head. The tug from the book diminished to a thin thread.

"That's right, you blighter. Mess with a Merriweather, will you?" My voice pulsed with menace. The Demented Dragonet flared to life, on the prowl and hungry.

"Let's see how that ends for you. You have your hooks in me? That means I have my hooks in you, too. We will see who wins, you manky old thing. How many lives have you ruined? I will return you to the ash heap of time, a blasted shriveled shard of used-to-be magic." My voice rumbled the cavern with power.

Marissa hovered anxiously about a foot above my palm. "That may not have been wise, Miss Becca. Not wise at all," she fussed.

I was too angry to be afraid anymore. "How do I seal this challenge, pledge my troth or whatever? What's the form of it? And what did you mean I might find a way out of this?"

Marissa glared at me. "Stop. Talking. Just stop. It hears you. Is there a way to seal this room so no one can enter except the two of us?"

"Sure. We leave the wards up, sealing it off from all contacts, mundane or magical."

Marissa told me to use my crossed athame and boline to hold the book open on the altar. We retreated to my bedroom, leaving the "Working in Progress" sign up at the entrance to the cavern, the wards locked with a flare of her magic.

My personal wards flared around my room at the flick of my hand, sealing it from all but the most persistent eavesdroppers in any of the five realms. Marissa launched from my shoulder, where my copper curls had offered her shelter from prying eyes. She landed gracefully on the headboard of my bed.

"Now then, Rebecca, we must ...."

"Again with the "we". Who and what are you, and what were you doing inside my avocado, which started this whole fiasco racing downhill in the first place?"

My power flickered in warning even as my hand dug into the left desk drawer for one of the protein bars I kept available for moments like these. The kombucha was long gone. No breakfast. I had shed blood twice and invoked my power. I needed food, now.

She sniffed, one of those regal things you see the Royals doing. Like someone farted and no one would admit to it. "I believe we have bigger problems than my origin story, Miss Rebecca. We nee..."

"No. We don't. Because there won't be a 'we' if you keep this up. For all I know you are a plasma pod of some evil creature working with the stupid book."

Marrisa indignantly drew herself to her full three inches, taking in a deep breath.

"As I already told you, I am Marissa Ranhel of the Maj Torindae, daughter of Queen Larstinga Ranhel, may she reign long in peace. The Maj Torindae are a council of magic workers dedicated to shepherding recent graduates from our alma mater, Saint Michaelmas, as they take their first adult steps into the wider world. We normally find our assigned charges after the graduation ceremony. You," she huffed. "You triggered a warning, and I was sent to keep you from making any blood contact with the book."

"Did a great job of that, Marissa. Any reason you couldn't have just sent a letter? Or waited for me on the counter before I picked up that knife?" I unwrapped and chomped on the bar.

"You had to bring me into your home, which you did with the groceries last night. I waited for what seemed an appropriate moment for introductions. Perhaps I misjudged your potential reaction."

I waved the newly-scarred fingertip in the elephant's direction. "Appropriate moment?! Potential reaction?! What the hell did you think would happen when you just popped out onto my palm? A brass band of welcome?"

Marissa waited patiently until I calmed down a bit. "In any case, we need to figure out how to deal with your doom."

I grinned. "I have that part covered. How do I pledge my troth to that thing? I want to be sure I am completed connected to it when I split the Gordian knot of its riddles."

At ten minutes to midnight, I used my athame to pin the left-hand page of the book in place. Using a quill and dragon's blood ink, I wrote across the existing words, then chanted aloud:

"You are called 'Bastard of Bistek'.

Your threats are weak, you'll never wreck

    my family, my friends, my very future.

I'll solve your doom, undo the suture

holding page to cover, curse to page.

    You caught the wrong young witch's favor

    hoping no one here would save her

    from this doom of bloodlines true.

    This mother's daughter you have screwed

    will rise to destroy you in her rage."

There was a sudden pulse of energy as the challenge was accepted and the curse fully engaged. I stood strong as my hair whipped around me, then settled.

"Now, Becca. Close the book around your blade and bind it with the scarf."

I made quick work of wrapping the journal in the heavily embroidered rose silk scarf Marissa had magicked out of somewhere. The book fought against the binding, it's every squirm risking my gleaming blade's slicing it to shreds.

Marissa and I traveled to my home on the next train. The book was shoved to the bottom of my valise, wrapped in the scarf and locked in a warded box.

I explained to my parents and brother what had happened and my solution to the deadly riddle. They agreed and we made preparations for the ritual that evening.

Nightfall found the five of us and the book out in our back garden within a warded circle. The wooden altar was bedecked with lantham leaves, five beeswax candles burning against the night, an unlit brazier, a censer filled with charcoal and incense, and four ritual knives encircling the book, bound by their black handles to a red silk cord. Each Merriweather had tied theirs to the cord from eldest to youngest in a knotted loop of power. Marissa hovered around us anxiously, finally taking her place on one of the candlesticks.

I stepped forward, my deep scarlet robes flowing to brush the grass beneath my bare feet. Blazoned in spun gold thread, the dragonet *passant* of my family crest caught the light of the candles. The censer flared to life at my touch in a cloud of sweet perfume. For the fourth time that night I walked the protective circle. Cast with salt, water, and fire earlier, the wards flared up as the smoke from frankincense and myrrh trailed behind me, spreading into a shell of power over and around us as I reached my starting point.

Replacing the censer, I opened the book to the curse. I drove my boline through the right-hand pages, pinning it to the wooden top of the altar. First things first. The book would have to wait its turn.

My mother stepped up to my left wearing a similar scarlet robe. A swipe of her hand called fire to the brasier. Coals burst into hungry flames.

"I, Angelika Brady Merriweather, summon my family to celebrate the coming-of-age of its youngest child. The bonds which held us together will be severed, to be woven again between equals.

"This night my son becomes a man. As is the custom of House Merriweather, he moves to his father's House. No man may carry our name past their coming of age, save for the time it takes for a spouse to bring his children to adulthood."

My father stepped beside my mother. He wore the emerald and black of House Bandyhort, their gryphon *rampant* embroidered in black silk on his left breast. The honed edge of his ivory-handled knife flashed. A few drops of blood fell on the knot of red cord surrounding his athame.

"Tonight, I, Monterro Bandyhort Merriweather, reclaim my name and House and take my son with me. Graced to be welcomed into House Merriweather, I return to the family and name of my birth, Monterro Brightborn Bandyhort."

He used his working knife to cut the red cord above and below his athame, breaking the circle. He untied the knot, released his blade and tossed the cord on the brazier. The scarlet silk flared, the burning blood adding a sweet coppery tang to the air.

The journal squirmed against the steel holding it to the altar.

Mother used her ivory-handled blade to draw blood and dripped it on the cord around her sacred knife. She sliced it free of the partial circle and untied the knot. Raising her athame in salute, she proclaimed, "This night I send my son to House Bandyhort. May he grow and flourish. May he always remember his origins and honor the teachings of House Merriweather. Blessed be the Bandyhorts!" Her blooded cord flared on the coals.

Power surged again, and the book flapped violently.

Thomas stepped between my parents, a robe borrowed from my father hanging loosely on his still-growing frame. His boline drew a few drops of blood to drip on the cord holding his ritual knife before he sliced it free and undid the knot.

He raised his athame and boldly declared, his voice cracking only a little, "Mother of my birth, my gratitude is eternal for all you have given me. Tonight, I claim my rights and responsibilities as a man. Blessed be House Merriweather, and hail to House Bandyhort, home of my father and myself. I, Thomas Merriweather Bandyhort, sever my ties to your House and claim my inheritance."

His blood-kissed section of the red cord flared in the brazier next to the ashes of the earlier two. The book flapped its pages against my steel as power shifted and swirled around us.

Stepping forward to untie the cord on my dragon-claw blade, I set the knife beside the book. Holding the remaining silk strands, I declared, "Merriweather born, Merriweather until I die. I honor my ancestress and all the women before me." I tossed the cord on the brazier. I was not changing Houses; no blood was required. The book raged impotently.

My turn.

I pulled a strip of hand-written parchment from my belt. Spreading it over the open book, I drove my athame deep into the left-hand side of the book, binding book and scroll as one, pinning both to our family altar. I sliced my finger on my boline and smeared blood across the scroll and the pages of the book as I read:

"You threatened my line by claiming two lives,
    such evil deeds cannot be shrived.

We ended the existence of Merriweathers two -
Monterro and Thomas whose hearts are true
To their family and lineage according to law

Claiming the name of their House, as you saw.

And you, you bastard book of doom?
I will bury your ashes in a tomb.
You've met your match and lost the right
To dictate to anyone after this night.

As a Merriweather I will always protect
my family and heritage in ways direct,
destroying you, returning the bane
you tried to force on those of the name
of Merriweather, honored and ancient Scion.

Blood calls to blood, now taste some of mine.
I invoke the fires of power sublime,
fuel it with power of my house true
returning your curse to destroy you.
Behold my doom. Your life is done!"

As Rebecca Bandyhort Merriweather cried out those last words, she unleashed a nascent pearl of power within her. It was her true inheritance from her many-times-great-grandmother, the ancient golden dragon Merriweather. Focused through her dragon-claw-handled blade and slammed into the evil book, the aurum fire left nothing but ashes drifting toward the ground as the Book of Choices learned too late not to make assumptions about lineage and names. The resulting silent blast knocked the candles over, snuffing out the flames.

Marissa Ranhel of the Maj Torindae had witnessed the rite of unweaving from the easternmost candlestick. The shock wave from the destruction of the cursed book blew her off her perch. She took a lap around the altar before settling with dignity in front of her charge.

A great belling roar shattered the sudden stillness of the night. Merriweather, watching from her hoard in the worlds between, welcomed her newest daughter.

Marissa looked up and smiled. She then made a leg, bowing gravely. "Well and truly done, young Merriweather. Well and truly done."

Now Becca's real training could begin.

ABOUT THE AUTHOR

Susan Imbs is a child of the sixties, born in southwest Michigan right on the Lake. She started her writing career in fifth grade when she was introduced to the limerick and wrote about a squirrel and a nut. She won the Michigan Young Writers prize five years later for an epic poem giving voice to the island in The Lord of the Flies. She has been creating poems, short stories and working on several longer pieces ever since.

She moved to Oshkosh in 2009 and settled into her current cottage in 2015, where she lives with Penny and Willow, her beloved Miniature Pinschers. She considers herself a semi-professional hermit and cherishes the quiet her home provides. A student of both spirituality and science, she is constantly seeking better ways to touch the flame at the heart of every soul.

Her publications include the Chicago Tribune Sunday Magazine, the Eads Bridge Review, several technical journal publications which led to a patent, and placed two years in a row at the Lakefly Writers Conference writing contest. Her most recent works can be found in the Fragments of Ourselves anthology.□

SECOND CHANCE

BY REDD HERRING

Part I - Reflection

He opened the door to the guest room. The musty smell made him wrinkle his nose slightly. It hadn't been used in a long time, since they started fighting. "Nobody wants to visit and listen to arguing all day," his father told him as he packed his bags. His parents were the last visitors, almost ten years ago. The room had not seen a soul since then. He laid his luggage on the bed and reached to open the curtains, but pulled back shaking his head. He was an intruder here now – not allowed to change things anymore.

He opened the closet, revealing an intricate web in the corner. He gently blew. It fluttered as if on an ocean wave. A small, dark spider revealed itself, in search of prey. It painstakingly worked every strand of the web, but found nothing to satisfy itself. It continued searching, as if more effort would change the outcome. He sighed and remembered doing much the same near the end. *Just try harder – work more, and it will all be fine.* He closed the door and left the spider to its business. "Just ignore it. It's what you do best," she used to tell him.

The top dresser drawer screeched as he slid it open. He felt the high-pitched complaint in his teeth and shivered. Memories of past arguments flooded him. He slid the fancy napkins, the ones only used on holidays to make everything look perfect, to the side. His fingers found pieces of the molded plaster handprints the kids made one summer. He fished out the shards and began assembling them on top of the dresser. Missing pieces left holes that glared out at him the way she did every time he did something to leave another hole in their lives.

He had apologized, shakily dropping to one knee to clean up his mess. "I've got it," she pushed in front of him. "Just have another beer, and let me take care of it." He reached

to help, but she shoved his hands away, "Stop! You're just
making it worse, like you always do."

He opened the middle drawer. It was filled with medals,
certificates, and other awards they had earned during their
school years. He held up an honor roll award his son received in fourth grade. He missed the ceremony, just like
every one before and after that.

"Been real busy. Working a lot lately. You understand.
Really sorry, buddy."

"It's OK, Daddy. I know you're busy," his son replied.
He also knew Daddy would be passed out by the time the
ceremony started. He was drinking the day his boy's first
child was born. It had been three years, and he still had not
seen his granddaughter. "Real busy, Dad. You understand."

"Sure, buddy."

He grabbed a track medal his daughter brought home
from her seventh-grade athletic banquet. The one she had
to show him the next morning, because he was too drunk
to pay attention when she came home with it. The back
read *Heart of Fire Award.*

"The coaches said I was the hardest-working one on the
team! Isn't that awesome?" She beamed with pride. "Dad-
dy! Are you awake?"

"Hmm?" He lifted his head. "Great. That's great, honey."
He rolled over. He could feel her staring at his back, but his
head hurt so much that he just pretended to sleep.

"Hope you feel better soon, Daddy." She touched his shoulder. *The last time he saw her was at the graduation party. He stumbled on the patio and knocked over the buffet table. His beer bottle smashed on the edge of the pool. Everyone had to get out while his daughter picked pieces of brown glass from the bottom.*

"I'm sorry, sweetie. Need to fix that loose stone on the patio."

"It's fine, Daddy." She continued to pick the glass out. She had not even changed into her swimsuit yet. *"Go on and take a nap. You look tired. I've got this." He had just nodded and gone upstairs.*

He kicked the drawer shut and stared at the framed award on the wall. *Salesman of the Year.* He went out with the guys at work to celebrate that night. That was the first one. He tried to explain it to her when she showed up at the police station.

"The guys took me out to congratulate me. Just a quick beer."

"It's two in the morning."

"Well, I think it just takes a long time to process the paperwork."

"You couldn't call a cab?"

"I didn't want to leave the car in the lot all night."

"Just tell me where you are. I have to get Mom to watch the kids while I bail you out. I'll tell your brothers to go pick up your car."

"I'm sorry," he shook his head. "Never happen again. I swear." He dumped all of the beer bottles into the trash can. "I'm done with it." He didn't have a drink for six days. On the seventh day, he got his second one – she left him in jail for a week. He was fired the next Monday.

He sat on the bed and sighed. The room darkened. The cloud passed after a few minutes and light streamed through the fabric again, illuminating his hand. He turned his palm up to look at the long, red scar on his wrist. That was after the third one. The one that left him with a limp and a suspended license.

He promised to go to rehab. He never did. He was passed out when she left.

There was a soft knock at the door. "Hi, sorry to interrupt."

"No problem. Just making sure I have everything I need." He stood and gathered his luggage. He looked at the dresser one last time. "Yea, I have everything I want. We can go now."

"The buyers are very happy, and you got a really good price."

"Did you set up the payments? Split three ways?"

"Yes. Are you sure you don't want any of the money?"

He shook his head. "Won't need it." He flicked the light switch, shut the door, and headed downstairs.

In the truck he took a long pull from the flask in the console. The whiskey burned all the way down. He picked his jacket off the passenger seat and eyed the old book he found in the dresser. "Never seen this before. Wonder where she got it?" He wasn't even sure why he took it. It just kind of felt like he was supposed to have it, but he couldn't explain why. He shrugged and covered it with the jacket. Maybe it would be worth a few bucks someday. He put the truck in gear and pulled into the street. He ran his hand along the cracked dash, lingering on the spot where his head hit it in the crash. "Well ole girl, I think I'll just let you take me wherever you want us to go."

Part II - Redemption

He turned the book over in his hands. The cover, worn and stained, felt almost oily to the touch. He took a long gulp of gin and tonic as he examined various scratches in the leather. He leaned in close on a few that looked like fingernail marks. He wondered if there were others, maybe like him, who had handled this book before. Nothing looked intentional – that is to say none of the marks seemed to be writing or symbols of any sort. With no words on the pages, the book was a complete mystery. He was not sure why he even kept the weathered volume after he found it in his old guest room, except that he *felt* it was what he was supposed to do. The next drink, that last one in the glass that was mostly gin, was always the best. It burned his throat, letting him know that he would suffer later. He lay the book on the old, wooden spool he used for a table and poured another, this time leaving out the tonic and lime.

What he was actually supposed to do that day two years ago was pack up his belongings and leave – and he did. As he was making one last check of the room, he found the book in the bottom dresser drawer under some guest towels. He thought it was an old high school yearbook at first. When he looked closer, he realized he had never seen this before. He was not sure where the book came from or if it belonged to his ex-wife. The real estate agent coming up the stairs prompted him to stuff the book into his suitcase. That moment flooded back on him with a rush.

There had been a soft knock at the door. "Hi, sorry to interrupt."

"No problem. Just making sure I have what I need." He stood and gathered his luggage. He looked at the dresser one last time. "Yea, I have everything. We can go now."

"The buyers are very happy, and you got a really good price."

"Did you set up the payments? Split three ways?"

"Yes. Are you sure you don't want any of the money?"

He shook his head. "Won't need it." He flicked the light switch, shut the door, and headed downstairs.

Now here he was, two years later, in a rented room behind the garage where he worked cleaning floors and doing odd jobs. It was small and smelled like gasoline most of the time, but at least the price was right and no one bothered him. Here he could relax with his gin and kill the hours. He tried to drown the memories of the car crash that took his family – his ex-family, actually – the week after he sold the house. He knew that if he were a better man, the whole situation would have been different and they would still be together – a whole family. No amount of liquor could help him forget. He refused to spend the trust money that was never disbursed to the three of them, so it sat in an account useless and wasting away.

"Just like me," he sighed. "Never was there when they needed me and can't help them now." He wished the alcoholic's empty wish: *If I had one chance to fix it all, I would definitely do it!*

He grimaced as he took a drink and looked down at the book again. He ran his fingers along the straps. There was nothing unusual about them. The rusted buckles looked like they would fall apart at first touch, but they were as solid as could be. He thumbed through the pages, like he had done a hundred times before, but saw no writing. He snapped the book shut and slung it at the cabinet door under the sink.

"I am sick of that damned book!" He slammed his hand on the spool, tipping the gin. He lunged to steady the bottle and braced himself with his other hand. "Ouch!" He looked down at the thin trickle of blood on his finger. "Man, that's one helluva splinter!" He moved to the sink to get a better look. He held his hand up to the light and squeezed the tip of his finger, pulling at the splinter. It finally gave way and a single drop of blood fell, landing on the open book on the floor.

A thick plume of dark smoke rose, causing him to jump back. The gilded pages began to turn on their own until the inside back cover was exposed. He picked up the book and brought it to the small table. He could see writing inscribed in red letters. "Now, I know I have been through every page of this thing and never seen any words at all!" He leaned in closer, but could not make out what it said. "Must be in some foreign language. Nothing like I've ever seen."

The letters burst into flames. The book spun and bounced on the wood. He took a step back and reached for a kitchen towel, slapping at the fire. The book rose in the air and hovered in front of him. "What do you want?" he yelled. The words on the cover glowed yellow and then red, almost jumping off the leather surface. "I don't understand the words!" The book lurched toward his face. He ran to the bathroom, trying to escape. He closed the door and turned the lock, then ran cold water into the sink. "I know I've been drinking, but this is insane." He leaned over to splash water on his face. When he looked up at the mirror, he could see the reflection of the door. It was on fire! He spun around and saw the book burning through the wood. It moved through the door, hovered for a second, then shot across the tiny room. It slammed into the mirror, falling onto the vanity top. The lights in the bathroom went out and the letters glowed red once again.

He moved closer, looking down at the book and trying to read the words again. "I just don't know what it says." He stood in the dark room shaking. The words pulsed bright red, then yellow, then green – over and over in the same pattern. He looked up. He saw the words reflected in the mirror, and he could read them!

Three are gone,
Caused by thee.
Undo what's done,
Death, the remedy.
Trade the one,
For the three.

He stared as the words continued to glow - red, yellow, green - repeatedly. His hands shook. "I know what I need to do," he fell to his knees sobbing. The lights came on and the book hovered in the air. He stood. "I know it was my fault – all of it! I need to make it right – for them!"

The words burned from the cover and were replaced with the outline of a hand. The edges burned like before – red, yellow, green. He nodded and wiped away tears.

He placed his hand on the outline. He felt something pulling him into the book. He screamed, more out of terror than pain, but he knew it was a fair trade. Everything was going to be alright.

***

She took one last look around the guest room.

There had been a soft knock at the door. "Hi, sorry to interrupt." The real estate agent said.

"No problem. Just making sure I have what I need." She stood and gathered her luggage. She looked at the dresser one last time. "Yes, I have everything. We can go now."

"The buyers are very happy, and you got a really good price."

"Thank you for your help." She wiped the corner of her eye with a tissue.

"Of course," the agent gave her a hug. "I was so sorry to hear about your husband's accident. He was such a good man and a great father."

"He was," she nodded. "He was always thinking of everyone else first. He left each of us a trust so we wouldn't have to worry if something ever happened to him. I used to tease him about always thinking of the worst-case scenario," she let out a slight laugh, "but he always said *failure to plan is planning to fail, my dear. The one thing you can **never** do is go back later and fix your mistakes!*" She flicked the light switch, shut the door, and headed downstairs.

ABOUT THE AUTHOR

Redd Herring has written as long as he can remember but only recently began publishing his work. Maybe he was busy sailing his ship, **Have Mercy**, across the seas of time and space, maybe he just wrote for himself, or maybe he spent too much time in the Crossroads Cantina trading stories for drinks - probably that last one.

Redd listens to metal music or watches sci-fi as he writes and tries his best to sneak in references to his favorites. If you have read "The Red Diamond" in The Golden Gull Anthology, you might be able to catch a nod to Alice in Chains, Mad Season, or Firefly.

Currently, **Have Mercy** is docked at a small farm in Texas, where the crew is learning to grow grapes and make wine before leaving on their next voyage. Redd is also in negotiations with Nemo, the Crossroads Cantina bartender, to get a juke box filled with metal tunes added to his favorite corner near the back door.

You can go to www.reddherring.com for a list of his works or just to send him a message.